# Tin Camp Road

ALSO BY ELLEN AIRGOOD

*South of Superior*
*Prairie Evers*
*The Education of Ivy Blake*

# Tin Camp Road

————        ————

## Ellen Airgood

RIVERHEAD BOOKS | NEW YORK | 2021

RIVERHEAD BOOKS
An imprint of Penguin Random House LLC
penguinrandomhouse.com

Grateful acknowledgment is made for permission to reprint the following:

"Mean Time" from *Mean Time* by Carol Ann Duffy. Published by Anvil, 1993.
Copyright © Carol Ann Duffy. Reproduced by permission of the author
c/o Rogers, Coleridge & White Ltd., 20 Powis Mews, London W11 1JN.

Library of Congress Cataloging-in-Publication Data

Names: Airgood, Ellen, author.
Title: Tin camp road / Ellen Airgood.
Description: First. | New York : Riverhead Books, 2021.
Identifiers: LCCN 2020019494 (print) | LCCN 2020019495 (ebook) |
ISBN 9780399163364 (hardcover) | ISBN 9781101610510 (ebook)
Subjects: GSAFD: Christian fiction.
Classification: LCC PS3601.I74 T56 2021 (print) |
LCC PS3601.I74 (ebook) | DDC 813/.6—dc23
LC record available at https://lccn.loc.gov/2020019494
LC ebook record available at https://lccn.loc.gov/2020019495

Printed in the United States of America
1st Printing

*Book design by Alexis Farabaugh*

*For all my dear ones.*

*And in memory of my brother,*
*Matthew Alvin Airgood.*
SEPTEMBER 13, 1961 – JUNE 12, 2016

So at the end of this day, we give thanks
For being betrothed to the unknown


—John O'Donohue, "The Inner History of a Day,"
*To Bless the Space Between Us: A Book of Blessings*

# Tin Camp Road

# One

Laurel Hill knew that a part of her would die if she ever had to leave Lake Superior. Its lapping was a heartbeat, one connected to her own. Without the sight and sound of it landing onshore and departing again, the turning of the water as constant as the earth's orbit, her soul would fade and tear, a sheet left out on the line too long.

She tapped the handle of her cleaning cart. The sky was as clear as a polished window today. The water riffled under the August sun; the air smelled of sand and lake and something else, something she'd never been able to pin down. Maybe it was Canada. Alaska, even. Maybe stray molecules of distant forests and mountains and prairies—cities, too—sailed down to Gallion on the northwest wind that almost always blew. Or maybe it was the smell of bigness, of eternity. Whatever it was, it was essential. She breathed deep to bring it into every corner of herself, then pushed on toward room 15, her sixth of the day at the Lakeshore Inn.

The cart's wheels grabbed at the parking lot's gravel and veered it off course. She yanked it straight to hop it onto the walk and trundled forward again. When she knocked on 15's sand-pitted door, no one answered, so she bumped in backward, dragging the cart along with her.

Inside, a backpack slouched beside the television, a framed photograph stood on the nightstand, and a bath towel lay folded on the sink. A note was tented on top of it, written on the envelope Paula Hoover gave the maids to leave out for tips. *Dear Housekeeping. I'm sorry about the coffee I spilled. Thank you*—miigwech—*for your service. The room is very pleasant and clean; I have enjoyed it.*

Laurel lifted the envelope's flap and stared at the twenty that lay inside. Tips of any kind were rare, but one this large was unprecedented. She nodded at the bill to welcome it to her always-too-small collection, tucked it in her jeans pocket along with the note—you rarely got thanked for doing work like this—and turned to the bed, pulling the coverlet off and tugging the sheets from the corners of the mattress. Then she stopped and took the envelope back out of her pocket. She picked up the pen Paula had them leave beside the phones—*Compliments of Lakeshore Inn, Your Upper Peninsula Happy Place since 1967*—and wrote, *You are very welcome, thank you!* below the original message. She reread her own. A period would have been better than an exclamation mark, but she propped it on the backpack anyway.

———

She was jabbing the vacuum hose into the far corner beneath the bathroom sink when the machine cut off. She jumped and banged her head on the vanity; Rip coughed and said, "Sorry. Wasn't trying to scare you to death."

Laurel rubbed her skull. "It's all right."

Rip had small, neat ears and snapping eyes she'd always suspected saw straight into her. Saw her evasions and the lies she told herself, inspected her failures more closely than she could ever bear to. "I came to tell you, Lydia called. She's not coming in today."

"What? Why?"

"Hungover, I expect."

Laurel almost kept silent, but she'd known Rip since she was a child and her mother cleaned these rooms. He used to give Laurel peppermint sticks out of the candy jars in the gift shop. The October of her eighth birthday, he gave her a kite that hadn't sold all summer because the packaging was torn. She and Mom and Gran took it to the beach and flew it until a gust of wind grabbed it and crumpled it into a broken-winged bird. They still had fun, though; losing the kite wasn't a tragedy. They dropped it in the firepit and used it to light the kindling. Gran made Laurel write Rip a thank-you note the next day, and twenty-two years later that note still lay tucked under the glass on his desktop. Laurel had moved away and returned a dozen times with her mother, but the note was still there. Rip was still Rip, managing the Hoovers' motel like he'd been doing for decades, and Laurel, the real Laurel, was still here, too. She straightened her shoulders. "You should just fire her."

3

Rip laughed, a single *hmmp*. "Should I, now?"

"There is no 'just'" was the secret motto of everyone who worked at the Lakeshore. The saying lived in her earliest memories along with the cedary aroma of the inside of Gran's sauna, the song of the peepers ricocheting from the swamps in the spring, the sight of Gran at the stove boiling cranberries or blueberries or any other berry that grew for jam. No just and often no justice. It was a fact life here taught you early and kept on teaching you, no matter how well you thought you'd learned your lesson. Laurel ducked her chin. "Yeah, no, I know better."

"Good. 'Cause if I fire her, who do I replace her with? You have a clone of yourself stashed away? Or else maybe your kid's ready to start working?"

"She's ten, Rip. Ten today."

"Is she." Rip grimaced the way people did when they wanted to convey that time flew without spending breath on the subject. And it did. Gran always insisted it sped faster and faster as you grew older, and at nearly thirty, Laurel knew she'd been right. "Anyway. Lyd's young and chafing at the bit for her life to happen. She'll grow up yet. The question right now is whether you can pick up her slack in the meantime."

"Oh, Rip, I don't think so. I promised Skye I'd be home by three at the latest—we're supposed to spend the day on the beach. All day and half the night. It's the Perseids."

"Is it. Well. 'The best-laid plans of mice and men,' eh? Ask the boss man on that one."

"What do you mean?"

"I don't mean anything."

Rip had a way of sounding final. She had never argued with him and never would; certain truths about yourself you had to accept. "What about Paula? I can't let Skye down."

Rip gave her the lowered-brow look that always made her feel simpleminded. "Mrs. H. has not been gracing this place with her presence overmuch of late, Laurel. Or have you not noticed?"

"I thought she was busy with their house remodel."

"Sure, that's what it is."

Laurel hunched her shoulders and kept quiet. No need to further expose her cluelessness. Rip ran his eyes over the room: pine-paneled walls, a bureau bearing an old-style television on its scarred shoulders, the bed made up with a pastel-flowered duvet. His gaze lingered on a water stain on the ceiling. The Lakeshore was not in perfect condition, but it was nowhere near as run-down as the Breakers up on the main street, so it was always busy in the season. And the Hoovers painted it at least once a decade and replaced the mattresses now and then, so in this town, on the northernmost rim of Michigan, it was respectable, or it had been. Since the county paved the back road from McAllaster a few years ago, the visitors came faster and thicker and were more demanding—more demanding, less appreciative, and in a bigger hurry. Not all of them, but enough that Laurel veered quicker than ever away from strangers. Rip knocked on the doorframe. "What do you think?"

Laurel twisted her hair around her hand. Her grandmother had called it her crowning glory but mostly Laurel kept it in a low ponytail, out of her way and less apt to call notice to itself. Long, curling, the color of cider vinegar, it was the hair of a storybook princess and didn't fit the rest of her: thin and angular, strong lines drawn quick. "I can't, Rip."

A look raced over his face, anger or annoyance or only weariness, but he shrugged. "I can't make you." Laurel stayed silent, unsure, and he brightened. "I'd throw in a pizza. You could call it in to Belle's, pick it up on your way home."

Laurel smiled. "You wouldn't have to do that."

"Call it a birthday present for the little one."

Laurel nibbled at a thumbnail but yanked her hand away. A habit she was trying to break. "Who will you get if I don't do it?"

Rip rubbed at his eyes. "Me, I guess."

"You don't want to be cleaning all these!" Rip was trim and brisk-moving, fit for his age, but he'd had a back surgery a decade ago and Laurel knew he had to be careful.

"I've done it before, it won't kill me." A grin flashed beneath his mustache. "Any luck, I'll find a quarter behind the headboard."

Laurel glanced outside. The sun bore down; the water glittered. She nodded before she could think better of it. "I'll call Skye. There's plenty of day left."

Laurel paced the three-foot path the phone cord allowed while she waited for Skye to pick up. At last, there was a breathless " 'Lo?"

"Skye? Baby, where were you?"

"Out on the patio. There's a frog, an eastern gray tree frog."

"Oh, a frog, that's great, I haven't seen a frog in a long time."

"Yeah, but it's a tree frog, Mom. Tree frogs belong in trees, and it's sitting on the cement in the sun. And he's so little. He's tiny."

"How did you see him?"

"I was out there reading and I just . . . noticed him."

Skye had noticed their dog, Harper, this same way. They were climbing Plank Hill one day late in April, going quick as they could on

6

the ice. It was one of the first days after they'd left Sean's, and Laurel was trying to distract them from their sorrow with fresh air and movement. Halfway to the corner, Skye pulled her to a stop and stood statue-still. Her eyes lit on an animal where it lay huddled in a drainage pipe the county hadn't installed yet. She moved straight toward him, stopped a few feet away, and squatted on her heels with her hand held out. "Oh, Mr. Dog," she said, grave as a train wreck. "You look like you've seen hard times."

When he lifted his chin, Laurel saw pale blue eyes, bright with smarts and maybe fury at the way the world had treated him. She moved to hold Skye back, but Skye was already scooting closer. "Oh, Mr. Dog. Dear Mr. Dog." She fluttered her fingertips, patient as a mountain, and after a moment the dog dragged himself from the pipe. Mud chunked his coat; one rear leg twisted beneath him. Laurel's stomach churned. She stepped backward, but Skye beamed and nodded encouragement as if he was a shy child going onstage for a piano recital. He limped to her and they studied each other. Then he licked her palm once, the seal on a covenant.

"This poor frog is out of his element," Skye said now. "That's not good."

"No, it doesn't sound good."

"It isn't. I looked—"

Skye cut herself off and Laurel filled in the sentence. Skye had looked the frog up on the internet, which meant she'd broken Laurel's express rule not to leave the yard except in case of a five-alarm emergency and had run down the block to use Lori Trevor's computer. In an ideal world, that would have been fine. But the world wasn't ideal. It was beautiful, amazing, and complicated.

"Okay, you looked it up. Then what?"

Skye huffed in relief. "I read all about him and I'm afraid he's dying. He's very still. And very gray."

"Didn't you say he's a gray tree frog?"

"Yeah, but not this gray. You have to be careful about moving them, so I didn't. I put a bowl of water down and made shade with tree branches. I put them over him like a tepee."

"You didn't break branches off anything, did you?" Harv Duke was particular about his rental's appearance, yard and all, though not so choosy about how the house actually functioned.

"Um, I might've. Off the maple. But it's not noticeable. Not very."

Laurel closed her eyes.

Skye breathed in and out in Laurel's ear. "I killed some flies and put them by him, too. He hasn't taken them yet."

"Ah. Well. I'm sorry, and I wish I was there to help. And that's the thing, it's why I called." Laurel sank onto the bed and picked up the framed photograph. Two women and a child gazed at her from their picnic spot on a beach; she stared back at them while she explained.

"Mom! No!" A bang echoed. Skye had punched the tabletop, a new and unwelcome habit. "You worked late last night. It's all you do, and it stinks. It stinks even worse since we moved out of Sean's. I hate sitting at Belle's all night while you do the dishes."

In the photo, sun cascaded over the women and girl and reflected off the water behind them; their matching smiles proclaimed they didn't have a care in the world. Laurel knew that couldn't be so. Everyone had cares. Everyone, everywhere. Still, she closed her eyes. It was hard to look at lives that seemed so much easier than her own, and she saw so many of them. People on vacation, people eating every meal out without blinking at the cost, people abandoning the remains of those meals in their fridges as if they were nothing. People with cars that started every time they put the key in the ignition, cars that didn't even have keys, they were so up-to-the-minute. Laurel didn't begrudge anyone these conveniences—she didn't think she did—but she hated to feel herself falling so short in comparison. "I'm sorry. It's summer. You know how summer is."

Skye sniffed.

"I work so I can take good care of you."

"I know."

Grudging words, but they made Laurel straighten. "I promise I'll go fast. Fast as a whirlwind. We'll have all kinds of day left, and we'll stay out so late watching those stars of ours, you won't even believe it."

Skye sniffed again and Laurel twisted the phone cord around her hand. She wished she'd told Rip no, but how could she? "It'll be great, you'll see."

Skye sighed. "Okay."

"And why don't you call Abby in the meantime, see what she's up to?"

"She's still at camp."

Laurel smoothed the bed's coverlet. "That's right. Well. I'll be as quick as I can. And we'll have fun later, I promise."

"Okay."

"I love you, baby."

"I know."

Laurel made her voice firm. "Stay in the house or the backyard. Not the front." In front, strangers—even neighbors—might see her and realize she was home alone. Lori Trevor wouldn't say anything, but someone else might. Even on Railroad Street summer people owned half the houses now.

"But it's boring."

"You'll survive."

"Why can't I go to Ms. Trevor's? She said it was all right."

Because Lori Trevor drank. Discreetly, but with a devotion that elbowed every other consideration out of its way. "Because you can't."

"Or Sean's? He's not at work today."

"I'd . . . have to talk to him about it."

"So, talk to him! Call him up. Please?"

"That won't work. I'd have to . . . see him. I'd have to see him, and I can't leave here."

Another bang, this one quiet. "I miss Margie."

Margie McMinn had babysat for Laurel ever since Skye was a toddler. In June she had fallen down the steps at church and broken her hip, and a week after that, she was gone. "I miss her, too, baby."

"I thought—" Skye paused. Laurel waited her out. "I thought, since she left you all that money, you could stay home more. Like, a lot."

Margie had left Laurel five thousand dollars. A staggering and unexpected bequest, and one that must not be squandered. "Oh, sweetie. It's a nice amount of money, but I can't stop working. It wouldn't last long." Laurel stood, making her voice bright. "Things will get easier. Summer's winding down, you'll start school soon. Fifth grade! You've been so excited about it."

"Yeah," Skye admitted.

"Better times are just around the corner."

Skye sighed. "Have you ever noticed how you always say that, but then the corner moves?"

# Two

Frogs were everywhere by the time Laurel got home. An enormous sidewalk-chalk frog crouched on the square of cement outside the back door they called a patio—this would wash off, so Laurel smiled at it—and on the dining room table, half a dozen watercolor frogs leaped across the giant sheets of art paper Jen gave Skye last Valentine's. Laurel smiled at those, too. A frog had been doodled in pencil on the scratch pad beside the phone, his expression both angry and quizzical (Skye must have drawn it while they talked), a free-form chalk frog inched across a piece of junk mail, and an ink-pen frog peeked from behind the toilet paper dispenser in the bathroom. Laurel frowned at this one. She'd have to paint it over before Harv saw it or there'd be hell to pay, but when she saw Skye, she only said, "Your frogs are awesome."

Skye lay on their bed with her ankles crossed and her hands folded on her chest. She craned her neck to look at Laurel. "The real one disappeared, though." She wore paisley leggings and a fuchsia T-shirt; her feet were bare and her toenails painted crimson.

Suddenly, Laurel glimpsed future-Skye: Grown up. Gone away. No longer looking to her mother for direction. "He must have had his food and drink and hopped into a tree," she said, settling onto the edge of the mattress.

"Maybe."

Laurel brushed aside a lock of Skye's bangs. "You okay?"

"Yeah." Skye took Laurel's wrist and felt for her pulse, the way she'd been doing since she was small. Sometimes it meant she was uncertain, other times deeply peaceful. Today it seemed like the latter. After a moment, she scooted herself up to lean against the headboard. "When he was gone, I decided to draw him, and I lost track of time. I just finished. I'm kind of exhausted."

"I'll bet. That's a lot of art to make."

Skye bounced her palms on the mattress, agreement and satisfaction in the gesture.

"I'm sorry I'm late."

Skye shrugged. "I smell pizza."

The pie was only twelve feet away, on the table jammed next to the tiny fridge. The table doubled as a counter, school desk, craft area, and office. Laurel could see it and every other inch of their home from here. Harv referred to this as an open floor plan and Jen called it Gallion Ghetto, but Laurel was just glad to have a roof over their heads. "It's from Rip, for your birthday."

"Nice!"

"Tomorrow you can make him a thank-you card. But right now, let's go."

"*Yeah.*" Skye slid off the bed and surged toward the love seat where her beach tote sat packed. A tight spot in Laurel's spine unkinked. She knew she worked too much, especially in the summer, and it scared her sometimes to realize what she put off for another day or even season. With Skye looking so distant and grown, a fleeting knowing that was quieter than a whisper filled Laurel: life was happening now, nothing could be postponed, the future wasn't real. But that was nonsense, she told herself. What she'd said earlier was true: better times were ahead. They just had to work toward them.

"You have your hat?" Laurel asked, rooting through the top bureau drawer for her own.

Even in August they would need hats to sit out beneath Superior's big, cold sky watching meteors rocket toward earth.

They unpacked their snacks and blankets at the firepit, a ring of rocks that Laurel and her mom had gathered when Laurel was young. Skye dug a baggie of dryer lint from her tote and placed it in the pit's center. She leaned twigs and wood from their cache beside the pit into a tepee, leaving an opening on the side so air could get in, and glanced at Laurel. Laurel gave her the thumbs-up. "You're a pro." Gran had taught Mom, Mom had taught Laurel, and Laurel had passed on to Skye this same skill: starting the bonfire from age eight on was a family tradition, a rite of passage.

Skye squeezed tiny squirts of lighter fluid on the wood. She closed the bottle and handed it to Laurel, squatted an arm's length away, and struck a match, holding it to the tinder until flames fingered up. Behind her, Laurel nodded. Skye had done everything right.

Skye rested on her haunches. "What is it about fire?"

When the tepee fell, she laid chunks of wood atop the now-crackling kindling and took off across the sand, the dog behind her. "Har-per!" she sang out. "Harper-dog! Harper is a lark, not a carp, not a narc. Harper likes to bark, in the park, in the dark."

Harper did bark then and Skye ran faster. She turned a cartwheel and landed on her feet and kept going, and Laurel's throat clogged. How had it been ten years since her water broke while she'd been doing the dinner dishes, thinking later she'd go out to the pasture with a blanket to watch for meteors? Her mother had been in Detroit with Wendell Hendry, recording a demo that never went anywhere; Laurel was alone except for the baby, who was, it had become apparent, intent on arriving *right then*. Laurel had dialed 911 and told the dispatcher to round up Gallion's search and rescue team because the ambulance from Crosscut would take too long. "Tell them get up to the Hill place fast," Laurel gasped. "Tell them Laurel Hill is delivering early."

"How early?"

"Three weeks." Laurel had dropped the phone. The contractions came in insistent waves; it was all she could do to get the shower curtain down and onto Gran's mattress; her own room upstairs felt like a continent away. She lay on her side and focused on not pushing, not yet, just as she'd rehearsed in case of this exact emergency but never expected she'd have to do. She had assumed Mom would take her to War Memorial Hospital in Sault Ste. Marie—the small city two hours away, which everyone referred to as "the Soo"—a day or so before her due date the way they'd planned, that Skye would come slowly the way first babies tended to. But Skye had been raring to go from the start, sure of who she was and where she was going before she ever left the womb, on a mission to see the world, to experience it in all of its bumpy wonder.

The team arrived within minutes. Alice Stonehouse flung her medical kit onto Gran's dresser alongside Great-Grandmother Greta's tin sewing box; Pete Jenkins grabbed Laurel's hand and helped her focus on her breathing. Finn Anderson picked up the dangling phone receiver to tell the 911 dispatcher they'd arrived; his wife, Meg, coaxed Laurel onto her hands and knees and stationed herself at the end of the bed. Laurel panted and sweated and pushed, staring at Gran's kerosene lamp—it had belonged to Gran's mother—hoping no one broke it in the excitement and wishing Gran were there. But Gran was gone, and with Mom away and Jen in college, Laurel and her four helpers were the ones to welcome this baby, this spirit who seemed real and not real at the same time. When Skye arrived, everything changed. Suddenly, the world was just beginning; it was astounding and indescribable.

"Mom! Watch!" Skye pelted back, Harper on her heels. She turned another cartwheel and landed with her arms in a V, and Laurel clapped and cheered.

"I'm worried, though." Skye rotated the marshmallow she had skewered on the end of a green stick. Darkness had descended; the stars burned and trembled. "He's an exile."

Laurel had been seeing them as God must, if he was watching: two tiny humans and one lame dog leaning toward a campfire. Would he even notice they were there? "Who's an exile? Baby, watch your marshmallow, it's going to fall."

Skye eased her stick toward herself and tested the marshmallow between her thumb and index finger. "My frog. I'm worried. He's an exile."

Laurel frowned. "No, baby, he's not an exile. He's just turned around for a minute."

"The map said he wasn't supposed to be here."

"You told me it said 'no data available.' So, we don't know. Maybe you're the first person to notice a tree frog here."

"But he was so gray."

"Didn't you say tree frogs change colors according to their environment, like chameleons?"

"I guess." Skye's voice was sticky with doubt. She ate her marshmallow and skewered another, rotating it above a cove of embers at the edge of the fire. "Thank you again for my present. I love it."

For weeks, Laurel had snipped and sewed and looped and threaded in every spare, hidden moment, to make Skye a satchel. She'd used worn-out jeans for its body and decorated it with calico owls cut from an old shirt of her grandmother's. She'd carved strap buckles from driftwood, had Casey at the rock shop drill a hole in an agate and hung it off the zipper pull with a ball-chain bracelet Sean had once given her, and taken the zipper itself off an old dress of Mom's, one of her elegant gowns from when she was trying to be a lounge singer and not the folk singer on endless tour in far-flung locales that she now was. Laurel was about to say she'd loved making it, when Skye went on in a confiding tone, "Abby's hoping to get a headlamp for her birthday. She can take the dogs out at night this year if her dad goes with her; she can drive her own team. Hamish and Corrine said I can go, too, if it's okay with you."

"Oh. Well. Probably."

"And also, she wants these boots we saw online. They're tall and rubber and pull on with little handles." Skye propped her stick on a rock and pulled at invisible tugs near one knee. "They're printed all over with flowers. She doesn't need them, she has two other pairs already, but I'll bet she gets them anyway."

And just like that, the cobbled bag with its salvaged parts—the lining from another fancy dress of Mom's, the owl's eyes jet buttons from Gran's wedding suit—was inadequate, the poor country cousin of birthday gifts.

Skye sighed, either with contentment or with envy of Abby's fortunes, and, after one more marshmallow, fed her stick into the fire and spread her blanket on the sand. The flames flickered and swayed; sparks jumped up. The legs of Laurel's jeans grew hot; her bones warmed. She should have felt one hundred percent relaxed, but she didn't, not until Skye whispered, "It's nice, isn't it? By the fire, under the stars?"

The water lapped; a late-flying gull landed with a clatter. From the woods a coyote howled once and fell silent. Laurel thought Skye was asleep, when she said, "Mom?"

"What?"

"Will we ever have to move, do you think?"

The fire lit Skye's face; her gaze was aimed upward and her hands cinched her head. Again, she seemed remote and grown in a way that Laurel wasn't ready for. "No. Why?"

"Ms. Trevor said Abbott's parents are moving down below for jobs."

"I haven't heard anything about that."

Skye's head swiveled toward Laurel; now instead of distant she appeared young and heartbroken. "It's true, though. It's supposed to be a secret, I guess that's why Abbott didn't tell me right away. His parents didn't want to ruin everybody's summer. Ours, I mean. Mine and Abby's and Abbott's. But now school's starting and they're going."

"Oh, sweetie." Laurel held her arms out and Skye scrambled into her lap. Abbott, Abby, and Skye had made up their entire grade since kindergarten. In McAllaster it might've been eight or ten kids and in Crosscut twenty or thirty, but here classes were tiny and functioned like families—the three children were as close as siblings. For one to leave was unthinkable, a rending of their fabric. Laurel breathed in the smoky, coconut scent of Skye's hair. "I'm sorry. I know you'll miss him."

Skye nodded.

"Why didn't you tell me sooner?"

Skye's shoulders hitched up. "I was trying to pretend it wasn't true." Laurel began to say *Oh, sweetie* again, but before she could, Skye said, "Like you do."

"What do you mean?"

Skye ran her thumb across Laurel's now-quicker pulse. "I guess the way you always look on the bright side, never on the bad."

Laurel's heart thunked like a tennis ball in a dryer, despite the apparently laudatory nature of this comment.

Skye leaned deeper into her. "Mom? Would you ever get back together with Sean?"

"No."

"Are you sure?"

Sean appeared in Laurel's head: smiling, guitar in hand, hair and beard scruffy. She closed her eyes and concentrated on the feel of her feet on the sand. "Yes."

"He's sad without us, though."

Probably true. But truer was that Skye was sad without him. "I know. But he'll be okay."

"And Aunt Jenny's sad about it, too."

Mad, was more like it.

"I don't want her to be."

"I know." Laurel didn't either, not mad or sad, but like certain truths about yourself, some situations you had to accept, no matter how unwanted or uncomfortable.

"It was all so perfect before. Auntie Jenny and I both said so on the phone the other day."

Laurel shifted to ease a sudden pain in her back, though it didn't release.

"Sean was kind of like a dad to me. You know? In the year we lived there?"

Laurel tangled her fingers in Skye's hair, gave an apologetic tug.

"Ouch, that pulls."

"I'm sorry."

Skye squirmed. "It'd be amazing, being a twin."

"Would it?" Mom and Uncle Milton were twins and as different as if they'd been raised in different galaxies.

"Do you think Sean and Aunt Jenny had their own language when they were little?"

"Not that I know of. I wouldn't ask him, though." Sean avoided talking about his childhood—both he and Jen did.

Skye's nod rocked Laurel's chin. "I'm making him a card when I make Rip's. To say I love him lots."

Laurel relaxed. "That's a good idea. But we should hush now, and watch the fire. And the sky. It's meteor time!"

"For sure we won't move?" Skye asked again a while later.

Laurel kept her eyes trained on the heavens. "Not planning on it. Know why?"

"Because we're Hills."

"Right. And what do Hills have?"

"*Sisu.*"

"Bingo. And where do Hills live?"

"Gallion!"

"Right again. We're Hills, and we have grit, and we live here, and that's the whole story." Laurel latched her arms around Skye's belly. Her mother had moved Laurel around plenty before she let her stay with Gran in Gallion, and Laurel had known she would never do that to her own child. In Gallion she was someone. She had roots and history, she had joy and freedom. She had family—half the people in town were family, not by blood but by action and affection—and context. Away from Gallion, she'd been no one. A quiet, poor kid with bad shoes and worse clothes and no idea how to care much about those things. A homesick kid who'd sat in half a dozen new schools in towns downstate and discovered herself to be untransplantable, a fish trying to live on a sidewalk.

Skye craned her head. "Promise?"

Laurel squeezed tighter. Here, Skye was a wonder, a little wise-woman. Out there, she'd get eaten alive. "Yes. I pledge and avow. To the best of my ability, I will keep us here, in heaven."

Skye pointed at the stars, a silent correction.

Laurel laughed. The misgivings that had flickered all day turned to smoke, burned up by the fire and crisp air and by Skye's easy return to happiness. "Close enough. Bet you can't find anywhere closer."

# Three

The hours spun past and clouds rolled in; by two a.m. the stars were hidden and the air smelled like iron. Laurel roused Skye and they packed their things, moving slow with cold and contentment. They'd eaten two slices of pizza and two hot dogs each and polished off half a bag of marshmallows. Laurel had seen forty-six shooting stars; Skye claimed she'd spied sixty-two and a half. Now it was time for bed. They ambled to the car—old, gray, inherited from Gran and not what it used to be, but still limping along—and Laurel stuck her key in the ignition. "Did we forget anything?"

Skye leaned against her door, already half-asleep. "It'll be there tomorrow if we did."

This was true. Even with all the changes, Gallion was a safe town. Safe, unassuming, a speck on the map with no special claim to fame besides beauty, and even that didn't compare to the towns farther west along the shore, the ones with crashing waterfalls and rocky cliffs and newer motels. Gallion had plopped itself down next to the water in 1859, home to a handful of fishermen and farmers (of potatoes; it was too cold for much else), some of whom were Laurel's ancestors. It hadn't changed much since then, though now its main industry was tourism instead of fishing and logging. But even with the resulting influx of traffic and visitors, of services and knickknacks for sale in every shop, of T-shirts and coffee mugs printed with a hundred varieties of the directive to visit Gallion, it remained a modest and down-to-earth place, a place about as big as a tackle box, and as efficient in its contents: four churches, two motels, one gas station, one market, one bar, one bank, one school, and one out-of-business café, where Laurel had washed dishes and bused tables when Skye was a toddler. That was it, and it was plenty. Laurel had suspected early on that most of the time what people really needed was within themselves. Gallion was quiet enough to hear that needed-thing whispering, wild enough to glimpse it if you looked. Not like the cemented-over places Mom dragged them to again and again when Laurel was young, chasing her dreams.

The ghosts of Laurel's former selves lounged and lingered everywhere as she drove along the silent streets. On the bench in front of Johnson's Gas where she and Jen and everyone—Sean, Jeff, Louise, Brian—loitered in the summers, nibbling candy and watching tourists. At the sledding hill they careened down, the park where they shot baskets and sipped clandestine cans of beer, the campground she ran through with the wind off the water like a hand on her back urging her along.

She turned off the main street onto Second and then again onto

Railroad. Half a block past the corner, she stopped. Their rental had been built as a summer cottage in the 1930s, when things—some things, anyway—were simpler. It was twenty feet by twenty, covered in green-painted cedar shingles, with cream-colored shutters and a red shingle roof. Sweet as it was, that roof needed patching, the windows were single paned, and the door locks didn't work. That didn't matter, though, not in Gallion. None of it did. Laurel jostled Skye's arm. "Wake up," she whispered. "We're home."

Inside, Skye heeled off her sneakers and plonked her bags on the floor. "I'm taking a shower."

"Leave some hot water."

" 'Kay." She disappeared into the bathroom but was back before Laurel had even stowed the leftovers away, a towel clutched around her body. "The water quit."

"You're kidding."

Skye shook her head and Laurel sagged. Four times now in the four months they'd been here this had happened. Harv fiddled with the pump but hadn't replaced it, and they'd learned to keep a five-gallon bucket filled. "We should've gone in the lake before we left the beach, I guess."

"Yeah."

Skye stood planted as a shrub, regarding Laurel as if she expected her to resolve the issue right now, but Laurel didn't see how she could. She'd call Harv in the morning and hope he'd take care of the problem this time. Beyond that she was helpless. Places to rent weren't thick on the ground in Gallion. Just the opposite. She grabbed a saucepan out of the drainer. "Sponge baths it is."

24

"Grah," Skye growled, a disgruntled old man. She cinched her towel tighter. "Can you heat enough for my hair? It's all sandy."

Laurel left the twinkle lights on and crawled into bed beside Skye half an hour later, her own hair still smoky with campfire. She'd been too tired to heat more water after Skye's. Her eyes roamed over their belongings: a rocker she'd found beside the curb in front of a summer house, a footstool Granddad had made for her when she was young, shelves she'd built from driftwood planks that she'd dragged home from the beach, the small oak dining table that had come from Gran's. They were lucky to have that. Lucky to have the bureau they stowed their clothes in, too. Her great-grandfather had built it out of bird's-eye maple, so it was worth real money, and Mr. Clark, who owned Gallion Savings and Loan, could've insisted they leave it for the auction when Mom lost the house, but he hadn't. He told them to take it and a few other things—Great-Grandma Greta's sewing kit and rolling pin, Great-Grandfather Aapo's shotgun, this bed they were lying in, the one Skye was born in—and wished them well, his eyes damp.

Sean had been there helping, since Jen couldn't make it, and now strolled into Laurel's head again, his eyes smiling and his grin easy. But then his cheer vanished. He wasn't smiling; he wasn't anything. He was blank, gone, unreachable.

Laurel pushed his image away and replaced it with a house. Her favorite daydream, the one she comforted herself with in the middle of the night, entertained herself with while she washed dishes at Belle's and cleaned rooms at the Lakeshore. With a house and some land, even just a little, they could have a garden. They could put vegetables up like Gran always had—can tomatoes, pickle cucumbers, grow dill to flavor them with—and keep a goat or a cow for milk. Learn how to make cheese. Plant apple trees, put in a rhubarb bed, have flowers everywhere. They'd dig a root cellar and keep potatoes and carrots all winter, build a henhouse and raise chickens for eggs. For meat, too, if she could bear to slaughter them. Probably she could. She usually could do what she had to when it came down to it.

Wiggling farther into the pillows, Laurel unspooled more daydreams. With a garden, they'd save money on food, and it would be better food, too: tastier, healthier, more nutritious. Plus, Skye would learn the things Laurel had learned from Gran: planting, growing, preserving, cooking—simple fare but good fare.

Laurel let her daydream lead her into a room for each of them. To a couch of their own instead of Harv's. To a woodstove with an easy chair in front of it. With a woodstove she wouldn't have to pay so much for propane and Skye would have the memories Laurel did, of huddling beside it on cold days. Plus, a fire warmed you twice, the way people said.

An image of herself and Mom and Gran bouncing out to the state land in Gran's pickup slid into her head and every atom of her being shied away from it. In its place she conjured up a kitchen with plenty of shelves, and hooks for pans, and walls painted colors she chose, and water that always ran.

She glanced at Skye. It was one thing to wash up in the sink or bathe in the lake in the summer, but when school started, Skye needed better. Even in Gallion it would be a cloud hanging over her if they didn't have water. The box with her envelopes of cash lay beneath the bed. She could repair the pump, even buy a new one. She was handy, she could put it in herself.

But Harv would never let her; he'd insist on doing it himself and then drag his feet about it. A bleak feeling slammed into her and she tried to shove it away. Felt the pulse in her feet, the sand pebbling her skin, the brush of the sheet on her toes. Soon her thoughts slowed and smoothed. A house. A house of their own. It would give them security. It would let them look people in the eye, give them standing and confidence. It would give them roots.

Laurel tugged a corner of sheet from beneath Skye and Skye's fingers encircled her wrist.

"Sorry I woke you," Laurel whispered.

"I was awake."

"You were?"

"I . . . forgot to tell you something."

"What?"

Skye's grip tightened. "Um. Harv stopped by. While I was painting."

Laurel had that falling feeling that sometimes startled her out of sleep. She propped herself up on her elbow. "What did he want?"

"I'm not sure. He didn't say."

Laurel sat all the way up. "Tell me what he said."

"Are you mad?"

"I don't know. I think you didn't forget to tell me he came by. You didn't want to tell me."

"Because you'd be mad," Skye whispered. "And it was my birthday."

"What did he say?"

Skye squeezed her eyes shut to recall. "He said it surprised him to find me home alone. That we sure had a lot of pictures hung. And that I hurt the maple tree. Somebody saw me getting the branches, I guess, and called him."

Laurel's heart hammered.

27

"I told him I was sorry! I explained about the frog, how it needed something leafy and not dead."

"Harv Duke is not going to care about a tree frog."

"He did, though! I gave him one of my paintings and he didn't act mad anymore. Not as mad."

Laurel released her breath in increments. "What did he say about Harper? And Frank?" Frank was Skye's gerbil, a Christmas gift from Sean last year, misidentified as a boy at first.

"Not that much. Nothing, really." Skye's words were a pileup in progress. "I don't even know if he noticed Frank. He said what's the dog's name and is he yours. So, I told him Harper and all about finding him. To kind of distract him from, you know, the tree branches."

Most likely Harv had known about Harper already, the way everyone always knew everything here. And none of this was Skye's fault. It was Laurel's own for leaving her alone. If only Margie wasn't gone, Margie and almost everyone like her. Much as Laurel tried to deny it, Gallion was changing. Women willing to look after a child six days a week for a pittance? As rare as agates. Rarer. "That was nice of you."

"I gave him a glass of lemonade, also."

"That was a good thing to do."

"He talked a lot, and I wished he would go."

The room was too bright now. Laurel leaned to pull the cord on the twinklers. "Talked about what?"

"Everything. How many tourists there are now and how high the taxes have shot and how those people who bought Great-Gran's place must be loaded, with all that work they did on it so fast. That most of all."

Harv Duke had always been a gossip. At Graham's he used to go on for hours over a cup of coffee and not even leave Jen a tip.

"I thought it was tacky of him, to talk about them like that."

"You're right, it was."

"He went back outside, finally. He climbed up on the ladder and poked at the roof. And he scraped at the paint where it's flaking down by the cement in back."

Laurel kneaded her neck. "I see."

"He isn't really mad at us, is he?"

Skye's voice was folded small; she tiptoed worried fingers up Laurel's arm. Laurel caught her hand. "I doubt it. Who could be mad at you?"

# Four

S wear to God, she should be at Cranbrook." Jenny stood in front of Laurel's fridge on the last Monday in September, licking toffee ice cream from the back of a spoon and staring at Skye's latest frog painting. She'd shown up Friday night bearing armloads of packages, weeks late but no dollars short, as if she wanted to make up for a summer's worth of coolness between them by showering Skye with gifts. "Surprise!" she sang when Laurel opened the door, shoving a fistful of foil balloons forward. She wore silver high-heeled sandals, skinny jeans, and a shimmery blouse the color of sunrise. She had brought no pajamas and no change of clothes, and now sported a pair of Laurel's sweatpants and a faded pink T-shirt that read *Get Going to Graham's!* in script across the front. After Skye had left for school, Jen had paced the patio talking on her phone for an hour, her expression stormy, one arm wrapped around herself. Jen-style, she dropped all this when she was finished and came back inside talkative, teasing, and pushy.

Now she tapped Skye's latest painting, a spiderweb with leaves caught in it and yet another tree frog crouched in the corner. The leaves looked real; the color behind the web was a swirl of blues and greens that suggested both air and water; the frog seemed on the verge of speaking. "She should."

Laurel folded a pink sock into its mate. Skye had worn them nonstop after she tore the package open Friday and Laurel had to pull them from her feet to wash them last night.

Jenny turned. "I'm serious."

"Jen. I couldn't afford Cranbrook if I robbed every bank between here and Bloomfield Hills. Besides, Skye's too young to go to boarding school."

"I'd have thrown a party if Faith sent me to boarding school when I was ten. The answer to my prayers, that's what that would've been."

"Mm."

"She'd be fine. She'd be great."

"Thus spaketh General Jen."

"Oh, I forgot for a minute, we're riding the Laurel Limited. Not going far, just a few stops. One little route, same old view." Jenny hooked her arm around Laurel's neck and bumped their heads together.

"Well, it's out of my league any way you look at it."

Jenny let Laurel go. "Scholarships, La. Greatest invention of the century. I'll bet she could get one, even for this term."

"School started three weeks ago, Jen."

"So, winter term."

"No."

"You guys should come and stay with me and Oren, then. She should, at the very least. The schools are great—all kinds of after-school programs—it'd be perfect for her."

"Are you crazy?" Even if Laurel had been interested, she would never move them in with Jen and a boyfriend, especially one with whom she was obviously feuding.

Jen blinked. "Good to know you trust me."

Laurel cleared her throat. "I trust you. But there's no way I'm sending Skye away. To anyone."

"Move, then."

"What?"

Jen narrowed her eyes. "Move, La. Re-lo-cate. To Traverse, where you could get a real job and have a real life and live like real, regular people."

Laurel tucked two more of Skye's socks together. She had given her this pair, one of those deliberate mismatches that were popular now, their colors the same but their patterns different.

"Hello? Anybody home?"

Laurel gave Jen the glare she sometimes deserved. "I'm home. That's the point. Skye and I are home and we're not leaving, not for Cranbrook or Traverse or anywhere else. And our life is real. Not to your tastes, maybe, but real."

Jen slid a finger along a rung of the rack where Laurel hung the laundry. Yesterday, Laurel had hauled water from the Lakeshore, heated it on the stove, and washed their clothing in the bathtub, and now those clothes were drying. She'd avoided Harv since Skye's birthday. Put the rent in his mailbox, watched for his car in town, and didn't go into Phil's Market or Johnson's or the post office if he was there. No water was bad, but reminding him of their existence might be worse. "There's nothing for her here. For either of you. Look at you." Jen shook a towel to force its bend smooth. "You're living like settlers, like pioneers, like that ad on TV about upgrading from cable. It's ridiculous."

Laurel hunted up two more socks to pair. "We have what matters." Community. History. Context. Beauty. And also, safety. Anywhere else, they'd be tree frogs exposed to the boiling sun on a square of cement.

Jen shook her head and Laurel wanted to drag her outside, point out the lake pounding onto shore a few blocks away. She wanted to make Jen breathe the air and smell the water and wave at everyone who knew her, truly knew her, not glancingly the way people did in other places. She wanted to coax her into hunting for cranberries and cranes, for frogs and phoebes. She wanted to make her notice the earth under their feet and wake her to the satisfaction of living on it and coping with its challenges. But there was no point. Jen was as stubborn about her opinions as Laurel was about her own. "My great-grandmother lived this way. Harder. Gran, too."

"Come on. You think they loved scrubbing all those clothes in washtubs? It's a waste of time. If it was just you, that'd be one thing. But you have to think of Skye."

Laurel's head snapped up. "I always think of Skye."

Jenny grimaced. "Sorry."

Laurel snatched a towel from the rack. It was still damp, but she folded it anyway.

"Forgive me?"

"Nothing to forgive."

Jenny rumpled her lips in a way that made Laurel forgive her a little after all. Turning to the fridge, Jen tapped a magnet that read *Love is a friendship set to music.* Laurel's mother had sent it. She was always sending magnets, to Jen's endless amusement. "How's your mom doing, anyway? Still up in Canada with her true love, Link?"

"They're happy." Laurel folded a T-shirt with a Superwoman emblem on it. *To Skye's-the-limit. From your one and only AUNT JEN,* Jen had written on the tag.

"Loyal Laurel."

Laurel inspected a pair of Skye's dungarees. A hole gaped in one knee. She set them aside for patching.

"They're dreamers."

"Is that so terrible?" Laurel asked.

"You would say that."

Laurel glared and Jen grimaced. "Sorry. Again."

Laurel liked the magnets, but it embarrassed her that she did. She also loved her mother, even if she couldn't entirely forgive her for her mistakes.

"Are they working?" Jen asked, still studying the magnets.

"They're always working."

"Are they earning anything?"

Laurel's cheeks heated. "They booked a bunch of gigs on the back side of Cape Breton Island this winter."

"Do they pay?"

A jolt of anger coursed through Laurel. But Jen eyed her expectantly, as if it was her business to know, and maybe it was. Still, she glanced away as she answered. "A little. And they get room and board at most of the taverns, and she says they'll run into great people, other fiddlers and singers."

"And I'll bet you won't be able to reach her for weeks on end."

Laurel bent her head to hide her irritation. "I'm an adult."

"I still say Lynnette's a tad bit flighty."

"Hard to believe you used to have such a crush on her."

Jen touched the *Love is a friendship* magnet again. "Her voice is fantastic."

"Yes, it is." That was part of the problem. Laurel couldn't help but understand the choices her mom had made, the dreams she'd trailed after.

Jen moved to the sink and gazed out the window. "It's just, I worry about you guys."

Laurel stopped folding. "Why?"

"You're on a shoestring. It's dangerous."

Laurel studied her friend. Narrow waist, curvy hips, cascading hair, and an edge-seeking personality to match: Jen was the one in danger. Laurel assumed from the moment Jen arrived that something had happened on Friday, something bad enough to make her appear unannounced from two hundred miles away. A fight with Oren, a flirtation with a stranger. "That's a little melodramatic," Laurel said gently.

Jen turned. "You told me Harv might jack up the rent, or take your deposit."

"He didn't, though. I doubt he will."

"You hope."

"I do." It was what Gran had taught her—hope was a choice you made.

Jen sighed. "Do you know, when I came into town there wasn't one car moving? Not a car, not a person. One dog, Edwina's beagle. It's appalling. It's too small a world, it's like solitary confinement."

Sometimes it was like that. Even so, Laurel said, thinly, "Thanks."

"I didn't mean you. But sorry. Again."

"Three strikes and you're out."

Jenny laughed, her eyes bright as spring grass. She came and flung her arms around Laurel and Laurel had to drop the sweatshirt she was turning right side out. "You'd never evict me, it's not in your nature."

Laurel breathed into Jen's sweet-smelling neck and returned her embrace, smiling. "Never assume," she said.

"Cranbrook, darling," Jen called, rolling down her car window. She wore her own clothes again and looked as sleek as a magazine ad despite three nights on Harv's lumpy couch and two days of sponge baths in kettle-heated water. "Or better yet, Traverse with wonderful me! Just cross that bridge."

The Mackinac Bridge, she meant. The big, beautiful Mackinac, dangling from its cables in a way that seemed impossible if you thought too hard about it and hooking the Lower Peninsula to the Upper, a gigantic train car coupling. Most of the state's inhabitants lived in the southern car; just a few hardy souls hoboed on the northern one.

"Four fifty's all you need for a one-way ticket." Jen plunged her hand into the change cup she kept in her console and came up with a fistful of coins. She held them toward Laurel. "Easy-peasy. You have what you need right here."

Laurel folded Jen's fingers back over the money. "That's right. I do."

Jen dropped the coins back into their cup. "Think about it."

"Aye, aye."

Jen pulled away, blowing kisses behind her.

Inside, Laurel frowned at the folded laundry. Jen was wrong: Gallion wasn't dreary and confining; Skye wasn't being cheated. They'd boiled life down to the basics, was all; what was most essential remained.

She stopped in front of the frog painting on her way to the bureau. The magnet holding it in place read *You can if you think you can* in yolk-colored letters. Laurel wiped a smudge of jam from it. Jen had laughed at it, but what was wrong with being told to never give up as you pulled your milk out in the morning? If she hadn't proceeded as if success was inevitable, where would Skye be?

# Five

Laurel measured oats and water into a saucepan, then tossed a pair of balled-up socks at Skye's head. "Time to wake up, it's daylight in the swamps." They were halfway through October now. Leaves were falling; the nights were sliced through with cold. Good for sleep, hard for waking. In truth, Laurel was just as inclined to burrow into her covers as Skye. She didn't—needs must when the devil drives, Gran would have said—but in her marrow, she yearned to. Skye groaned. Laurel zoomed a paper airplane she kept handy for this purpose at her head and returned to the oats. They churned to a boil and an earthy scent rose from the pan as it had in Gran's kitchen when Laurel was young. She listened for movement. "No kidding," she called. "The oatmeal's done, the clock's ticking."

A series of clattering thunks sounded as Skye rolled off the mattress; she always had a stack of books piled beside the bed. She shuffled over to Laurel in the hand-knit socks Laurel's mom had sent from Cape Breton and pink flannel pajamas printed with rearing horses and lariat-swinging cowboys, another birthday gift from Jen. Her eyes were half-closed; even her shoulders seemed sleepy. Laurel smoothed a lock of Skye's sideways-poking hair. "Rise and shine, it's a brand-new week. Time to take some sustenance."

Skye scrubbed at her face with her palms like a long-distance trucker awaking from a too-short nap, then scooped raisins into her cereal and sat. Laurel carried a mug of coffee and her own bowl to the table. "You finished your homework?"

Skye tipped her head toward her satchel. "It's in there."

"Need me to check it?"

Skye fished out folders, workbooks, and a notebook and returned to spooning up oats, methodical and still blank with sleepiness, and Laurel drew the stack closer. Checking her work was a formality—it was always done, and always right—but following the bread-crumb trail of Skye's thoughts was a chore Laurel never tired of.

She opened the math workbook. Pluses and minuses, $x$'s and $y$'s, figures and brackets marched down the page in close ranks; every equals sign was the barrel of a drawn shotgun. Laurel's mouth filled with a metallic tang. Mrs. Denise Fisher of Kalamazoo, Michigan, had made her sit in the corner when she handed in an unfinished math test in the fifth grade, certain she was malingering. Laurel had taken her punishment in silence rather than admit she was stupid and not stonewalling.

Skye reached across the table and tapped the page with her spoon. "I adore math."

Laurel smiled to herself. "I know you do."

"It's a puzzle you can always solve."

"Mm."

"It makes your brain feel good."

Laurel squinted one eye shut and Skye hitched herself forward. "Well, because it always makes sense. It's like music. Your brain just enjoys it. You solve an equation and it's like Lego pieces snapping together in your head. You can kind of feel it." She patted around on her skull with one palm, as if there might be a door she could open to reveal the workings, a place Laurel might shine in a flashlight and see toothed gears turn. "It almost makes a sound, you know?"

"Sure." Laurel had flunked math her freshman year at college. First math, then with a swiftness that still made her stomach hurt if she thought about it, biology and history and finally even English.

"It's fun."

"Whatever you say." Laurel moved on to the science workbook and read a fill-in-the-blanks about comets. A comet was a celestial object, Skye declared in firm, round script. It had a nucleus of ice and dust and often a long tail of gas. Its orbit was eccentric; its head appeared fuzzy and its heart bright.

Laurel's own heart glowed. Here was her girl, learning as she and her mother and grandmother had learned, in Gallion's old redbrick school with its clanking radiators and high ceilings and windows that let in acres of sunlight and sweet air and daydreams, its marble staircases and photos of every graduating class lining the entry hall. The class of '59 was Gran's, twenty-two seniors with somber smiles; the class of '82 Mom's, with seventeen; the class of 2005 with Laurel and Jen and Sean and Jeff Hoover, plus Brian Carney and Louise Griffith, who had married each other and moved out west and become astronomers. Maybe that was what Skye would do, though there wasn't any Brian—courtly, quiet, thin as a railroad track and smart as fresh paint, as Gran used to say—for her to marry.

Skye finished her oatmeal and clattered the bowl into the sink with the rest of the dishes Laurel was stockpiling until it was worth heating water. "I'm getting dressed."

"Take the kettle. Don't forget to wash behind your ears."

Skye shot her a look. "Mom. Please."

She stomped away and Laurel read a Language Arts report, "Amazing Animals in Our World."

The tortoise is one of earth's longest-lived creatures. A group of them is called a creep.

The owl has very good night vision and its ears are excellent. Their groups are parliaments.

A giant clam can weigh four hundred pounds and live to be one hundred and fifty years of age. That's a long time. (15 x 10 (my age) = 150.) Areas where there are a lot of clams are called flats, and the oldest clam ever found was called MING THE MOLLUSK. Ming was 507 YRS OLD!! Tragically, the scientists who were studying Ming killed him (her?) when they were figuring out how old he (she?) was. They opened Ming's shell to count the rings on it and Ming couldn't stand it.

Elephants are awesome. They purr like cats and also cry, play, and laugh. When they pass a place where a loved one has died, they stop and stand still for a long time. Their hide is thick, their ears are thin. Their groups are herds and they remember everything.

One of Laurel's own middle school reports had been about elephants; it still lay tucked in a box somewhere. She smoothed the paper, a sense of rightness spilling into her chest like water filling a bucket.

A few minutes later, Skye came out wearing jeans turned up at the cuffs and a shirt the color of split pea soup that they'd found at a thrift shop over the summer. She plopped onto the couch to tie her boots. Another secondhand find: bulb toed, ankle high, leather. She yanked the bows tight and pulled on a cap, blue-and-white-striped cotton, and her transformation into a miniature farm laborer out of some 1930s documentary was complete.

"Nice lid," Laurel said. "Where'd you get it?"

"Sam gave everybody one when he came to do music last week."

"Sam Lovell?"

Skye snugged the hat down. "The Sam who's married to Mary Lynn."

The Sam and Mary Lynn who bought Gran's house last spring—the latest in a line of new owners in the last half dozen years—and turned it into a bed-and-breakfast. At the start of the school year, they'd joined a handful of other adults in town who volunteered to share their skills with the students. Sam did music one day a week; Mary Lynn taught cooking. Lori Trevor, still instructing Gallion's high schoolers in English and Spanish as she'd done since Laurel was young, always urged Laurel to lead sewing classes or coach track or cross-country, but Laurel always told her she didn't have time, which was true. Even more true was that she couldn't have borne to coach running and couldn't imagine teaching sewing. It would make her nervous to stand up in front of a roomful of even familiar people, and convincing anyone that sewing was interesting—that it mattered and wasn't a dowdy craft out of an antiquated time when people didn't know any better, the way Jen frequently teased—seemed impossible.

It was good that skilled people like Sam volunteered, though. Laurel often heard him playing when she stole past Gran's into the woods beyond. (She shouldn't go there, but sometimes she had to.) To her he sounded like a professional, a pianist performing at some grand hall. She made herself smile at Skye. "Why'd he give you hats? You and Abby, you mean? Or everybody?" There were just the two of them in fifth grade now with Abbott gone, but twelve total in fourth through eighth, so few this year they were taught in one room.

"All of us. I don't know why. He's kind of funny."

"Funny in a good way?"

"Mostly, yeah. He's just—" Skye scrunched up her face, then shrugged, dismissing the puzzle. "Different. Kind of distracted. But he's good at the piano." She snagged her lunch from the counter. "Off to the mines."

Laurel suppressed a grin. "Be careful out there."

"Always."

Skye tromped out the door and Laurel moved to the window to watch her. At first, she clumped along slowly in the heavy shoes. Then she stuck her arms out and spun, making looping circles as she progressed toward the corner, her head tipped up to the sky like she was drinking it in.

"Mom, Mom!"

Skye barged through the patio door midway through Saturday afternoon, back from a night at Abby's. Laurel glanced up from hemming a pair of Levi's for Sharp, the bartender at Belle's. "Hey. What's up?"

Skye flourished a pamphlet. "Ms. Bainbridge came to visit Corrine this morning, and she had this in her purse—she's been carrying it around all fall. She wants you to read it."

The flyer advertised *Cedar Lake Academy, Summer Arts Programs*; the photo on the front showed a girl's hands shaping a piece of pottery. Slowly, Laurel unfolded the glossy paper. The left side listed the courses available—writing, dance, music, visual arts—and the right provided contact information. The gist of things lay in the center: program length, program dates, age range, tuition. Five thousand dollars for a two-week session. More than what they'd live on for the winter.

"Ms. Bainbridge says I should go there. Her nephew went for trumpet last summer and she drove down for his concert. She said it was wonderful."

"Hmm."

Skye's head bobbed in excitement. "She said I'd love it and I'd learn so much and that she thought you'd want to know about it. She hoped if you had lots of advance notice we could save up or something. And that I could try for a scholarship, though there aren't that many and they're only . . ." Skye squinted, trying to remember whatever word Ginnie Bainbridge had used.

"Partial?"

Skye clapped her hands to her cheeks. "Yes. Oh, Mom. Wouldn't it be amazing?"

Laurel laid the pamphlet down and patted it with the tips of her fingers. "Yes, it would. It surely would be."

"Do you think I could go?"

Laurel began picking out the stitches she'd put in the jeans for something to do with her hands. She could never afford this camp. Even if Skye got a scholarship. She'd never be able to earn enough, and the money from Margie was their security. She had to save it for something big—a college fund or an emergency, one she hoped would never happen but still must be planned for. Or, her real dream, the start of a down payment on a house.

Skye leaned against her. "Mom? Do you think so?"

Laurel plucked at the frays of thread left from the broken stitches. She answered without meeting Skye's eyes. "We'll see."

# Six

aurel pulled on work boots and ragged jeans and headed for Crank Masters's place on a cloudy Tuesday midway through November. The breeze whirred in the pines, and a half mile out of town, a black bear bounded across the road in bunching hops, a last dash before curling up in its winter burrow to hibernate through the lean months, a thing everyone here had to do one way or another.

When Laurel arrived at Crank's house, a tan-sided box framed by swampy woods, he was sitting on his porch pushing a rusting glider back and forth with one toe. He waved his cane in greeting. "Thought you weren't showing up. Thought I had the day wrong."

Laurel shoved her hands in her back pockets. "The car wouldn't start. I turned the key and nothing, just a click."

"Oh, boy."

"It's been doing that. Once I got a jump; the other time it cured itself by afternoon."

"Uh oh."

Laurel shrugged. Getting the car checked out would be a pain—nobody mechanical lived in town now with Abbott's dad gone—and she didn't want to dwell on it. The problem might go away; it only happened now and then. "Anyway, it's a nice walk. I saw a bear. Just past the dip in the road near the clear-cut."

Crank's face cracked into a grin. "Did you, now?"

Soon Laurel had the splitter chugging. She wrestled stump after stump to the platform and dropped the wedge through their centers while Crank observed from a webbed lawn chair he'd dragged into the yard. "Lot of work for a lady."

On a day like this, the air damp, the sky vast, the town more or less empty of anyone but locals, the oldest man in Gallion bundled into a puffy coat and earmuffs so he could keep her company, Laurel could think of no job she'd rather do. In the distance, Lake Superior knocked and crashed, a watery giant busy at his labors, banging rocks, shoving driftwood and timbers torn from ships and docks and pilings this way and that. Nearby, a jay squawked, as insistent on his message as anyone. Laurel winked at Crank. "Who says I'm a lady?"

Crank cackled, but then his expression turned sober. "I always wondered why you never finished college, a girl as smart as you. And all that talent."

Laurel pulled her gloves off to wipe her sweaty palms on her jeans. "You never saw my report cards. And running's no great talent. Set a bear out after anyone and they'll do it. Pretty quick, too."

Crank flapped a mittened hand in dismissal. "It's a hard life here for a woman alone. Or a man. A young person, leastways. Me, now, I've had my fun. You, though—"

"I'm not alone." Laurel yanked on her gloves again. "I have Skye."

Laurel worked until the last stump fell into wedges and every wedge was stacked under Crank's lean-to under an ever-steadier drizzle. The three twenties he handed her for this effort crackled in her pocket as she headed home, her boots splashing. She banged on the WELCOME TO GALLION sign at the outskirts of town, a hello punch to an old friend. The roadside grasses rustled; the breeze push-broomed clouds across the sky. By the time she reached Johnson's, another bank of clouds had rolled in. More work for the wind to do. The water was dark, the cries of the gulls forlorn. She waved at Edwina, who stood talking with the man who delivered their gasoline, and at Mr. Owens, who was cleaning windows at the Breakers. "Bill! Hullo!"

Bill Owens smiled at her and wagged his fistful of crumpled-up newspaper.

Laurel marched on past Graham's. It had been the Coffee Cup when she was young; you could still see the ghost of the sign painted on the side of the building, red block letters inside a black border. The Grahams had painted over it, but only one coat, and white, and it never took. It hadn't mattered—they'd gone under in less than a decade. Only Belle's and Johnson's could be sure of surviving; alcohol and gasoline ran the world. Even groceries might not save you. Phil did all right, but that was because he inherited the store from his parents. Also, he was smart enough not to try anything fancy.

She turned onto Railroad Street, first smelling smoke from someone's chimney and then seeing the windows of home glowing. She lingered outside, rain seeping down her collar. Skye stood at the stove, a dish towel tucked into the waistband of her jeans and a bandanna Laurel had never seen before tied on her head. Her lips moved, her head turned. She was chatting with Harper. Laurel hurried for the door.

Inside, she breathed deep. "Wow, smells good. What is it?"

"Risotto."

"Sounds fancy."

"It isn't. Mary Lynn showed us today."

"Ah." So far, all the dishes Mary Lynn Lovell had taught the kids were odd and fussy: Escargot, the snails out of a can. Sourdough bread from her own wild starter. Vichyssoise, nothing but potato soup served cold. And now risotto, whatever that was.

"It's rice," Skye said, reading her thoughts. "In broth, with vegetables. You cook the onions and celery super slow, so it brings out the flavors, which it doesn't if you cook it fast. Faster seems better, but Mary Lynn said it isn't always."

Laurel crossed the room and dragged a shoebox from beneath the bed. The first of Crank's twenties she slid into an envelope labeled *Petty Cash*, for groceries and any little things Skye might need. The second disappeared into one labeled *Monthly Expenses*, ready for the next batch of rent and utilities. Years ago, she'd drawn Old Man Winter blowing out a puff of cold air on the third envelope. That money was for the thin months. December, January, February, March, April if the weather was crummy. Even May in cold years. Nothing remained for the fourth envelope, *The Future*. It held only the deposit slip from the savings account she'd opened when Margie left her the surprise inheritance. It might always stay thin, a thought that was an anchor

49

chained to Laurel's leg if she let herself entertain it for too long. She nudged the box back under the bed and scrambled to her feet.

"How was Crank?" Skye asked. "Cranky?"

Laurel smiled. Crank was never cranky, the joke of his name. "He kept me company while I worked. Left the door open, so we'd hear if you called." She lowered herself to the table and closed her eyes. Tried to feel each length of bone inside her body, every muscle, every vertebra and tendon and joint. The physical therapist she'd seen for a strained tendon in college had said that was one way to manage pain. To accept it. To embrace it, even, dive right in and swim around in it.

Skye set a plate mounded with risotto in front of her and Laurel breathed deep. "Smells fantastic."

"I made salad, too." Skye pulled a bowl from the fridge and plunked it on the table: crisp leaves of romaine, rings of red onion, a scattering of croutons.

"Wow." Laurel plucked up a lettuce leaf. "Where on earth did you get romaine?"

"From Phil's."

"Ha." Groceries in Gallion didn't run to romaine, not in November. "Did Corrine bring it home from the Soo?" Abby's mom often drove to Crosscut or even Sault Ste. Marie to shop because she liked Greek yogurt and baby spinach and whole-grain bread. And romaine. None of which you could get here.

"I got it at Phil's. Mary Lynn talked him into carrying it."

Laurel raised her brows. "Let's see how long that lasts." She snapped her napkin out and said grace, then took a bite of salad. It was exotic to have the summery flavor of romaine in her mouth at this time of year. "Tastes great."

"Thanks."

"Thank you so much for making dinner. It's a big help; I'm beat."

"You're welcome." Skye took a dainty sip of water.

Laurel wiggled her fork at Skye. "So. Did you have a good day?"

"It was okay."

"Learn anything cool?"

"The risotto."

"Where did you get the bandanna? From Phil's?"

Skye touched her head with her fingertips. "Mary Lynn gave one to everybody. They're just little gifts, for fun."

"Sure."

"You'd like Mary Lynn, Mom. If you knew her."

Skye sounded so much like Gran that Laurel's face heated up. "You're probably right."

"I probably am."

Laurel ate a spoonful of risotto. "This is excellent. I'm so proud of you for being such a good cook and a hard worker."

"Thanks."

"I'm sorry you have to be here by yourself sometimes."

Skye grimaced. "I'm ten, Mom."

"I know. You're ten, and you're very capable. Everything always goes fine."

Skye tilted her head to the heavens. "Miraculous. Finally, you admit it."

"Today was no exception, I take it?"

Skye rolled her eyes. "Except that Harv stopped by and stayed forever. Again."

Laurel went still, her fork half-scooped into her rice. "He stopped by?"

"Just like last time. Somebody knocked, and the door opened and there he was."

"What did he want?"

"I don't know. He said a million things, but not that."

Laurel gripped her fork tighter.

"Mostly he talked about the Lovells and the bed-and-breakfast and how much money they must be making. He's rude."

"He can be."

Skye said nothing more and Laurel put risotto in her mouth, but she didn't taste it.

She was scrubbing around the stove knobs with a toothbrush when someone knocked the next morning. The door hinges creaked and Harv Duke appeared. "Good morning!" he boomed. He was somewhere past sixty, tall, with a paunch like a fanny pack strapped low on his stomach.

Laurel set the toothbrush down. "Hi."

Harv inspected the Christmas cactus that sat on the counter, then snapped off a piece. "Don't these things carry lice or aphids or something?"

"It's a houseplant, Harv. It belonged to my grandmother." She stuck her palm out and he rolled his eyes but handed over the section. She eased it into the soil and tamped dirt around it. "I put the rent in your box. Did you not get it?"

"I got it. Though, a word of advice, you shouldn't deal in cash for everything the way you do. Anyone could've come along and taken it, and it'd be your say-so against mine it was ever there." Harv opened her fridge, shut it again. "But no harm done."

Laurel picked up the toothbrush. Better to be armed with it, a task at hand, proof of her industry. "Was there something you wanted?"

Even if he raised the rent a hundred dollars, two hundred, they'd survive. And it was good he was here. She would tell him about the pump.

Harv crossed his arms. "I might as well tell you the bad news. The missus and me are going to vacation rentals."

The toothbrush clattered to the floor. "What?"

"You know, rent to tourists."

"Harv, you can't."

"Sure, we can. Everybody else is. Look at those folks who bought your gran's place."

Laurel sagged against the counter. "But now? It's the end of the season."

"Nah, the season never ends, not if you've got friends. I got buddies from downstate coming after Christmas."

"*Christmas.*"

"So, we need you out by then. The sooner the better. I need to bring in a new couch, a better fridge, refinish the floors."

"You're kidding."

Harv lifted a shoulder.

Laurel's ears rang. "Harv, come on. Skye's in school."

"No guarantees, you knew it when you moved in."

"But—"

"If you can be out by the middle of December, we'd sure appreciate it."

Laurel gaped at him. "I'm paid up through the first of January."

"I'm pretty sure I remember saying no pets, and I counted two both times I stopped by. Two pets, the walls covered in nail holes, graffiti in the bathroom, my landscaping torn up. I didn't expect you'd be so hard on the place, Laurel. And then there's the fact of you leaving your daughter alone here. The wife and me, we don't want any part of that."

Pain blew through Laurel's back and she gripped the counter's edge to keep from laying hands on him. That or begging. "Skye's never here alone for long, and she always knows where I am and how to get ahold of me, I promise you that."

Harv made a noise she couldn't interpret. Was he accepting her explanation or dismissing it?

"I'll putty the holes up when we go—or now, if you want. Putty and paint. And I'm sorry about the pets, I promise they're not destructive. Harper's better behaved than most people, and gerbils are super clean. They don't smell, Frank's never out of her cage, not running loose, anyway, and—"

Harv shook his head.

Laurel pressed her palms into the plea she'd resisted earlier. "Harv, please. We need this place. I'd pay more, I would."

"You have five hundred a week? 'Cause that's what we can get, easy. I've done my research."

He didn't have to make the excuse about the dog and the gerbil, or Skye home alone. All that didn't matter anyway, Laurel understood in a flash that made her stomach ache. The fact that he could rent by the week if he wanted had doomed them from the start: he'd had it in mind all along. The rent she'd paid would fix the roof and the locks, replace the fridge and the couch. Jen would've known it in an instant, but not Laurel. She was as naive as Jen thought.

Harv rapped the table. "Money, money. It makes the world go around."

Tears started in Laurel's eyes. "You're kicking a child out at the start of winter?"

"Hey, now, don't be putting this on me. Everything else aside, you know I said no lease. I said no lease and you said no problem. Remember how fast you took that deal?" He clicked his thumb and middle finger together and Laurel clenched her fists. Why had she not believed him?

# Seven

The fancy fridge dropped ice inside itself, the parlor mantel clock bonged, and the half-wild cat Mary Lynn was trying to domesticate streaked past Laurel's ankles in its daily bid for freedom. Laurel splayed one hand against her chest, a gesture both firm and gentling, and stepped into the kitchen.

It was her third time at the Lovells' since taking the job of being Mary Lynn's all-around dogsbody for the bed-and-breakfast. A gig she'd heard about at Belle's the day after Harv dropped his bombshell. She had been busing the few lunch tables and worrying about the future while Mary Lynn ate a burger and Sharp polished pint glasses.

"I'm about at the end of my rope," Mary Lynn had told him. "The doctor didn't make us understand what could happen. We thought, sure, a month or two, things'll be different—strange, I guess is how we put it to ourselves—but now here we are, five months later, and strange is the new normal. But what choice did we have?"

"Yeah," Sharp said.

Laurel nestled a plate into the bus box. Everyone knew Sam had undergone brain surgery in June, but she didn't know any details. Would you even be yourself afterward? Did your soul get disturbed, or was that a foolish question?

Mary Lynn squirted ketchup into her basket. "We wouldn't have started here if we'd known what would happen, but we didn't. And now I have winter coming and I don't know what I'm doing, getting ready. Plus, there're guests due this week, a couple sailing in. Sailing! In November! Even I know that's crazy."

Sharp clinked glasses onto a shelf. "It's been mild. They'll be all right."

"I have an appointment in the Soo, and there'll be dinner to cook and laundry to wash, the sauna to clean, a hundred other things, and Sam is just useless. Gosh, listen to me." She smote her own forehead. "I don't mean to be cruel. But I thought I could handle it, just little old me, and I can't. I need three hands or something. And a Vulcan mind meld with an expert in up-north living."

Sharp hadn't looked Laurel's way, but Laurel wiped her palms on the seat of her jeans and stepped closer anyway. "Hey, Mary Lynn?" She hadn't known where they would live in less than five weeks, but she had known that more income would be essential.

And now here she was.

The first minutes were always the hardest. *Gran?* some voice inside her would call out. *Mom? Are you here? Am I here somewhere, the original me, the one who never pictured things going this way?* But once she was busy, it wasn't so bad, or that was what she told herself and anyone else who asked: Jen, Phil, Sharp, Edwina. Even Lydia when Laurel walked past her the other day, lounging on a chaise in her parents' side yard as if it was another room of the house, which she often did, even in cold weather. The Makin place was small; there wasn't physical or emotional space for three adults. Laurel had told Lyd and everyone else that it was weird: her childhood home, changed just enough to be discombobulating. Like wearing old glasses when your current pair broke.

That was true, but the whole truth was bigger and harder. Tears often sprang to her eyes as she washed dishes and ran laundry, laid fires and swept floors. Especially when she swept floors. Gran and Great-Aunt Pam had been ten and eleven, respectively, the year of calamity when they put these floors down. That November, a heart attack had felled Gran's father as he walked in the door, clutching an armful of wood. Then the family home burned to the ground on Christmas Eve, ignited by the tree's candles. The men of the town helped Gran's brothers raise the walls of a new house in January, and each day after school Gran and her sister nailed down the ends and pieces of flooring the mill had donated, not one of them over six inches long. They scavenged the nails from the ashes of the old place, straightening each one so they could use it again. Nail after nail they straightened and pounded, day after day in the freezing weather. Thinking of what they'd been through and lost, and what she'd lost, too, made Laurel mad and sad and she didn't even know what else. But even with Jen she didn't talk about it. There was no point. Not in talking about it or thinking about it or even feeling it, no matter what that college physical therapist had said about pain.

Laurel hung her coat on a maple peg carved by a great-uncle and turned to the note Mary Lynn had left her. She'd scrawled a quote across the top: *This couldn't be just a lake. No real water was ever blue like that."—Dorothy Maywood Bird,* Mystery at Laughing Water. *Check it out!* Mary Lynn. So starry-eyed. But it was hard not to like her, as Skye had predicted. She was like a character out of a British novel, the horsey maiden aunt, the big-boned, odd one who raised bird dogs and had a secret broken heart. Or not so secret.

The book the quote came from lay next to the note, along with its mailing envelope and invoice. Forty-five bucks for something with *79¢* printed right on its battered cover. *Roughing it at camp is mixed with the thrills of solving an old family mystery!* a banner above the title proclaimed.

Laurel returned to Mary Lynn's note. *Guests arriving in the afternoon. Two in a boat, hope they don't sink. (Is it always so windy here?) Make up front bedroom—w/flannel sheets! Clean sauna & guest bathroom. Do laundry & hang outside, except towels. Towels=dryer= FLUFFY.* A circle like a kid's drawing of a cloud encircled "fluffy." *Start roast. Make salad and apple crisp & I'll bring whipping cream. And keep an eye on Sam, okay? Yes, Sam, that means you. Sorry, sweetie. I'll be back no later than 4, I hope. I'll leave my cell on but I doubt there'll be service most of the way. ?!*

Laurel gnawed on a thumbnail. She, too, hoped that Sam would be back no later than four and that nothing bad would happen to him in the interim, because even jolly Mary Lynn might not overlook Laurel having let her husband back his motorcycle out of the barn within five seconds of her arrival and zoom off into the distance. He hadn't even been wearing his helmet.

Sam zoomed in again just as Laurel was starting the salad. He parked the bike and sauntered toward the house as if no doctor had ordered him to stay away from motorized vehicles for a year. Inside, he scooped a handful of cranberries from the bag Laurel had sitting open on the counter. She still thought of these as Gran's cranberries. Mary Lynn had picked them from the bog Gran had always haunted and then dried them in Gran's dehydrator. Laurel had forgotten to snatch the dehydrator out of the house before the auction all those years ago, and so it had sat there, like the kitchen table and Gran's bird feeders, through two different owners who'd held brief, sporadic summer tenancies before the Lovells showed up. "Hey, howdy."

Laurel kept her face blank, though she felt relieved and annoyed in equal measures. "Hey."

"Smells good in here." Sam untied his boots, his movements languid. "The guests show up? The sailing people?"

"A while ago."

"They inside?"

"In the sauna."

If there was such a thing as natural ownership of a place, then the sauna, this one humble building on the earth's broad face, should belong to Laurel. It was a log hut with a tiny window beside the door, and her great-great-grandparents had lived in it while they cleared the land and built the barn and the first house. Lived in it, bathed in it, doctored in it, did the laundry there. Gran was born inside it and she had stuck Laurel in it to have every cold she'd ever come down with steamed out of her while she lay staring up at the plank ceiling. It would forever seem strange and wrong that all she had the right to do now was light the fire and clean out the ashes.

Sam leafed through the mail, looking trim and well dressed in his moss-green sweater and faded Levi's. "Huh. Great." He padded toward the parlor. A minute later, the music began. He was all the way through a crashing run of notes when Mary Lynn pulled in. A moment after that, the bus showed up and Laurel relaxed; the hiss of the bus's air brakes was a shot of joy into her veins.

Skye loped up the drive and burst in the door. "Hi, Mom!"

Laurel hugged her. "Baby, I'm so happy to see you. But you have to be quiet when you come in; there're visitors."

Skye's mouth rounded into an O. "Oops," she whispered. "Sorry."

"It's okay. Just—we're not at home, okay? Gotta be on our best behavior."

"Oh, nonsense." Mary Lynn appeared, quiet in her sneakers. "This is not some chain motel. At a B and B you expect family, you expect life."

Skye wriggled from Laurel's arms and sailed to hug Mary Lynn. She was chunky, with short brown hair and big hands, and was always smiling, though to Laurel the smile seemed like a veil cast over a deep sadness. The sorrow in her eyes faded as she held Skye, however. She lifted her off her feet and swung her side to side. "And I can't imagine a visitor who wouldn't adore you, Miss Blue Skye. As anyone would be mad not to. Mad as a hatter. Want to go pick apples?"

"*Yeah.*"

"Good deal. I'll change—I can't take another minute in these jeans, they've got too tight somehow—and you see if you can coax old Barnum in while I'm gone. Take some tuna. Supposed to be cold tonight; I thought I'd make him a bed beside the stove."

Laurel took a packet of wild-caught albacore from the cupboard. The cat, an ancient tom who nominally belonged to an old lady, Opal Manninen, on the next farm down, would burrow into the hay in any available barn and like it better, but there was no harm in letting Skye take the tuna out, or not much harm, anyway. She handed the pouch over and lifted Skye's owl satchel from her shoulder. "He doesn't come, you bring it back in. We'll save it for next time."

"Can't I leave it out for him, even if he won't come to me?"

"That cat can catch more mice than he knows what to do with, and if you leave it out, something else'll get it, a coon or a skunk."

"Maybe they're a hungry coon."

"Mary Lynn spent five dollars on that tuna. Waste not, want not, kiddo, that's how things really are in life."

Skye clattered out and soon Mary Lynn reappeared, glancing toward the parlor where Sam still sat playing the piano, an antique upright they'd had refurbished and brought in by special delivery in the summer. Rumor around Gallion priced it at over six thousand dollars. "Everything okay while I was gone?"

"Yes. Fine."

Mary Lynn cracked the oven door open and inhaled. "Nothing like old-fashioned apples for baking."

"No."

"You'll eat with us in the dining room tonight, you and Skye?"

"Oh— No. No, thank you."

"I don't want you to eat in the kitchen! It'd make me feel strange." Laurel swirled the dishcloth on the already-clean counter and Mary Lynn plowed on through her silence. "Please? I want my guests to know you two. You're part of this thing; you're not just an employee."

Mary Lynn made air quotes around the word "just" and Laurel smiled politely. There was no just, but Mary Lynn didn't know that. She couldn't; she didn't live in Laurel's world. "Whatever you like." She slid the salad bowl into the stainless steel fridge, which had double doors and a viewing window. Quite a change from Gran's old avocado-colored Whirlpool.

———————

Laurel and Skye headed home after helping to wash the dishes. The evening was brisk, the sun about to set, and they ambled along hand in hand, bathed in the golden last light of the day. Piano music followed them and Skye lifted her free hand and waved as if to conduct it. Laurel tapped Skye's thumb with her own. "You need a tailcoat and tie."

Skye rolled her eyes, then tugged free and jogged forward to turn a cartwheel, landing on her feet with her arms spread. She wore a purple velvet dress over the paisley leggings today, brown chukkas she'd found at a Salvation Army, a denim jacket with a sheepskin lining. Her scarf was long and fringy, her hat a black cloche with a rhinestone button on the side. "You're a picture," Laurel called.

Skye rolled her eyes again.

"Sam sure plays a lot," she said when Laurel caught up. The wind carried a faint melody to them.

"Yes, he does."

"Why, Mom?"

"He likes it, I suppose. He's good at it."

"But aren't you supposed to sit at the table for the whole time while you eat, if you're Sam? I mean, if you're the host person or whatever?"

"There's not one rule for everything. People are different. Sam's different."

Skye grabbed up an apple from the roadside and lobbed it at the Esso sign on the side of Opal Manninen's garden shed. It smacked the O with a thud and her eyes glinted with satisfaction. "I like Sam."

"He seems like a good guy." He did. He had a crinkly smile that made you want to smile back; he rinsed his dishes if he made himself a snack; he did not track across clean floors in dirty boots. But the only thing he seemed to care about besides playing the piano was riding his motorcycle. And with Mary Lynn, he was hopeless. She was always turning to him, to smile, to touch his arm, to tell him some dumb thing. He'd say, *Uh-huh* or *Oh?* but if you watched, you could tell he wasn't paying attention.

"I guess their life is just about perfect, huh?" Skye skimmed her hand along the tops of the daisy stalks that lined the road. "They have all those nice things. That piano! And her dishes— Wouldn't most people save them for special instead of using them for everyday?"

"Yep."

"Plus, that lamp on the sideboard—wow."

The lamp was art deco, a naked woman holding a globe above her head, and valued at two grand, according to the talk in Johnson's. The house was full of such treasures. A kitchen timer that shouted 1920 but kept perfect time, a scrimshaw letter opener Mary Lynn brandished with a carefree flourish, a blue teapot that appeared ordinary but wasn't—the sailboat woman had whispered its value to her husband after dinner: over three hundred dollars. For a teapot! Persian rugs adorned the parlor floors; vintage (and mint) Fiestaware filled the cabinets; framed paintings hung all over the place. Some even had lights shining on them.

"I think I like her Michigan stuff best."

"Me, too." Laurel was striving to keep her distance—from both the Lovells and their B and B—but in the face of Mary Lynn's Michigan collection, resistance was futile. She had decorated the mudroom with vintage advertising for Vernors ginger ale and Vlasic pickles, for

Fords and Cadillacs and Oldsmobiles, for Carhartt coats—*You can bet on America and Carhartt work clothes!*—and Wolverine boots, *The 1000 Mile Shoe.* Antique tins lined the tops of the kitchen cupboards—Velvet peanut butter, Pioneer sugar, Better Made potato chips, Sanders candy—and inside sat their modern-day counterparts, waiting to be served to Mary Lynn's guests along with stories about their founders and histories that bubbled from her like concoctions simmered in the coziest, most durable cast-iron kettles.

Pewabic tiles and pottery lined the fireplace mantel; hardbacks by Robert Traver and James Oliver Curwood, Edna Ferber and Nelson Algren, packed a bookcase; framed photos of Francis Ford Coppola and Joe Louis and scores of Motown singers covered one wall of the narrow front porch, now renovated into an all-season entertainment room with a fully functional vintage stereo and a big-screen television for movie watching.

"It's good to have a theme," Mary Lynn had told Laurel one day, straightening a painting of a lonely pine tree poking into a big, hazy sky. "It's good to know where you're from and what you're about."

Despite herself, Laurel had leaned forward with a shock of recognition, an internal *Yes* she didn't want but couldn't deny.

"And their own business." Skye now whacked the hapless daisies with a stick. "Can you imagine anything more perfect?"

"Our life is about perfect, you goof." Laurel tugged them to a halt at the corner of Plank Hill and they gazed out over the water. The lake was steely blue and so was the mirrored sky; a pink belt of sunset ran between them. She draped an arm over Skye's shoulder. "Pretty."

Skye drew a line in the air like she was pulling down a shade. "It changes so fast."

Even while they watched, the sun plummeted out of sight.

Skye burst forward, but Laurel held her back. She had to tear the Band-Aid off. "Listen, baby. I have some bad news."

Skye's expression turned dark as Laurel explained about Harv and their rental. "This stinks."

"It does."

"We have everything the way we like it."

"I know."

"Moving is going to be a pain."

An understatement. "Yeah."

Skye whacked at the roadside grasses. "I never liked Harv."

"Me neither."

"I have a question." Skye strode ahead and Laurel hustled to keep up, her heart banging with dread.

"Yes?"

"Can I ride the bus up here tomorrow?"

Laurel blinked. She'd expected something weighty. "I don't work tomorrow."

"I want to help Mary Lynn make cider." Skye grabbed her hand. "There's a ton to do. We have to gather the apples and clean them, and figure out how to work the press."

"She has an apple press?"

"She stopped at a yard sale today and couldn't resist, though it cost more than it ought to've, given what she was getting."

"Did it now."

"She said she'd clean it up tonight so we can play with it. I can't wait. The cider will be tasty and special instead of pasteurized and blah. It'll have flavor, it'll be real. Which what you buy in the store isn't."

"No," said Laurel. "Of course not."

"It's all strained and diluted—" Skye shuddered. "Anyway, this'll be good. Plus, we can let it go tingly, which the store kind won't. Isn't it cool?"

"Oh. My. Yes."

What a pity she'd splurged on a gallon of the inferior type at Phil's that morning.

# Eight

"Mom, what're you doing?" Skye leaned over Frank's cage, dribbling sunflower seeds into her food dish. "I thought we were playing Boggle."

Another week had passed and the answer to their housing dilemma had yet to materialize. Laurel dug a sweater from their bureau. Cashmere, Lord & Taylor. She had found it at St. Vinnie's years ago and accidentally shrunk it in Jen's dryer so that now the sleeves were six inches short and the waistband rode up under her breasts, but Laurel still liked it. She always wore it over a fitted T-shirt Mom once sent her, white with a lace hem, so even shrunken it was stylish. "I'm figuring out something to wear. Friday night, right? Time to kick up my heels."

"Is that why I'm going to Mary Lynn's?"

"Yep. Gotta stash the baggage." The day before, in line at the market, Mary Lynn had overheard Laurel talking to Phil about needing a sitter—Abby was going out of town for the weekend—and she had jumped in and offered to do the honors. There'd been no graceful way to refuse and no real reason, either.

Skye came close and brushed a finger across the cashmere. "What with it?"

"What about this?" Laurel held up a slim black skirt Jen had given her years ago. Skye approved it—*sexy!*—and by eight Laurel was decked out: skirt, sweater, and the spike-heeled boots she hadn't worn since last November when she and Sean went to the American Legion fish fry in Crosscut, one of their last dates.

Skye made a frame with her hands, tilted it like a camera. "Someone special going to be there?"

"Not that I know of." Laurel tapped her head with last week's *Shopper*, within which she had found not one apartment, trailer, room, or cardboard box to rent in a twenty-mile radius. "It's time to go now, though. Get a move on."

Skye crammed clothes into her My Little Pony suitcase and hauled it to the door, and Laurel nibbled at a thumbnail. The bag was ripped in one corner and Skye was long past the My Little Pony stage, but it did still function as a container for overnight things, so it would have to do for a while longer. She tucked her thumb under her fingers. "You grabbed your toothbrush, baby girl?"

"Yes." Skye shuffled her feet into her boots.

"Pajamas, underwear?"

"I'm not a baby, you know."

"What's that supposed to mean?"

Skye sighed and Laurel let it go. "Homework?"

"I can do it Sunday."

"You'll take it with. Don't want Mary Lynn thinking I'm a slacker mom."

Skye glowered. "That's not what she thinks."

Once they were outside, though, she slid her hand into Laurel's and whapped a chunk of ice down the driveway with the side of her foot. "I wish Harper could come."

He couldn't; Sam was allergic to dogs. Even Laurel's and Skye's clothes made him sneeze if they weren't fresh laundered. "He'll be fine, I won't be too late. And I'll get you the minute I'm done at the Lakeshore tomorrow, don't worry."

"I won't. It'll be fun at Mary Lynn's. We're having a Yahtzee marathon. Plus, Mary Lynn has a telescope; we're going to look at the Galilean moons around Jupiter."

"The what?"

"The Galilean moons. Galileo discovered them, Galileo Galilei. Isn't that the most poetical name you ever heard? Anyway, there're four moons. Io, Europa, Ganymede, and Callisto. They were all named for girlfriends of Zeus, Mary Lynn said."

Skye sprinted forward to kick the chunk of ice again and Laurel began humming the tune that had appeared in her head, an old Flirtations song she'd never liked about heartache and being kicked when you were down.


At Belle's, Laurel took a stool near the draft pulls and ordered tonic water with a twist of lime from Sharp. A moment later someone laid a hand on her neck and massaged. "Long time no see, Laurel Tree. We are two ships that do not pass in the night."

Laurel smiled into the mirror at Hugh Findlay. "I saw you Wednesday. I worked late, remember?"

He made a mock mournful face. "Only a look and a voice, then darkness again and silence."

"Pretty. Is it the Hiawatha guy? Longfellow?"

"'On the shores of Gitche Gumee, / Of the shining Big-Sea-Water,'" Hugh confirmed.

"Can you still recite the whole thing?"

"Think so."

"Impressive."

Sharp shot Hugh an amused look from where he stood filling pints. "You still got it, Huge."

Hugh Findlay had been heavyset as a kid, but the middle-school nickname referred to his brain, not his size. Other than taller and thinner, he was much the same as he'd ever been. His brown hair ran halfway down his back in a smooth ponytail; his hazel eyes shone cheerily behind his John Lennon glasses. He even had on his Clash T-shirt, the one with Paul Simonon smashing his guitar to the stage, which he had ordered out of the Rockabilia catalog when he was fourteen and Laurel eleven.

Life was so different then. No internet, few cell phones, and the only radio the already-decades-out-of-date WCMZ, though on clear nights you could sometimes pull in a station from Canada, two hundred miles across the lake. Ordering anything had been an event, filling out the form (first in pencil, the second draft in ballpoint) and mailing the envelope, waiting and waiting for the desired item to arrive. The shirt was gray more than black now, riddled with tiny slits from age and washing.

Laurel patted the stool beside her and Hugh settled on it, dragging a paperback from his jeans pocket and plonking it on the bar. On the cover, reflective glasses dominated an impassive face; white type across the center read *Kafka on the Shore*. She smiled. Trust Hugh to be reading something obscure the way other people read sports magazines. He flipped the book over as if embarrassed and Laurel sipped her drink without saying what she thought: Don't be. Claim this rare and special shard of you. A lot of people don't have them, or anyway, don't reveal them. She ran her eyes over the room, then shut them and uttered a brief prayer for the divine intervention she needed.

Hugh tugged on her ponytail. "You okay?" When she said she was, he nodded. "Don't believe you."

Laurel dipped her head onto his shoulder. Before Jenny moved to town, she and Hugh had spent endless hours playing in the woods and bogs, shooting bows and arrows, fishing, berry picking, hunting for frogs—to observe, not to kill. They'd amble miles down the shore of Superior, race their bikes along the empty gravel roads, listen to music, watch movies on Hugh's VCR, fix snacks in his mom's kitchen or Gran's, do their different homework at the same time. Time would go transparent, then vanish altogether.

But sneakily, the three-year gap in age between them started to matter. Laurel became a slightly boring little kid; Hugh morphed into someone foreign and faintly off-putting. He began hanging out with Joanne Forte and the Bellamy brothers, who were all older than him; she grew entwined with Jen.

Laurel would always love Hugh, but now he made her sad as much as anything. He'd been so smart and sweet and funny as a child, full of energy and wacky, fabulous ideas. A Skye-like person, really. But when he started hanging with the older kids, he got into trouble. It was small-time stuff, a minor break-in and some booze lifted, nothing a lot of teenagers didn't do. Even Jen and Laurel had done it. The difference was that Hugh got caught. He ended up in front of Judge Peters in Crosscut and did a month in jail and lost his scholarship for State. Then his mom died and he couldn't keep up the payments on their house. After that he stayed on people's couches or in Belle's storeroom in the cold seasons, camped out on state land the rest of the year. He'd bathe in Lake Superior, cook over a campfire. These days he had a place a dozen miles south of town near Halfway, a camper on someone's land he paid rent on, and for work cooked at Belle's, plowed, and cut firewood. That was fine if he was happy, but Laurel didn't think he was. His friendly eyes often seemed dulled these days. Still, whatever he did with himself and his time was his business. He would have his own reasons for keeping the life he had, just as she had hers.

They listened to the jukebox in companionable silence. When Sharp waved a pizza order under his nose, Hugh rapped her temple gently with his knuckles and ambled away to prepare it.

Three hours later, Laurel dragged her coat on, her good mood drained. She had asked everyone and found nowhere to rent. Ditto to finding extra work, except for another pair of pants to hem for Sharp. The Clash came on the jukebox. *Breakin' rocks in the hot sun, I fought the law, and the law won*—Hugh's theme song since that bad summer.

"C'mon, Tree, stay a while longer," he called from the kitchen as she wrapped her scarf around her neck. "Shoot a game of pool with me."

"I can't, I'm sorry."

"Make you a plate of nachos, my treat."

Nachos were their go-to snack as kids. They'd sprinkle shredded cheddar on Tostitos and zap them in his mom's microwave. They'd been living large, stepping out into the great big future instead of being hick kids subsisting at the edge of the grid. Laurel bobbled the tip of her scarf at him. "No, thanks. It's time to go."

Outside, the stars sparkled and flickered like a million messages from a trillion miles away. Mysterious messages, though, and maybe it was only one instead of millions. Maybe it was a singular impersonal truth, encompassing her and every other atom in the universe, every soul and chunk of rock and blade of grass: Life is delicate and dangerous, it's gritty and gorgeous. No one can save you from it. You're as alone as Crank said; everyone is.

Laurel zipped her coat and started for home, her heels tip-tapping on the pavement in a way that sounded silly in her ears. It had snowed while she was at Belle's and her high-heeled boots only allowed her to creep and mince. When she reached Railroad Street, she looked up again, but without Mary Lynn's telescope she didn't have a chance of seeing Galileo Galilei's beautifully named moons.

# Nine

James Taylor woke Laurel the Sunday before Thanksgiving. He had seen fire and he had seen rain; he had seen sunny days he thought would never end. Laurel reached over to silence the radio alarm, set to WCMZ as always, still the only station that came in here, then reeled it back in instead. The song played on and the smell of simmering tomatoes lingered in her nose. She closed her eyes and saw Gran as she'd been moments ago in a dream: standing at the old stove that matched the avocado-colored fridge, smashing tomatoes through the canner's cone-shaped colander. "We ought to go see *Twister*," Gran had said. "I saw in the *Shopper* they're replaying it for discount night tonight."

Sixteen-year-old Laurel had stood on tiptoe at the cupboard, rummaging for the Wheaties. "I heard it's scary. Totally realistic, you're in the tornado." She poked the small of Gran's back. "You think you can handle it, old lady?"

Gran had snorted. "I'll 'old lady' you, youngster. You'll be the one hiding under the seat, I'll lay money on it."

Laurel burrowed deeper into her pillow.

But she was not a teenager in her childhood bed. She was thirty years old and living in Harv Duke's soon-to-be vacation rental with Skye asleep beside her. "Gran, Gran," she wanted to call out, a child lost in a parking lot. "Come back. Oh, please come back."

This would do no good, Gran would've been the first to say it. Laurel threw off her covers. Light flooded through the window. It had snowed again!

She jostled Skye's shoulder and Skye groaned. "Stop, I don't want to get up, it's too early."

"Yes, you do."

"No, I don't."

"Wrong!" Laurel tickled Skye's neck and Skye smacked her hand away. Then she scooted up against the pillows and inspected Laurel.

"Why do I?"

"Because we're going hunting."

"For real?" Her eyes brightened and Laurel's heart lifted even though she hated hunting. Skye's first easygoing response to moving had morphed into something more complicated lately and they needed a distraction.

"It snowed in the night. You should see it."

"What about work?"

"Rip gave me the day off, remember?"

"Oh, yeah. Yay!"

Laurel swatted her leg. "That's right, yay. I'm all yours, so hurry it up."

Skye tumbled from bed and headed for the bathroom while Laurel put two apples in a sack along with a few granola bars and a bottle of water. Next she lowered Great-Grandfather Aapo's shotgun from over the door and filled her jacket pocket with shells, then found string in the junk drawer and grabbed a bag of carrots from the camping cooler on the patio. She'd unplugged the fridge the week before. It was cold enough to keep things outside now, and any little she could cut a bill she would.

She handed Skye a granola bar before they headed out. "I'll fix a real breakfast when we get back."

Skye poked the bar into her coat pocket. "Sean says not to eat before a hunt. He says the animals can smell the food on you."

"I suppose."

"Could we invite him to come with us, do you think?"

Laurel gazed at the maple Skye had shorn the limbs from in August, deciding she wouldn't tell Skye that she'd seen Sean at the post office the other day. They'd exchanged careful pleasantries; she told him nothing of her troubles and he'd told her none of his, if he had them.

"Mom? Can we?"

Laurel clenched a shell in her pocket. Everything would be easier if she could say yes, both to the hunting and to what might follow. Sean owned a cabin and had a job with the road commission. He made good money and worked days most of the time, which would free her up to work nights at Belle's. Nights when there was an open slot for a server and the tips were good. Jen would be happy, and so would Skye, at least most of the time. In a way, so would she and Sean, or at least happy enough. But that kind of thinking was lazy and wrong, and would lead to no good. "Sorry, baby. No."

Skye took a sharp breath and huffed it out and Laurel patted her shoulder.

Ten minutes later, she pulled off at the edge of a swath of state forest. Sun streamed through the windshield and glittered off the snow. "The rabbits'll like this," Laurel said.

Skye pushed a nail through the fat part of a carrot and looped string around each end. A trick Sean had taught her. They'd find a spruce thicket flush with rabbit tracks and hang the carrots from low branches. After a while, the rabbits, made lazy and unguarded by the sun, would venture close to investigate. Their noses would quiver and their eyes would go intent; they'd sit up on their haunches. And then, when they were nibbling—*blam*. Laurel winced.

Skye glanced at her. "What?"

"Just waiting 'til you're ready."

Skye rammed her last carrot into the bag. "I'm ready."

They crunched into the woods. When a dozen carrots dangled above the snow in a mile-long loop, they leaned against a tree fifty feet distant from the first bait to wait. From the car, Harper—never trained to hunt and disruptive of the undertaking—barked. He sounded lonesome and insistent: he had important information to convey and they should come back to hear it right away.

A rabbit stood on its hind legs to reach a carrot and Skye took the shot, their first in half an hour. They fetched the kill and hiked on to where another bait dangled.

Skye shot again and the rabbit crumpled. Laurel closed her eyes. One more and they'd go. Three was plenty for a stew, and cleaning them was even worse than killing them, divesting them of their fur like peeling off a jacket.

"Mom, what are we doing for Christmas?" Skye asked.

"Hanging stockings and having a tree, I guess." Though where she'd put a tree without a living room, she didn't know. "We'll make something good for dinner. Why are you worrying about that now?"

"Um. The thing is." Skye took a deep breath. "Did Mary Lynn ask you yet?"

Skye undid her seat belt the moment Laurel turned off the ignition. Laurel shook her head. "You stay here."

"I want to see if the flying saucer Mary Lynn ordered for Frank came."

"The what?"

"The flying saucer. It's an exercise wheel."

"It's not plastic, is it?" Gerbils would chew anything plastic and kill themselves eating the pieces.

"Of course not. It's wooden and really cool and I want to see if it came yet."

Laurel folded her fingers into her palms. She must not be side-tracked into talk of exercise wheels. "Not right now."

"Why not?"

"Because I said not."

"You're mean."

"Maybe so, but you still have to wait here."

"It's not fair!" Skye shoved her door open and Laurel hopped out her own door fast. She pointed at Skye. "I'm not joking. You stay here. This is between me and Mary Lynn."

Skye flung herself against the seat and Laurel counted to five, staring at a jay that had landed on a nearby branch. The blue of its feathers came straight out of a paint box. It tilted its head and studied her with a beady eye. Laurel acknowledged its gaze, then headed up the drive.

Inside, Mary Lynn was pulling something from the oven. The scent of cinnamon and sugar, like Gran's streusel, made Laurel momentarily dizzy.

Mary Lynn turned. "Laurel." Her voice was as warm as the cake she cradled in two plaid oven mitts. "Where's Skye? Everything okay?"

"No."

Mary Lynn froze. "What's wrong, is it Skye?"

"No, Skye's okay."

She dropped the cake pan and put a mitted hand to her sternum. "Oh, thank God."

Laurel wanted to disdain the response for being melodramatic, but she couldn't, because Mary Lynn, clumpier than ever in a vast red sweatshirt with *Cornell* plastered across the chest in cracked vinyl letters, so obviously meant it. The thought ran through her head that she was lucky to have someone else in the world, someone near, who cared about Skye so much. Then she remembered what Mary Lynn had done and launched into the speech she'd been composing ever since they left the woods.

When she finished, Mary Lynn looked stricken. "I told her to let me tell you myself."

"She's ten years old, what did you expect?"

"You're right. I'm sorry. And it's not just a pleasure trip, if that helps."

Laurel clenched and unclenched her hands. They were sticky with blood from the rabbits. "What is it, then?"

"It's complicated. That's why I wanted to tell you myself."

"So, tell me."

"We're moving."

Laurel blinked.

"For the winter. Sam . . . wants to."

"What do you mean? You can't—" Laurel motioned around the room: the mammoth stove and fridge big enough to cater parties from, the antique tins and advertising, the fresh paint everywhere. The bookings, the effort, the care that had gone into it— This was their life. All of their lives.

Mary Lynn grimaced. "I know you didn't know Sam before, but since his surgery he's not the same." The mantel clock in the dining room bonged twice into the quiet. "He truly is a different person, just housed in the same body." She pulled a face and it was hard not to make the same face back. "He wants to play the piano now. It's all he wants."

"I don't get it."

Mary Lynn stared at the coffee cake. "And I can't explain it to you."

"I know he plays a lot."

"All the time. The same few pieces over and over. He's determined to master one particular Rachmaninoff sonata." Mary Lynn folded one of her oven mitts in half and squeezed it tight. "He was a tax attorney before. Completely left-brained. Now he wants to study piano, go back to school for it. I finally told him if he got in somewhere, I'd go along with it. For a while, anyway. And he did. A program in Albuquerque accepted him for the winter term. We're driving down at Christmas to find an apartment. The plan is that we'll just—I guess—stay."

"That's terrible."

"I don't know what it is. Maybe it's a great adventure."

Laurel squinted at Mary Lynn.

"After the surgery, I was just so relieved he was okay—I was sure I'd never ask the universe for anything else, ever. I made that deal, you know?"

Laurel nodded. She could imagine.

"It was terrifying. A brain tumor. But then it was, I don't know, weirdly anticlimactic. He was home within a few days, wandering around the house in a couple of weeks. Life snapped back to normal and I started asking for things again."

Laurel made a sympathetic face this time. Her anger had drained away.

"I wanted more business. And a new stove, right?" Mary Lynn wrinkled her nose at her range, so heavy she'd had the floors reinforced beneath it. It boasted two ovens and eight burners and an apple-red finish and had cost over ten thousand dollars. Laurel had looked it up online at the Crosscut library one day out of a fascination she didn't like in herself. "I started planning a café for the summers, a food stand without seating, or no indoor seating, so I wouldn't have to worry about bathrooms and zoning."

"That's a lot to take on."

Mary Lynn stuck her chin out. "Life is a lot to take on. And two rooms to rent out won't do much. But Sam fell in love with this place the moment we saw it, and I liked it, too." She pressed her lips together. "Anyway. Two guest rooms aren't enough, and besides, I wanted to explore our options, expand. Do jams and baked things, sandwiches and soup. Specialty things, seasonal, local, with a brick-fired oven. Down the road, of course."

"Uh-huh."

"I know. I get ideas, they get out of hand." Mary Lynn closed her eyes. "Anyway. I was on a roll. I even hired an architect to draw up the plans. But when Sam asked for this, I remembered my promise. So off we go."

The kitchen cupboards, coated in a vintage shade of green Mary Lynn called Gingko, hung where they had when the house belonged to Gran. The floor was the same, thank goodness, and so were the red Formica countertops, but everything else was different. The fridge, the range, even the light fixtures, which were reproductions of lights from the thirties and much prettier than the originals, which had been plain porcelain bases with 60-watt lightbulbs from the Ace Hardware in Crosscut screwed in. Everything shone; the room hummed with ease and sweetness. Laurel's mind began to race—maybe she and Skye could stay here for the winter. Maybe Mary Lynn would hire Laurel to keep it open while they were gone. If she would, could Laurel do it? Could she manage everything, greet the guests, cook fancy food for them, visit with them the way Mary Lynn did? She would try if Mary Lynn would consider it. For Skye she would try. For Skye she would do anything.

But then Mary Lynn said, "Of course we'll close it down for the winter."

The words might as well have been potatoes or parsnips, the way Mary Lynn plunked them down. "But what if—"

Mary Lynn seemed not to hear. "I've already scheduled the plumbers to come drain the water and blow out the lines. I'm not risking burst pipes."

Maybe Laurel and Skye could stay here even if it wasn't open. And water didn't matter; they could buy it bottled at Phil's for drinking and cooking, haul it in buckets from Johnson's or Belle's for baths and dishes and flushing the toilet. She tried to shape the sentence that would ask this favor. Before she could, Mary Lynn continued.

"We're getting a new furnace installed while we're gone. And the attic insulated. The roof's about shot, you know. So no heat beyond the minimum until that's done. I figure we can leave it at forty-five and call it good. Warm enough for the piano; not so warm it'll ice up the roof."

Laurel's hopes crashed, a kid's block tower knocked over with a swipe of a hand. She told herself to ask, to beg as she'd begged Harv twice now, but her pride wouldn't let her. She didn't want to admit her destitution and chaos to anyone, but she couldn't, *wouldn't*, admit it to Mary Lynn, this well-off woman from downstate who Skye so adored and esteemed. "Well. That sounds pricey."

"So it goes. We'll get the work done and, I guess, be back in the spring."

Mary Lynn moved the oven mitts with one of her square-fingered hands, hands that had struck Laurel in these few weeks of working for her as graceful and competent, peaceful somehow, despite Mary Lynn's being so generally awkward. Mary Lynn met Laurel's gaze. "In the meantime, I hoped Skye could ride along with us on this exploring trip. She's such a gem, we both love her. I'd started to think Sam had lost his knack for loving anyone or anything except the piano and his motorcycle."

Laurel nodded and thought she shouldn't have.

Mary Lynn laced her fingers together. "You'd be doing us the biggest favor if you'd let us have the pleasure of her company over Christmas."

Laurel hesitated, then squared her shoulders. "No. Thank you for offering, but I can't let her. It's too far for too long and she's too young."

The sunset cast a red-orange glow through the windows and gilded their possessions that evening. Laurel set a bowl of stew in front of Skye, but Skye pushed it away. "I don't want that much."

"It's not that much."

"This bowl is huge."

The bowl was pottery, hand-thrown, discovered at a Salvation Army a few years back in a set of three, two of them unchipped. Laurel always thought their swirling, earthy browns and blues made any meal more appealing, but apparently not. She spooned stew back into the pot and Skye clapped her palms on her thighs. "You barely took out any."

"Life is hard, baby-cake." Laurel took one of Skye's angry, damp hands. Bowed her head, closed her eyes. "Thank you for this meal we are about to eat. For this roof over our heads and this floor under our feet. Amen."

"Amen," Skye muttered.

Laurel smiled despite her own glum frame of mind. She'd often not listened when Gran recited this prayer before every dinner, but the words had lodged themselves inside her anyway. Saying them as an adult always infused her with at least a momentary flush of peace.

Skye lifted stew to her mouth, and Laurel followed suit. "Good?"

Skye raised a shoulder. "I don't like the bones left in."

"You don't? First I've heard of it."

"I've never liked the bones. I just never said."

"Well, I stand corrected."

Skye jabbed at the rubbery cartilage at the joint end of a leg bone. "That's why. That grosses me out."

Laurel thought of explaining cartilage's benefits as taught them by Coach in high school. It was a connective tissue, tough and flexible but easy to damage. It held things together and softened blows, and if you wrecked it you were screwed—Coach didn't use that word, but that was what he meant. "I'll take the bones out next time. But this time, eat up."

"I hate the potatoes cut so big, too, and carrots make me want to puke."

Laurel's head snapped up. "Watch what you say to people, you can hurt feelings. Even mine."

Skye scowled. "I'm sorry."

"Your apology is accepted."

Skye thunked her spoon into her bowl. "I wish I could have what Mary Lynn made when I stayed over. It had Parmesan cheese. Fresh Parmesan, the kind you buy in a hard hunk at the grocery store."

"No grocery store in this town."

"I grated it for her."

Laurel sighed. Skye must have wanted to go out west very badly.

"You use a zester. It's like a potato shredder, only smaller."

"I know what a zester is."

"It had asparagus in it, too. Wild like we picked with Grandma and Aunt Jenny last June."

Laurel looked up in case this was a peace offering. Jenny and Mom had been visiting and the four of them had hatched a plan to sneak up to Gran's and see how the asparagus was doing. Sam and Mary Lynn were still making trips back and forth from downstate with a moving van and were more like rumors than real people; the place had seemed like theirs, as it had been forever, until Mom's mess-up. Seagulls had called in the distance; the breeze was gentle. Skye whistled "Greensleeves," Mom hummed along, and soon Jenny and Laurel joined in. They had all been peaceful and satisfied with the plain fact of life that day.

"And it had chicken, with no skin. I hate skin," Skye said.

Laurel always left the skin on chicken. "If you've got the money, honey, I've got the time."

"Mary Lynn's kind of chicken's good for you." Skye mashed a potato against the side of her bowl. "It's de-ranged and it's just better."

"Free range. And it might be better, but it costs five times as much as our kind. Hush up and eat."

"You're mean."

"I know. Mean Joe Greene, that's me." Laurel mimed a bear attacking, hoping for a grin. Skye frowned and nibbled glumly at her stew.

# Ten

L aurel ducked outside and fished the tub of leftover stew from the cooler three days later. It was D-day; they had to eat this before it spoiled.

"I want to be a Viking when I grow up." Skye sat cross-legged on the couch, a book she'd brought from school on her lap. She raised her head from the encyclopedia-sized tome. "Oh, your hair's all wet."

"Sleeting," Laurel said. "Coming straight down."

Skye gave a sympathetic shiver. "Anyway, the Vikings were so cool. And their boats—"

The phone began to ring. "Hang on." Laurel dropped the stew and grabbed the receiver and, as soon as she heard who it was, inched as far from Skye as the cord would allow. Keeping her voice low, she talked and listened. In the end she said, "Okay, yes, thank you, I understand."

The caller disconnected and Laurel stood rubbing her neck.

"Okay, so there were knarrs and karves and faerings and long-ships." Skye ticked the varieties off with her fingers. "Vikings sailed all the way to Greenland in a knarr, Mom. Just twenty or thirty people in a boat, and their cows or whatever. The big ones could carry a hundred and twenty-two tons. That's, like, a hundred and sixty-two of Sean's truck."

Laurel widened her eyes. "Wow."

"I know. And they rowed them by hand. Every boat had a different number of oars. Listen." Skye bent over the book again, one hand stroking Harper's head. He groaned and leaned into her. "'A faering had two pair, a longship might have sixty men rowing, and a knarr relied mainly on its sail.'"

"That's interesting." Laurel rummaged under the counter for a pot.

"And did you know that Greenland isn't green?"

Laurel did. "It isn't?"

"No, it's all ice, with walruses and polar bears and stuff. Erik the Red called it that, Greenland, to get people to go there and live." Skye clicked her pen and Laurel imagined her as an adult in a laboratory or loft, figuring something out, directing some project. "He said if it had a nice name, people'd want to live there."

"Tricky." Laurel fished a leg bone she'd missed from the stewpot, her face hidden.

"What's wrong?" Skye's voice was abruptly tight.

"Nothing."

"I don't believe you."

"No, it's true, it's good news. Sue Lerner is not renting to us."

"Why is that good news?"

Laurel strangled the tears she wanted to cry. "Because her place is tiny and ugly and the bedroom's up the loft stairs, where Harper couldn't go. And what else? It's a mile out of town and impossible to heat. That vaulted ceiling. A nightmare."

Skye scowled.

Laurel had tried everything in the last few weeks. Put out feelers with everyone, scoured the *Shopper*, the internet, the *Crosscut Gazette*. She'd begged Harv yet again, to no avail, and had even talked to Lori Trevor. That had been awkward. Ms. Trevor was understanding and sorry and, like Sam, allergic to dogs. Sue's place had been Laurel's last hope. What came after that? Better understanding, a finer solution? She pointed the soup spoon at Skye. "Also, she lives next door. Right next door. And you know how she is. Plus, she said she'd insist Harper stay outside at all times."

Skye nodded as if she might deem these worthy reasons to celebrate not moving there after all. "So . . . then what?"

"I don't know. I'm thinking."

"What if you can't think fast enough?"

"Then I'll . . . rent us a room at the Breakers."

"Broke-Down Breakers?"

"That's not nice."

"Aunt Jenny says it."

"That doesn't mean you have to."

"It's gross in there. It smells like cat pee. And it's dark and dingy and the blankets are weird, they're plasticky."

"It would only be temporary."

"But it's depressing, and we'd be there at Christmas. Where would we put our tree?"

They always cut a tree from the state land, chose the biggest that would fit into wherever they were living. They decorated it with ornaments as old as Great-Gran (who had snatched an apronful off the tree as it caught fire, a wonderful and terrible family story) and as young as Skye; they sang carols, drank cocoa, made cards and construction paper chains. They even strung cranberries that they put outside on New Year's for the birds to eat. "We'd—we'd put up a wreath or something."

"A wreath!" Skye's face was contemptuous. A wreath was nothing. It was worse than nothing.

Laurel stirred the stew, though it didn't need stirring. When she looked up, Skye was staring at her. She had probably been staring the whole time Laurel tended to this unappetizing food that neither of them wanted. Laurel cleared her throat. "Wash your hands. It's almost ready."

Skye crossed her arms. "You know what I wish?"

"What?"

"I wish we had our own house. I wish we were rich."

"We are."

"We are not."

"We're rich in the things that matter. Health. Love. Friends. Curiosity."

Skye jerked her chin high, her eyes blazing. "Oh, that's dumb, that doesn't help anything."

"Those things matter."

"This still stinks!"

"I want to have our own house, too, but everything's so expensive, and just getting by is—" Laurel stopped herself. Burdening Skye with worries and problems was the last thing she wanted to do. "Things will get easier. But for now, this is how it is."

Skye scrubbed at her eyes with her palms. Then she patted Harper's head three times—he had been gazing at her all along, his chin on her knee—and returned to her book.

"I love you more than anything on earth, baby."

Skye glanced at Laurel. Her face had an adult hardness that Laurel did not like seeing. "I know you do, Mom. I get that."

Laurel stared into the semidarkness of their room that night. Outside a truck with a bad muffler roared by. The streetlight flickered off—the room was plunged into real darkness—and on again. Skye's breaths were deep, but Laurel struggled to draw her own. Something invisible but heavy as the world lay on top of her.

Skye hauled her Vikings tome to the table with her at breakfast. Pages swished; her spoon clinked; Frank scrabbled in her bedding. Laurel sipped her coffee. When Skye finished her cereal, Laurel spoke. "Guess what. I've changed my mind. You can go to New Mexico. It would be such a great experience for you, a real adventure."

Skye ran her finger along a line of text and narrowed her eyes. Laurel couldn't read her mood, aside from skeptical. And Skye's mood was Skye's business, she reminded herself. Laurel could only flounder along as best as she was able, make the decisions she had to, try to make them worthy and good, even if sometimes it took a while to come to them. "And by the time you get back, I'll have found us some-place to stay. To live, I mean."

Skye arched her brows and Laurel wanted to weep. Not only at the situation and her inadequacy, but at Skye's silence and the wall going up between them. A wall built of hard times, of a knowing beyond her years. Exactly what Laurel wanted to shield her from.

"Am I telling Mary Lynn, or are you?"

Laurel raised her thumb to her lips, but pulled it away again. "I will. I work there today. Mary Lynn wants help getting everything cleaned before they—you—go. So, I'll talk to her."

"I'll ride the bus there after school, then."

"Okay."

Skye jammed books into her satchel. "See you."

A moment later, she yanked the door open and let it bang shut behind her.

# Eleven

The knock came early. Laurel pulled the door open and Mary Lynn fluttered her fingers. "Hey ho. Here we are, ready or not." Snow swirled and a gust of cold air twined around Laurel's ankles. She clutched her robe shut. She'd overslept. Today of all days. She hadn't even brushed her hair yet. She ushered Mary Lynn in, hurrying to offer coffee, or tea, straightening a pile of papers on the counter as she passed it, wishing she hadn't left yesterday's dishes in the sink. Last things to do had kept cropping up, was all.

Skye galumphed across the room in her bulb-toed boots, her various pieces of luggage dangling off her shoulders, and minutes later she was climbing into the Lovells' Subaru, the duffel bag Mary Lynn had given her bumping behind her. The bag was hot pink with black straps and Mary Lynn had claimed it was something she'd had around forever and never used much. Laurel doubted that. It reeked of plastic and the fold creases were still in it when Mary Lynn handed it over the other day.

In the car, Sam sat in the passenger seat fiddling with an iPod; piano music drifted from the earbuds. He turned and did a fist bump with Skye when she tapped his head, made a hat-tip gesture to Laurel, and rapped his knuckles on his heart. Despite herself, Laurel smiled at him.

"Shove your bags over into the cargo," Mary Lynn told Skye. "I left room near the front so you can get at them whenever you want. And I put some pillows there, too."

Skye began rearranging her space and Mary Lynn fiddled with her seat settings. "You have everything?" she asked when she had things set to her satisfaction. Skye said yes and then Laurel knew it was happening. Skye was leaving. Harper stood beside her with his tail low. Laurel dropped a hand to his head.

"You're sure? No last-minute additions or subtractions? You're ready to roll?"

Laurel wanted to say *No!* but Mary Lynn wasn't talking to her.

Skye aimed a hopeful smile into the mirror. "The only perfect thing would be if Harper could come?"

"He can't, though I have no doubt he's a perfect gentleman."

"He really is!"

"Sorry, Charlie."

Skye drooped. "O-kay." She leaned to give Harper a last pat.

Laurel hugged herself against the cold, smiling and smiling.

Mary Lynn started the car and Skye cried, "We're going! Isn't it exciting?"

Laurel laid her palm on Skye's warm neck. Skye-warm, not

feverish-warm; she had always been a little radiator. "It's fantastic. I never took a trip like this when I was your age." Or ever, Laurel thought, as she squeezed Skye's shoulder and shut the car door.

Skye rolled her window down. "Make sure you give Frank lots of sunflower seeds."

"*Some* sunflower seeds," Laurel said.

"They're her favorite, and it's Christmas!"

"She won't be neglected, don't worry."

"I won't. And you don't worry either. Don't worry and don't be sad, I'll be back before you know it."

Laurel squeezed her eyes shut. "Time will fly."

"Remember, Harper likes ice cubes in his water."

"His wish is my command."

Skye gazed long into Harper's eyes and he gazed back. She gave him a firm smile. Next, she studied Laurel. "Don't work too hard. Take breaks."

Laurel had postponed packing up their home until after Skye left. "I won't and I will."

"Merry Christmas!"

Laurel gripped the door's edge. "Merry Christmas, baby. Call me every day, all right?"

Skye slipped her phone out of her coat pocket and waved it. "I will."

Laurel took its twin, flip phones she'd gotten in Crosscut a few days before, from her robe pocket. "I'll have this on me at all times. Call whenever; call a lot."

"Okay."

"Have fun."

"I will!"

"Behave."

Skye made a mock glum face. "O-kay."

The car rolled inches forward. Skye shot her hand out the window and Laurel grasped it. Then Mary Lynn beeped the horn and picked up speed and she had to let go.

Late that afternoon, Hugh Findlay hefted the back half of Laurel's bureau into his pickup alongside the bed frame and mattress and oak table. She'd asked him at Belle's the previous week for an hour of his time and muscle; now he clunked the tailgate shut. "So, you're out of here."

Laurel tucked a blanket around the dresser edge. "Yep."

"And you're going . . ."

"To be fine."

He drew his hair into a new, smoother ponytail, watching her. Laurel gazed at the triangle of Lake Superior visible in the distance between the Makins' house and the summer cottage next door to it. The water undulated, slow, cold looking, and vast, and her problems were tiny in its face; she was one human in a parade of humans who'd trudged across this planet. Something would work out. The lake in its endless foreverness promised that.

Hugh puffed out a breath. "Okeydokey, then. Off we go."

Laurel climbed into the passenger seat. "Niels said there's space alongside Hope Callahan's sailboat." Gran's old beau, Niels Hermansen, was letting her rent the corner near Hope's sailboat for twenty bucks—for a week or for the winter, whatever she needed, he'd said.

Hugh rolled his eyes but shifted into gear without asking any more questions.

———————

By eight thirty, she'd finished ferrying the last of her boxes to Whittle's Mini Storage. Almost everything they owned was now lodged there: the bed and dresser and table and also their pots and pans and plates and bowls, their craft supplies and Laurel's sewing machine, Great-Gran's sewing kit and kerosene lamp, their books and shelves and the bulk of their clothes. Hardest of all somehow, the twinkle lights that had glowed down on them so many evenings like tiny whispering hopes.

Laurel drifted through the house once more. Oh, what would become of them, really? She snuffed the thought out. Something would come up. It had to. She set Harv's key on the kitchen counter and pulled the door shut behind her.

After that she didn't know what to do. She ended up at Belle's because there was nowhere else. Even the churches were locked at night nowadays.

Inside, she took a table near the potbelly stove and brought out her book. Pretending to be absorbed in someone else's made-up world seemed like the best way to avoid conversation. Only after the last devoted beer drinkers straggled away did she tuck it back into her bag.

Sharp stopped beside her on his way to check the johns. "You okay?"

Laurel's back ached and her spirits were as low as a sunken ship. "Yeah."

"You get moved out of Harv's all right?"

She hadn't shared the details of her situation with anyone, not even Jen—too much opportunity for Jen to say "I told you so"—but plenty of people knew, or thought they did. She hesitated, then said yes.

"Found a place yet?"

"Um. Kind of."

"You end up in a pinch, let me know. I got a couch."

"Thanks, Sharp." Laurel flashed him a smile and pulled her coat on.

Outside, the air smelled of snow and gas fumes. A half dozen snowmobiles pulled up; the riders dragged their helmets off and groused about getting in to town too late for a drink. Laurel weaved through them and climbed in the car. Frank huddled in her bedding; Harper gazed at her unblinking; the plants looked numb. Laurel blasted the heat and the defroster and, after a minute, eased onto the main street and then drove up Plank Hill. Soon she was backing into Gran's—the Lovells'—driveway, alongside the barn.

An hour later, Frank was making the soft peeps that meant she was nervous and Harper lay wedged alongside Laurel with his head on her lap. She stroked his ears. "We're fine. We can do this." The weather was mild for December—it was above thirty tonight—and she would run the car now and then. She could sneak in a few showers at the Lakeshore while she was working, hang out at Belle's and Phil's and Johnson's during the day, join the old guys there around the table in the back, drink coffee and gossip. They'd like that. She could go to church on Sunday, which she did now and then in the slow seasons anyway, and attend the lunch after, volunteer to do most of the cleanup. Everyone would be busy with their holiday plans, and if she stayed cheerful and didn't complain, no one would notice that she was homeless. They'd assume she was filling time with Skye gone. And she was; this was only temporary. A solution would materialize, even if it was a room at the Breakers. She wasn't dipping into their savings for that any sooner than she had to, though.

Despite her resolve to stay positive, before long the cold had seeped into her feet and butt in such an insistent way she could think of nothing else. The energy in each molecule of her watery self was decreasing; her atoms were all drawing together, *huddling* together, as she turned from liquid to solid.

She pictured going into Phil's as soon as he opened in the morning. She'd buy a granola bar or an apple, but take her time about it, and chat up Phil, who'd talk forever once you got him going. When Belle's opened at noon, she'd go there. In great detail, she imagined washing her face and hands with hot water in the women's room. She would order a mug of cocoa and take it to the table beside the stove, start the book at the beginning and make sense of it, even get lost in it. It wouldn't be so bad.

She gazed at the star-pricked sky. Picked out the North Star, which Gran had shown her when Laurel was Skye's age. They'd come out to the field together, Gran in jeans and her mackinaw, Laurel in parka and pj's. Mom was living downstate then and Jenny wasn't there either; Big Jim had vetoed it that weekend. Laurel kept asking Gran why, in the nagging way of kids, and finally Gran said, "Come on, get your coat on. And your boots. We're going for a walk. Time you learned your bearings."

They made their way across the pasture. Arrived at the rock in the field's center and leaned against it with their heads tipped back. Gran hauled Laurel close and pointed out Polaris. "So you'll always know your way around this big old world." Her peppermint breath puffed in the cold air, and Laurel looked into her eyes. Her voice had sounded strange, grave and weary, but now Gran only pointed in the other direction and changed the subject. "Orion, now, he's the hunter. See his bow? He's after the bull, Taurus. He's protecting the Pleiades girls."

Laurel peered into the heavens, trying to see the story Gran was telling.

"That's his dog there at his heel. Canis, they call him."

"I want a dog."

Gran chuckled. "I know you do. Maybe we'll get you one here soon."

"Really?"

Gran made a noise, an *ahh*, then said, "Why not? We have room enough, and I venture to say food enough, too."

Back inside a half hour later, she challenged Laurel to a game of Ping-Pong. They played across the kitchen table and Laurel laughed until her eyes streamed when Gran's hits ended up in crazy places: the gravy boat on the sideboard, the cocoa pan on the stove, the flower vase with a bouquet Niels gave her in it. The next day, they drove to Crosscut and came back from the pound with Orville, a middle-aged brown dog with white spots who had died just before Gran had.

Laurel put her fingertips on the window, as though she were reaching for the sky. Oh, Gran. What would she say if she saw Laurel now?

# Twelve

aurel pulled Belle's door open and the smell of French fries spilled out. She shivered from the shock of warmth, then sagged into the relief of it. It had been half a week of winter camping now. Every day she convinced herself she was okay, no need to take Sharp up on his offer of a couch or answer the question Hugh never asked. Every night she regretted her own stubbornness. Still, she kept at it, taking drives instead of hanging out at Belle's until closing because she knew she'd confess everything if she sat there too long. She didn't want to do that. She was a Hill. Hills were from Gallion. They had history here; they had meaning and standing and grit. They were not homeless and broke and unable to take care of their daughter at Christmas.

She unwound her scarf and plucked off her hat. Janis Joplin wailed from the jukebox; bottles clinked; voices and laughter rose in a roar like distant surf. "Laurel!" someone called. "Merry Christmas! Where's the Skye-ster? What're you doing down here?"

She moved through the crowd, a needle and thread weaving herself into the fabric of it all: the town, the people, the mingled fragrance of fries and pizza and hot cast iron. Sharp had the potbelly in the back burning along with the furnace. She took in the sounds of music and dishes clanking and voices she'd known her whole life, voices of people who'd known her mother and her grandparents and their parents even. "Passing time," she answered over and over as people asked what brought her to Belle's on Christmas Eve. "Skye's on vacation, having an adventure." Eventually the sad spot in her chest, that mucky sinkhole, dried out a little.

She ended up at a table with Jeff Hoover—the son of George Hoover, the Lakeshore's owner—who'd been three grades ahead of her in school, and also Moira Parks and Luke Carlson, whose families had summer places there. As usual, Jen had boycotted Christmas, a custom she'd started as soon as she was old enough to drive away from town. She avoided any holiday meant to involve family and feasts and goodwill. *Fairy tales*, she always seethed. Sean wasn't there either. He loved Christmas as much as Jen hated it, but the way the snow was coming down, he'd be out plowing. It was just as well, because seeing Luke at the table made Laurel's heart bump faster. Luke's ears were too big; his hair was too short; he was muscular but too skinny, the same as always. And as always, she warmed to him like he was a fire and she was a chilly traveler. She folded the feeling away. It was a fine shawl that spent its life in a trunk: saved for good, for special. For never.

"How've you been?" Luke talk-yelled into her ear.

A match-strike of happiness flared inside her. "I've been good!"

Jeff bought a round of flamers and one of shooters; Laurel drank the flamer to be festive and sipped at the shooter even though that was the opposite of what you were supposed to do. Moira finished both shots fast and swayed to the bar and came back with a round of Sex on the Beach. Laurel hopped her chair a few inches closer to Luke's as he sipped the drink from Moira. "Girlie," he muttered, his nose wrinkling. She laughed and he leaned in close. "What've you been up to?"

Laurel tapped him on the chest. "You first."

He frowned like she'd suggested something suspicious, but told her about his job selling medicines for a pharmaceutical company, about the current research into MS, which his mom suffered from, and about an idea he had of buying a house or a condo. Soon he stopped and gestured at her. "Your turn."

He had a tiny cut on his chin, from shaving, she thought. His sweater was cloud gray; laugh lines radiated from his blue eyes. Her hand lifted as if to smooth at one of those lines with a fingertip and she pulled it back into her lap. "I've been okay, I've been busy. With Skye, with work, nothing new."

She talked, quietly at first, but soon with animation. Finally, she was not cold and alone. Not only not alone, but with Luke. She told him the not-pathetic version of everything and Luke laughed or frowned in all the right places, and at last the sense that she must go everywhere with her head ducked and her shoulders tensed faded.

The order bell rang, Hugh slid a pizza into the window, and Lydia hurried to grab it. She carried it to the Johnsons' table, where Edwina sat with her dad and brother, who must be up for the holidays. Moira laughed in her too-loud way at something Jeff said; Luke tossed a wadded-up napkin at them. Laurel smiled at him and he grinned back. Abruptly, her eyes filled. These were her oldest friends and neighbors all around her tonight. She was nestled in among them, a Christmas ornament in its box, all of them fragile but each held in place by the others.

"You guys want to take a drive?" Jeff asked a minute later. "I know a place in the middle of nowhere. Nobody'll bother us, we can do whatever we want."

Moira looked around with manufactured surprise. "We're not already in the middle of nowhere?"

"And doing what we want?" A tree decorated with silver balls sat on the bar, the colored lights strung around the mirror blinked, and on the jukebox, Perry Como crooned that there was no Christmas like a home Christmas, which was right.

"Yeah, but I have some stuff." Jeff arched his eyebrows. "Good stuff, stuff you don't want to get caught with."

Luke studied Jeff. "Don't you and your folks always do your tree Christmas Eve?"

"We don't do a tree anymore, not since they bought the house in Crosscut. Ma hates the needles on the carpets and Dad won't agree to an artificial one. Says it isn't real if you can't smell it." A bleak expression crossed Jeff's face, transforming him from a cocky, familiar man into a kid who'd raced into the living room Christmas morning to find that there were no presents. "They can't say ten civil words to each other; it's World War Three. I'm thinking it wasn't smart for them to buy that Best Western up in Waiska. Really not smart. But that's my folks." He laughed as if this was funny and reissued his invitation.

Moira said it sounded better than sitting in Belle's, Laurel said nothing but wished Jeff would give up the idea, and Luke sighed very quietly. In the end, everyone decided to go.

Outside, Jeff and Moira climbed into Jeff's Blazer. Luke opened the passenger door of his Wrangler. "Want to ride with me?"

Laurel did, but Harper gazed at her through the Sable's side window and Frank would be peeping sadly. Plus, the plants had to be miserable. "No, thanks. I won't stay long."

"Yeah, I'm not into it either. But old times, right? Old friends, keep the connections?"

"Right."

They trailed Jeff south down the highway toward Crosscut, then east on a graveled county road. Harper glanced at Laurel, then back out the window. Jeff's Blazer trundled on, ten miles in, then fifteen, and then they were on the road up to Hasp: a motel called Stumps—a handful of swaybacked one-room cabins and a gas pump with a permanent placard dangling from it that read NO FUEL—and a bar called Stumps 2. Jeff pulled up in front and left his Blazer running. He came out a minute later carrying a thirty-pack and eating a candy bar.

The convoy resumed. They passed Jenson, a carbon copy of Hasp except that the gas pump worked, then drove north for a few miles and turned onto a narrower dirt road. The Sable bounced and groaned and Laurel gripped the wheel tight. She should turn back. She didn't know why she didn't.

After a while Jeff pulled onto a still-narrower track. A hand-painted sign nailed to a tree at its corner read *Tin Camp Road*. Their progress slowed. With a sinking feeling Laurel realized exactly where they were going. She didn't know why she hadn't thought of it before. The trees grew so close on either side, Laurel could've reached out and torn branches off. After another twenty minutes, Jeff pulled into a clearing. Before them was a trailer, ten feet by thirty, silver with a band of turquoise painted at the top and bottom, along with shark fins that pointed to the roofline. Laurel remembered when Baldy had painted those fins, trying to make the small trailer seem jaunty and tropical. Everyone piled out and Jeff pointed with his beer can. "Sweet, eh? It even has its own meteor."

A huge rock sat in the yard, and Jeff stumbled toward it. He fell into the snow and started making an angel and Moira dropped next to him. She began making her own angel; Jeff rolled on top of her and she shrieked.

Laurel walked close to the rock and Luke followed. "That's no meteor," he said. "If something this big fell out of the sky, it'd break into a million pieces."

"Or else make a huge hole." Laurel put both hands on it. The rock felt colder than she remembered it being, and harder, somehow. It squatted in the clearing like a fact you couldn't avoid no matter how much you wanted to. A boulder such as this didn't ease into the landscape; it didn't drift in and land like a feather. It came down hard. It was the geological equivalent of losing your gran and your home and getting pregnant without knowing the baby's father all in one year.

Laurel sighed. She had been seventeen the first time she saw this rock. Wearing her Brooks and running shorts and singlet, her hair damp on her neck. She'd gotten turned around on a cross-country route during a meet with Waiska, and when she saw the rock, she veered toward it. As she stood panting beside it, her hands on her knees, an old man, dressed in jeans and swampers and a jacket zipped to his chin, appeared from around the trailer's corner. The stubble on his face was white, his skin fair. He seemed stern, at first. Then, when she'd passed whatever private test he was administering, he was merry. He pumped a dipper of water for her and pointed her back the way she needed to go.

Laurel had returned a handful of times to see him. A few times when Skye was an infant waving her fists in the air like a boxer, and several more over the years as Skye became a toddler with a cowlick of black hair and already-wise brown eyes, then an eager kindergartener, and swiftly a sober-minded second grader. How strange that this was where Jeff led them.

"You okay?" Luke asked.

Laurel shoved her hands in her pockets. "Never better."

Jeff and Moira dangled from the branches of a pine now, scrabbling at its trunk, trying to climb higher. Luke winced. "We should've realized he was this lit. Jeff never could drink."

"No." Laurel slid her phone out. The screen showed two bars of service and she brought Skye's number up. But she shouldn't call again. When they talked earlier, Skye was fine, she was great. A bedtime check-in might make her homesick. She tucked the phone back into her pocket.

"Screw it, I can't get any higher." Jeff dropped from his branch and Moira dropped beside him. "Come on, let's go inside." He picked Moira up and towed her toward the trailer; she squealed and broke loose and ran to the door and tugged on it.

"Hey, quit it," Luke called. "We don't need to break into somebody's place."

"It's nobody's place." Jeff yanked on the padlock until it broke free. "You guys coming?"

It was cold. And in a way, Jeff was right, unless someone in Baldy's family had shown up and either taken over the property or sold it, which Laurel knew was unlikely, based on what Baldy'd told her. She followed the others inside.

Moira rotated in a circle. "Oh my God, it's claustrophobic. I'd be insane within ten minutes."

"No, it's sweet." Laurel touched the birch-paneled wall. Two chairs and an end table crowded each other beside the front window; a love seat filled the adjacent wall. Across from it was a small woodstove Baldy had installed. "Nothing like a wood fire for warmth," he'd said as he showed her around, his eyes gleaming with pleasure at the amenities he might offer his visitors, visitors who did not and most likely would not ever exist.

In the kitchen, a squat, round-bodied fridge stood beside a one-binned sink, and a narrow cooktop elbowed a short stretch of counter. Beyond that were two bedrooms separated by a minuscule bath. A double bed consumed half the first room, but it felt intimate instead of small: cupboards hung near the ceiling, a window looked over the woods, and a dark horizontal row of paneling midway up the birch gave a wainscoting effect. The room in back sported a bunk with a built-in ladder instead of a double bed, but was otherwise the same: pretty, cozy, inviting. Laurel patted the mattress—firm—and slid the closet door open on oiled runners. Baldy's work. His eyes had sparkled beneath his watch cap as he escorted her from one room to the next, his steps brisk and proud.

Back in the kitchen, she ran her fingers over the countertop. Red with a boomerang pattern, like Gran's. Her throat tightened. Gran would not have liked to see her breaking into a deceased friend's place with Jeff and Moira on Christmas Eve while Skye was halfway across the country. She turned. She was getting out of here; she'd make the others go, too—

Luke slung an arm around her neck. "Cool, huh?"

Laurel leaned against him.

An hour later, her eyelids drooped. Jeff had built a fire and the trailer was warming. "Go on, lie down," Luke said, patting his leg. Laurel paused—he nodded—then slouched into the couch's armrest and put her feet on his lap. Soon she was dozing. The talk wound like a lazy river. Everything mixed and connected in her head in a way that seemed meaningful but probably wasn't: Sean and his problems since he came back from overseas; Moira's job hostessing at a fancy dinner place downstate; the roll bars Jeff wanted to put on his Blazer; a book Luke was reading about water, how people needed it and not just in an obvious, drink-it-every-day-or-die way, but in an inborn, involuntary way. A spiritual way that was also practical, because people were made of water and had come from water.

That's right, Laurel thought devoutly. She curled closer in on herself.

The talk meandered on until Jeff suggested going outside. "Let's conquer that rock. I have a paint gun in the truck, we can write on it—*Merry Christmas, suckers, Gallion was here.*"

"What's the point, it's nice in here," Laurel heard Luke say, though faintly. Sleep had nearly taken her over. The warmth was precious, and it was a relief to have people nearby, even Jeff at his worst and Mannequin Moira, as Jenny had always called her.

"It's nice out there, too." A hand jostled Laurel's calf. "Wake up, Tree." Jeff's voice. "Shake a leg."

She tensed, resigning herself to going back out into the cold, but then a blanket settled over her. "She's out," Luke said. "Leave her alone, let her sleep."

A flume of cold air rushed in the door and woke her when they came back in. "Guys, listen," Jeff said in an urging way. "It's nobody's, it'll be awesome. Picture it: flames leaping. Way up."

"Burn, baby, burn," Moira answered, and Laurel opened her eyes to see Jeff clasp her close.

"All that'd be left is a pile of ashes—nobody'd know how it happened." Jeff glanced at Moira. Her face was avid and his eyes glowed bright. "It'd be primal. Let's do it."

Luke shook his head. "No way."

Jeff dug in the cupboard under the kitchen sink and came up with a bottle of lamp oil. "It'll be great."

"Put it back, Jeff."

Jeff danced the bottle in the air; Luke grabbed at it and missed. "Dude, listen—"

Jeff unscrewed the lid. "Come on, *dude*. It's Christmas, the season of light, right?"

"Drop it, okay?"

Jeff wagged the bottle again and oil flew out. Luke jabbed his shoulder. "I mean it, knock it off."

Jeff set the bottle down. "Fine, loser."

Luke screwed the lid back on. "We should go."

"Mr. Nice Guy." Jeff sounded both disgusted with Luke's straightness and resigned to it. "Moi, let's get out of here."

Laurel finally breathed, glad Luke seemed in control of the situation. Jeff had always been crazy when he was drinking. She stretched her arms above her head and Luke looked down at her. "You coming?"

"Just waking up."

He hesitated, smiling at her, and Laurel remembered a long-ago morning in Gran's kitchen when she'd flipped through a magazine, daydreaming about wearing a seafoam prom dress and dancing with Luke in the gymnasium. She'd wanted bright blue GoJanes for shoes. How much it had seemed to matter. How little it really had. And Luke hadn't come north for the dance, just as she'd expected he wouldn't. But maybe now he'd turn from the door—

Luke tapped the frame. "I should go, my parents will wonder. And I have news for them tonight." His face flushed. "I'm engaged!"

Laurel blanched. "Oh, wow!" she said quickly. "That's amazing. Congratulations. And yeah, go, hurry, it's late." She made a shooing motion, deeply embarrassed that some part of her was still the high school daydreamer, as clueless as ever about what anything really meant.

"You sure you don't want me to wait?"

"Yes! I'm the one who lives here. Go."

Luke went.

Laurel stayed behind to refold her blanket and pick up the leaves and twigs they'd tracked in. She wished she could get rid of the smoky odor. The Motel Five-and-a-Half, Baldy had called the trailer, patting the siding. He'd said it was a 1954 Custom Palace Ranchome, nodding as if she'd know how great that was. He lived in a cabin through the woods a quarter mile away; the trailer was on the property when he bought it and he'd kept it as a guest house, though as far as Laurel knew, he never had overnight guests. "It keeps good and warm, you're welcome to make yourself at home, you ever want to come and stay," he'd said. He'd gestured like a doorman rolling out a carpet, as hospitable as an uncle.

Outside, Luke's Wrangler had vanished. The Blazer's taillights blinked and exhaust chugged from the tailpipe; Jeff's window hummed down. "You okay to get out of here?"

"Yeah. Fine." Laurel placed a cautious foot on the metal stair.

"Tree?"

"Yeah?"

"Rumor has it my folks are splitting. Not too sure Dad'll keep both places open this winter, if they do."

Laurel stopped in midstep.

"I think he'd go over to Waiska. It's busier over there, you know? And the place is in better shape."

"I— Yeah."

"I'd hate to see you blindsided."

Laurel made herself smile at him. This was not that bad. She never earned a lot from the Lakeshore in the winter. "Thanks. And I'm sorry to hear about your folks."

He thumped the side of his truck and pulled away, bouncing and bobbing on the uneven track.

In the Sable, Harper raised his head from the circle he'd curled himself into on the passenger seat, and Frank was quiet. Laurel put her key into the ignition. Then she paused. She gave Harper a long look—apologetic, confiding—and pulled the key out again. It was warm inside, and cozy. And Baldy would not have minded. In fact, he'd invited her.

# Thirteen

aurel woke to the brightness snow makes of morning. She kneaded her neck and pulled the blanket closer. The warmth inside was a world unto itself, but Harper scrambled to his feet and gazed at her, his tail stilled in midwave. "Merry Christmas, buddy," she said, her voice creaky. "You want out?"

He trotted to the door and Laurel followed, wearing the blanket like a cape. Fern-shaped swirls of frost etched the window. She put a fingertip to one and melted a peephole but couldn't see much. She opened the door and drew in a surprised breath.

The pine boughs drooped with snow; the lines of her car had turned soft. She looked to Harper like they'd swap exclamations, but he brushed past her and down the steps. She exchanged the blanket for her coat and followed. The snow rose halfway to her knees, fluffy and sparkling.

At the car, she buried her fist in her sleeve and brushed the windshield. Harper stuck his head into a drift, then lifted his leg to pee. When he was finished, he trotted to another spot and dove his head under again.

Laurel wished she had a compass, though she knew the way out. It was traction that she needed for the miles of two-track stretching between here and Gallion. Chains would be good, not that she'd ever used chains, but she'd never put herself so far out in the woods in winter. She'd need a shovel if she bogged down, and she didn't have one of those either.

Harper bounded across the clearing. A pine let loose a branch of snow on his back and he barked an exclamation. Laurel laughed and suddenly felt cheerful. The snow was powdery and she'd been a good driver from the moment Gran taught her to drive the lawn tractor at age eleven. She would put a few small pieces of wood on the fire to get everyone good and warmed up, and then they'd head off.

She leaned against the car and studied the silent woods, the endless acres of trees, sky, snow. A tight spot that had hunched inside her ever since August—ever since the August Skye was born, in a way—relaxed and unfolded.

Maybe this was why Baldy lived out here on his own, even old as he was. He'd never said what had brought him here. Not just here, to this tract of forest, but to this way of living, which seemed lonely but might not be. Waiska was six miles north of Baldy's place, and she remembered from high school track meets that there was a laundromat and a bar and a gas station there. Also, the casino and the tribal college were close; the reservation started ten miles east of town. It was civilization as much as Gallion and maybe more so. His place felt remote, tucked in as it was and coming on it like she had, but that was misleading. Maybe his life had been misleading, too. Maybe everyone's was. And maybe it wasn't lonely to him, or maybe the loneliness was worth it for the peace of the place. It had a silence that was deeper even than Gallion's.

Back inside, Laurel added twigs from the woodbox to make the fire blaze. She liked that Baldy had kept wood for his nonexistent guests. It was a sign of his merriness and his optimism. Soon heat shimmered around the chimney; steam rose from her clothes and filled the air with the scents of wool and cotton. Laurel hoisted her boots onto a footstool. She would never be a risk-taker like Jen or accomplished like Mary Lynn, but being stranded miles from anywhere in the dead of winter was not a huge deal. If she got stuck, she'd walk somewhere to get help, that was all.

When the fire blazed, she wandered through the trailer again. Everything was snug and tidy: the lamp oil back safe under the kitchen sink, the bedding zipped into plastic storage bags in the closets. Baldy had kept the Motel Five-and-a-Half shipshape. "Plenty of propane," he'd bragged, tapping the tanks. "I always keep a winter's worth on hand, for the stove and the lights." He wouldn't use the gas heater that came installed in the Ranchome, though; he'd said too many people died in their sleep that way. Aside from that, everything was convenient and at the ready. "The place is high and dry. Anybody ever stayed for much of the winter, they'd be snug; we'd just have to keep the roof raked."

Laurel warmed herself through, fed the pets, and tromped out again. She started the car and turned it around so that when she left—she'd go soon, or anyway, soonish—it would be ready. The track they'd come in on from the west last night met a main road half a mile or so to the east. It led up to Waiska and down to the main highway. She would drive home the long way, ninety miles instead of thirty, but that was fine. Time was one thing she had plenty of.

Skye was full of talk about a place they'd been to see the day before, Mesquite Canyon, when they talked a few hours later. "We took a sightseeing drive and there's a camp there, Mom, a summer camp. It's in the foothills of the Zuni Mountains. Isn't that a romantic word? Foothills?" She sighed. "Anyway, they have sessions for kids my age. Mary Lynn said maybe I could go. She said she and Sam could help pay for it."

"Hang on—"

"You go on expeditions. It's all about ecology and archeology and art. Mary Lynn wants to talk to you about it."

Laurel tightened her grip on the phone. The wind blew out of the northwest steady as a stream of bad news. The sky glowered freighter gray and snow whirled in the clearing. She inched a few steps around the curve of the rock. Her face and hands were freezing. "I don't—"

"It seems so cool. Could I go?"

"I can't answer that right now."

"But—"

"We'll talk about it when you get back."

"O-kay. But do really think about it. It would be super great."

"Even better than Cedar Lake?" Laurel made her voice cheerful and teasing, but what she felt was desperate.

"I don't know. I can't compare, because I've never been. But it'd be amazing."

"I'll think about it."

"Mm-kay."

Above Laurel, a tree limb screeched against a neighboring trunk. The wind moaned and the snow in the clearing whipped into tornadoes.

"Mom, where are you?"

Laurel pressed closer against the rock. "It's beautiful today. Fat clouds, like ships, and snow dervishes."

"Mom. Where. Are. You?"

Laurel must not tell Skye about her strange, lonely Christmas. "I'm in the woods, it's—"

"Why?"

"No reason. It's pretty." Laurel looked up at the limbs of a maple pressed against the sky. The small branches were twisty; they'd been turning toward the sun their whole lives.

Skye made a frustrated sound. "I knew I shouldn't have come. You said you'd be fine, but you're not fine, are you?"

Laurel had left Sean to protect Skye from his moods when they were bad, from his outlook on life in the low times. She'd wanted to keep Skye from having to grow up too fast and know too much, from getting into a habit of watching and wondering, of caretaking and constant wariness, but she'd failed, or anyway, lately she was constantly in the process of failing. The only option that remained was to slog onward. "I'm fine. I'm more than fine, baby girl, I'm excellent."

"I guess," Skye said after a moment.

Laurel laughed. "What are you, jealous? Your old mom is out and about, having adventures and surviving without you, is that the problem?"

Another jolt of silence. "I'm not jealous."

"Okay, good. Now you tell me stuff. What's the weather? Is it warm, is it sunny?"

A voice murmured in the background. "Mom, I'm sorry, but I have to go. Mary Lynn wants to try a breakfast place and she read there's gonna be a line out the door."

"I won't hold you up, then. 'Bye, baby girl." Laurel held a hand up to shield her face, trying to shelter herself from the wind, but the wind changed direction again and found her anyway.

# Fourteen

I n the Dollar General, Laurel considered Tide but put the jumbo-sized Xtra into her cart instead. In front of the dish soap display she chose Home Essentials over Dawn; in the pharmacy aisle the no-brand aspirin over the Bayer; at the hand soap display the yellowy-gold one-dollar option over the lilac-colored soap called lavender-moonlight that came in an octagonal container. After spending twenty minutes choosing the cutest of the now-discounted cards and wrapping paper, she circled back to begin her Christmas shopping. Tomorrow, at last, Skye was coming home. Laurel had brimmed with anticipation when she woke that morning; she'd flung the blankets back and beelined to Crosscut.

Now she filled her cart with the bags of her purchases and pushed the swaying load outside. The sky was as gray as a garage floor today, typical Crosscut. It didn't matter. She popped her trunk and packages slipped and slid from the cart. She snatched up a bag containing a bright pink sweatshirt just before it plunged into the parking lot's glop. The shirt was basted together more than sewn, but she would fix that. She jammed it in alongside a jumbo can of popcorn. That had been an impulse buy; the cute tin was what she wanted, not the popcorn inside.

Soon she slopped around to the driver's-side door, sidestepping the lake of slush beneath it. She'd wrapped duct tape around her leaky left Sorel earlier in the winter, but even so it wouldn't be smart to march into trouble if she could avoid it. In the car she gave Harper a biscuit and fed Frank some seeds, then ate her own peanut butter sandwich before pulling away.

Her phone rang five miles north of town. She checked the number and steered onto the shoulder; she would run out of service in the swamp if she kept driving. "Skye! Hello! How are you, what are you doing? Tell me everything."

Skye launched into travelogue. They'd gone out to breakfast, Bruno had given her a T-shirt, she'd said goodbye to Abuelita, who'd given her a can of their special hot cocoa mix, and played with Benji and Dobs one last time.

If Laurel was a cartoon character, a bubble with a question mark inside would have hovered above her head. Skye galloped on. After breakfast they'd headed into Downtown Books and Skye spent all the money she had left on a book that looked excellent, a hardcover because she'd decided she couldn't wait for it to come out in paperback, and also into a hat shop, where Sam bought a cowboy hat, a nice one, and then they saw a hair salon that said walk-ins were welcome and she and Mary Lynn got haircuts.

"You what?" Laurel shouldn't feel dizzy, she'd had that sandwich, but she did.

"We got haircuts. It was so fun. Mary Lynn thought we should call you, but I said you wouldn't mind. You don't, do you?"

"Oh. No, sweet girl, why would I mind that?"

"I knew you wouldn't. Anyway, after that we found a camera shop. They had telescopes, too, and Mom, Mary Lynn bought me one. A telescope! The lady in the shop said it's a good one, and Mary Lynn agreed. It's so cool. It's black and it says 'Orion SkyQuest' on it. That's all. The shop lady said you never want to buy a telescope that advertises its magnification because that'll be a cheap, useless telescope, one that never works."

A noise came out of Laurel, an *Ah* that might have been an interjection conveying understanding or else a gasp of pain. In the slag heap of the gifts she'd bought at Dollar General, there was one fine thing, or there had been: a telescope whose box advertised its magnification, 35x to 40x, which had seemed like a lot.

"Mom? Are you okay?"

"Yes! I'm good, I'm perfect. Tell me more about this telescope."

"It was on sale for Christmas, three hundred dollars instead of four. Mary Lynn said it was such a good deal, she couldn't let it go by. She says to tell you she hopes it's okay she bought it. It is, isn't it?"

Laurel couldn't catch her breath. She rolled down her window and watched an eagle rise from the tip of a dead pine. It was far off, but she recognized it by its stately flaps and by the blurred flash of its white tail feathers. With a good telescope, she probably could've counted each one.

"Mom, are you still there?"

"I'm still here. I'm not going anywhere."

———————

In the airport parking lot, Skye dove into the back seat to greet Harper, and it was many minutes before Laurel persuaded her to climb in front and strap her seat belt on. Finally, they began the journey back to Gallion.

Skye bubbled with stories. Laurel had heard the highlights on the phone, but now she got the details. Skye rode a mountain in a tram and felt seasick at first but then the view cured her. She bought tamales from a street vendor and her lips burned from the fresh chili peppers, so much hotter than anything they had here. She talked to a Hopi woman about silverwork and they exchanged addresses. "She was so nice, and her work was beautiful. Sam bought me a bracelet from her." Skye stuck her arm out. A silver bracelet dotted with nubbins of turquoise encircled her wrist.

Laurel gaped at it. "That's nice. Kind of, um, too nice?"

"Mary Lynn said you'd worry about that, and Sam said if she could get me a telescope, he could get me a bracelet. But, Mom?" Skye touched Laurel's arm.

"Yes?"

"I know it's special. I'll keep it forever and I'll take good care of it, I promise."

"I believe you." Laurel did.

"We did so much. It seems like I was gone forever."

Laurel winked at her. "To me, too."

Sam and Mary Lynn and Skye had gone into an adobe house that was a museum; they sat in the back pews of a church where Sam liked to listen to the music; they made friends with the proprietor of the café where they had their coffee and cocoa in the mornings. The café was Café de las Flores and the proprietor was Bruno. His mother, who everyone called Abuelita, helped Bruno there, though she nipped home every few hours to let her dogs out. The dogs were terriers named Benji and Dobs, and Skye adored all of them.

*Wow*, Laurel said. *Interesting. Cool. Amazing.*

Seventy miles passed, then eighty. Gaps of quiet opened between Skye's stories, like rests in a piece of music. Laurel tapped her leg. "Getting tired?"

"Just thinking." She turned. "I took a bunch of photos on Mary Lynn's phone and she printed them for me. When we get home, I'll put them up on my corkboard and get everything out—paints, pastels, pencils, everything—and paint them. I can't wait. We're going to our place you found now, right?"

The day before on the phone Laurel had told Skye she'd found a place for them and that she'd tell her more when Skye was back in Michigan. Skye had accepted this lie that wasn't a lie. She trusted Laurel and she was too busy in far-off New Mexico to worry, so immersed in her adventure it hadn't even occurred to her to ask if that place was the Breakers. Perhaps it had seemed unthinkable, out under the big western sky.

A semi loaded with logs roared past. The car shuddered and Laurel gripped the wheel hard. "Skye. Listen. Here's the thing."

Laurel had barely finished explaining before Skye interjected, "You're kidding me."

Laurel shook her head. "Afraid not."

"But, Mom. The Breakers. That's ghastly."

Laurel blinked at this new word. "No, it's not. It's—quaint. You know the rooms are all kitchenettes, so we can cook, and we're at the end, so you can see the water, and Mr. and Mrs. Owens gave me a good deal. 'Cause they love you." Which was true, but likely also true was that the rate, one fifty a week instead of the almost six hundred it would've been on a night-by-night basis, was as much because they were usually half empty: small rent trumped no rent at all.

Skye tucked her hair behind her ears and it untucked right away, too short now to stay in place. "Great."

"They have cable," Laurel said. "We'll have movie marathons on the weekends, run to Phil's for snacks. We'll dash out and get 'em and be back before the commercial's over."

"This is our life we're talking about, Mom. I doubt movies and snacks are our highest priorities."

"I know it's our life. But this is temporary."

Skye tapped the armrest. Buzzed the window down an inch, three inches, then back up. Stared ahead for a while. At last she said, "Snacks, huh?"

Laurel slid her eyes sideways. "We'll live it up. I'll get chips." In general, chips were a no-no in her book, along with most other store-bought snacks. "And Ho Hos." These weren't a no-no, exactly, Skye relished them too much for Laurel to forbid them, but they went only into her lunches, one package per day every school day of the year, every year since first grade. Skye never tired of them, and on this, Laurel never economized.

"Like, extra Ho Hos?"

"Ho Hos galore."

"I still don't like it."

"Me neither. But we'll settle in there." She reached to tug on a lock of Skye's newly shortened hair.

———————

Skye shuffled out of the bathroom in her pink pajamas two hours later looking creaky and wilted. Laurel glanced up from unpacking the burgers she'd brought from Belle's. It was after eleven when they finally reached town, and she was too tired to cook; Hugh was nice enough to fry these even though the kitchen was closed. "What's wrong?"

Skye kneaded one shoulder. "I don't know."

"It was a long day. You're all worn out."

"Maybe."

Laurel palmed her forehead and Skye leaned into her hand. "I'm so hot."

She must've picked up a bug on the plane. Or else the energy she'd bounded home with drained out of her the moment she learned Laurel had moved them into Broke-Down Breakers. Laurel massaged her neck. "Okay, cowpoke. Into bed." She patted the mattress and Skye climbed under the covers.

She woke at midnight, coughing chestily. Laurel snuggled her close, wishing she had a sauna to light so she could steam this out of Skye the way Mom and Gran had steamed ailments out of her.

"I feel crummy," Skye said sadly.

"I know," Laurel answered, equally mournful.


Hours plodded past. Night turned to day and day to night again. Laurel asked Mrs. Owens to watch Skye midway through the second morning. She drove to Whittle's, where she dug the humidifier out of a box near the top of a pile. She dodged the rest of their possessions.

She didn't want to see their bowls and blankets and books, the bed or rocker or footstool, the sewing machine or the box with the twinkle lights in it. Their old life seemed idyllic now, an unattainable oasis.

In the room, the humidifier emitted faint mist and hummed endlessly, a low background chorus to their sad state. Skye coughed and dozed; she tossed and turned and complained of aching everywhere. Even her skin ached, even her eyes. She opened books and closed them without reading, flicked the television on and changed channels every few minutes. Laurel fed her baby aspirin and toast and broth; she kept cool cloths on Skye's forehead and rubbed Vicks on her chest. She murmured comforting things when Skye woke from bad dreams and read aloud from the Vikings book if the dreams had been nightmares. She sat on the chair wedged between the wall and the bed, or else on the bed. She did little except tend to Skye. She could put her mind to nothing else.

At daylight on the fourth day, Skye slept deeply. One fist curled beneath her cheek, the other dropped off the edge of the bed to rest on Harper's skull. Laurel laid a hand on her forehead. It was no longer scorching. She tucked the blanket closer around her and Skye opened her eyes.

"Sorry," Laurel whispered.

" 'S okay."

"Feeling better?"

Skye pushed her shoulders up. "Maybe. I think so."

"It'll be nice today. Sunny."

"Huh."

Laurel smoothed her hair. Skye rolled onto her back and looked at the ceiling. It had a stain Laurel had thought looked like a brindled schnauzer in the hours she'd spent staring at it. "Penny for your thoughts, baby."

"I kind of hate it when you call me that." Skye's tone was contemplative.

"Call you what? Baby?"

"Yeah. Because I'm not one anymore."

Laurel dropped into the chair. "That's true. I'll try to stop."

"That would be good."

Laurel tapped Skye's nose. "I have another penny or two. Got another thought?"

"I do," Skye said slowly. "I wonder about it a lot."

Laurel's skin prickled. "Yes?"

"Why is everything so hard all the time for us?"

The humidifier whooshed; the fridge hummed. Harper stood with his chin on the mattress beside Skye's knee and he tilted his head in mutual inquiry. Laurel narrowed her eyes at the line of the light shining between the curtains. "I don't know," she said finally.

Skye wiggled her toes, watching them in the easily entertained way of the recently feverish. "It seems like we're always waiting for something that never happens. Like it never will happen. Like it's a corner way up ahead that never gets any closer."

A truck released its air brakes outside. The grocery semi at Phil's. Laurel skimmed her hand up and down Skye's leg.

"Will it ever get better? Will it ever be different?"

Laurel sat up straight. "Yes. We're going to have an excellent year."

Skye gazed at her and Laurel nodded despite her urge to glance away.

———

The next morning, the sky shone robin's-egg blue and the shadows of buildings and street signs inscribed sharp lines against the snow. Tiny old Gallion with its peeling paint and swaybacked roofs was quiet but expectant, as if anything might happen.

Skye was getting ready for school. She leaned in the bathroom doorway, her mouth full of toothpaste. "Corrine and Hamish gave Abby a new phone for Christmas. She said the case is so cute, it's all flowers. And a new coat and snow pants."

"Purple, right?"

Skye nodded. "And more boots. She said they're so warm."

"Nice."

"She really wanted them."

"She got what she hoped for, that's great."

Skye bent over the sink to rinse her mouth. "Mom, what would you have, if you could have anything?" she called.

"You mean if I had three wishes and a magic lamp?"

"Yeah."

"Hmm. That's a tough one."

Skye reappeared. "Is it?"

Laurel laughed. "No. If I could have anything, I'd have what I already do."

"What's that?" It was a line Skye had been told a million times and still loved hearing.

Laurel fished on the nightstand for her trusty paper airplane and launched it at her daughter. "You. I'd have you. Now go on, before you're late."

Through their room's west window, Laurel watched Skye zigzag down the middle of the street, avoiding three snowmobiles that buzzed up to the gas pumps at Johnson's. Hugh stepped out the side door of Belle's, where he would have been mopping or cleaning the beer lines. He climbed into his pickup and sat slumped behind the wheel, motionless and peaceful-seeming.

After a moment, he yanked the shifter and pulled onto the street, exhaust fumes puffing. Skye stopped when he came abreast of her and waved at him with sweeps of her arm. "Rock on!" Laurel heard her holler, her voice faint through the glass.

"Rock on, little sister." Hugh gave her the hang-ten sign. "Stay loose!"

Laurel's heart thrummed slow, steady; her blood pulsed evenly through her veins. She felt the one great truth in her life, that Skye was everything.

# Fifteen

Laurel turned from the window, brushing against the table where they'd been eating and where Frank's cage was perched; it rocked beneath her hand and Frank peeped in fear. The table would have to double as Skye's desk starting tomorrow. Where would she put Frank? On the floor? In the sink?

In the bathroom, the towel bar flapped loose on one end and several of the shower's tiny puce tiles were missing. Laurel turned the spray on with faucets like outdoor spigot handles. Turned it off and yanked her hair into a tight bun. She stared at herself in the mirror and haunted eyes stared back.

A moment later, she dropped into the main room's one chair, which was covered in cracked black vinyl. Frank peeped, Harper sighed deeply, and Laurel plucked Skye's duffel from the floor and unzipped it. The smell of Skye wafted out: sage, with a hint of her coconut shampoo. A sketchbook lay on top of her sweaters and jeans. In it, drawings in pen and colored pencils filled the pages. The Hopi jeweler sat smiling on a blanket; Abuelita cradled her dogs. Sam lounged on a park bench; Mary Lynn held a bag of pastries aloft. The church towered; the tram clattered; the string of chili peppers shimmered with heat.

Laurel tucked the book away. She rounded the bed with its plasticky coverlet, jiggled the nightstand's wonky drawer, and yanked out the phone book.

"I was wondering if you need help in Waiska this winter," Laurel said a minute later, standing in the northwest corner of the parking lot where there was a signal, her back to the wind. "Jeff mentioned it Christmas Eve."

"I didn't *need* help then."

Laurel ducked her head as if George Hoover could see her. "I must have misunderstood. But *do* you need help over there?"

"It happens I do. Two girls quit this week, a receptionist and a maid. It's like a virus once it starts."

Laurel's stomach churned. "That's great news." She put conviction into her voice because it was time to be a new person, a *sure* person, for Skye's sake. Then she realized it might come across wrong. "For me, I mean."

George Hoover laughed humorlessly. "And I guess you calling is good news for me."

"Would it be full-time?"

"I'd say close. It stays busy, with the casino and the college so near."

"Is it days? I'd need days, I have Skye."

"I'll make it days to get some help I can rely on. I'd need you to start right away, though, by this weekend."

The phone slipped; Laurel clasped it tighter.

"What do you say?"

Laurel took a breath like she was diving into water.

At dinner she reached across the rickety motel table and speared one of Skye's green beans from her plate. "I have news," she blurted out.

"Oh?" Skye raised her brows; Gran gazed skeptically out from her eyes. Fond but stern.

"It's exciting, but I won't lie, it's also alarming."

Skye waggled her fingers toward Harper and Laurel pretended not to notice. Harper was forbidden from eating scraps, but he enjoyed green beans whereas Skye didn't.

"I have a new job."

Skye's head snapped up. By the time Laurel finished explaining, her expression telegraphed horror.

Laurel grabbed her hand. "I want us to think of it as, I don't know, an exchange program. Like we're moving to a foreign country for a while."

Skye's face rumpled. "But, Mom, school."

"I know. It's not perfect. But you are so smart. *So* smart. And you'll learn so much from it. Lots of kids travel with their parents for work. It's good for them. They get a whole new perspective, wider horizons."

"But I don't want to move. We're Hills, we live here." Skye thumped the table and their plates rattled.

"I know. But we're doing it."

"Why?"

"Because I think if we do . . ." Laurel had debated mentioning the camp all day. Should she give Skye the camp to look forward to or not risk disappointing her? "I think if we do, I can save more money. Then before summer, we'll find somewhere else to rent, somewhere better than Sue's or Harv's ever was."

"But where would we live? In another motel room?"

"I've decided the best thing is if we live at Baldy's."

Skye gaped at her, a green bean pinched between her fingers. "Baldy's. As in Baldwin Chapter, that guy who died when I was little?"

Skye had been seven. "It'll work out." At Christmas she'd seen that everything was still in place, as if no one had been on the property since Baldy passed. Firewood, kindling, propane, axes. Snowshoes, lanterns, a sled. Even the lamp oil. Most of all, seclusion. No one would notice them camping out back in there. The county plowed a pullout on the main road where she could park. The two of them could trek in and out the half mile, borrow Baldy's snowshoes when the snow grew deep. Not all that much could go wrong. And as for what could go right: she could save enough to send Skye to camp. It was what she had to do, what might change Skye's life, lift it up like a balloon.

"Trust me."


Skye trudged out of Waiska Consolidated cradling the box that held her knarr on a Tuesday afternoon two weeks later. She was a slow-moving freighter, and the other children were waves breaking around her. The younger ones rampaged toward the street and the buses; the teenagers ambled with indifferent dignity; the middle schoolers flip-flopped between the two approaches. The sun was bright, the kids' coats and hats a collage of colors against the snow.

Laurel blinked back sudden tears. She was such a foolish person! But the scene seemed charged with a message about life's brevity and also its eternalness. It might have been her shuffling out of school in heavy boots, might've been Jen striding ahead in an ice-blue coat with a fake fur ruff on the hood and Jeff sneaking up behind to stick a sheet of paper on her back that read *Kick me!* How much the same it all was. And how different. Hasp and Jenson were too small to have their own schools, and the reservation's population spilled into the school district, so there were ninety children enrolled in Waiska instead of Gallion's thirty. And all of them were strangers.

A teacher called out a greeting, another intervened in some minor roughhousing, a dog raced from a yard and scrabbled at a giggling middle schooler, barking. Skye stared at the sidewalk, placing each foot with care, her mouth pinched.

Laurel tugged at her work smock. She wished she'd yanked it off before she hurried here. It was dark blue, well used, and too big. It kept her own shirts clean, a good thing now that they had no washer and she snuck their clothes into the Best Western's machines every so often, but Skye found it ugly. Most days Laurel left it at work instead of listening to her criticisms: it's something an old lady would wear, it washes out your face, why can't it at least be cute like the scrubs some people had? Laurel volunteered that she thought it looked like a painter's smock, but the sneer in Skye's eyes made her wish she'd kept that to herself.

As Skye neared the car, a boy bumped into her, laughing with a friend, and shock washed over her face, then indignation. She clutched her box closer. Laurel tapped her horn and leaned to push the passenger door open.

"Hey, baby. I got off work early." Laurel put her arms out, wiggling her fingers until Skye relinquished her treasure. "That is some boat." Mary Lynn had sent it from New Mexico and Skye had spent most of her free time since they moved assembling it.

"It was a kit, Mom. Not that hard." Skye dropped into her seat and pulled the belt over her lap.

"I don't care. It's wonderful."

Skye stared out at the school, a single-story building of reddish bricks with a tan pattern belted around its center.

Laurel tried another tack. "Nice and warm in there, I'll bet."

"Gallion School has more character."

"Is that what it's called when you have to wear your boots inside in the winter?" In fact, Laurel had never minded wearing her boots straight through the school day in cold weather. Things like that were points of pride for Gallion kids. No school was smaller than theirs, or older, or remoter, and no students tougher.

"I don't know."

"It's new, is all," Laurel said in a bright tone she disliked in herself. "You'll get used to it."

Skye shook her head.

Laurel's voice softened. "You're a Hill, remember? You have *sisu*." Finnish for grit, stoicism in hard times.

Skye thumped the window glass. "Yeah, like you said, we're Hills. Hills live in Gallion. I don't even know how we ended up here."

"Oh, now. Exchange students, remember? Adventures, new horizons?"

Skye heaved a weary sigh. So far nothing about Waiska was as romantic as Laurel had painted it. Gallion and Waiska were only thirty miles apart—at least in the summer when the back roads were open—and they were about the same size. Gallion was on the water

137

whereas Waiska was two miles inland, but still they were so similar that it all should have been easy and familiar, but so far, it wasn't. The place didn't fit right.

The stone Lutheran church loomed over the street gloomily instead of sitting quaint and pert like Gallion's white clapboard version. The school was new and crisp instead of old and creaky; the streets were wide instead of narrow; the Veterans Memorial listed no familiar names. Hahn's Market was dingier and mustier than Phil's, though that was no palace either, and their brands were different, Aunt Millie's bread instead of Sara Lee, and no Progresso soup or any decent cuts of meat. Also, the dairy products sat in a bank of coolers at the back instead of on the north side—Laurel had yet to remember this when they shopped—and they weren't cold enough. Her heart was not with the program, but her gut said it was too soon to tell, and her head said she was the one who'd signed them up for this, so she had better keep their spirits from flagging. "We have to give things a chance," she told Skye. "We have to keep our minds open."

Skye ran her palm up and down her seat belt.

"It's not forever. Tell me what happened."

"Nothing."

"Baby—"

"I am not a baby!"

Laurel froze. "You're right, I'm working on it."

"Thank you."

"So . . . How'd show-and-tell go?"

Skye yanked herself around to face Laurel. "Not good."

"Uh-oh."

"Yeah." She patted the knarr as if soothing a browbeaten puppy. "I took it up to the front before lunch."

Skye waited as if Laurel would speak, so Laurel said, "Yes."

"And I gave a little talk explaining."

"Yes."

"And then there's always a question-and-answer part."

"Yes?"

"And people asked things. Like, how long it took and how much it cost and whether I ordered it from Norway."

Laurel nodded.

"Stephen Spears wanted to know if it would float, which I'm not sure, but I told him it was a good question." *Yes*, Laurel began to say, but Skye didn't let her. "Peter Walker said it was cool, which was nice of him but wasn't a question, and asked if I planned to make another one. I said I might and called on Joe Allen Phizer. He waved his hand the whole time like his head would explode if I didn't call on him, so I thought I better make him wait—people need to learn self-control, right?"

"Sure."

"But he didn't even ask anything! He said flat-out that girls don't like boats. According to him, only boys like boats. Boats, models, hunting, about a million other things I like. He said my knarr was stupid."

"Stupid! How dare he? Where was your teacher during all this?"

Skye gave an emphatic nod. "Oh, she was there. She clamped onto him like one of those pincer games at the grocery store and marched him into the hall. When they came back, his face was red and he wouldn't look at anybody."

"Good. But I'm sorry for what he said."

"Me, too. I worked so hard on it, Mama." Skye's sturdy fury crumbled; she gasped as she spoke these last words.

Laurel banged the steering wheel. "Joe Allen Phizer's wrong. It was an ignorant thing to say, and I'm sorry he hurt your feelings, but you can't listen to him. He's jealous."

Skye sniffed.

"Did anyone say anything nice about it? If they didn't, they're all jealous."

Skye wiped at her cheeks, though she hadn't cried. "Mrs. Fox said it was a striking example of concentration and focus." She glanced at Laurel. "That's good, right?"

"It's great."

"She said it could go in the showcase next month if I wanted."

"Fantastic. I never had anything in a display case, ever." In all the schools she'd attended all over the state of Michigan, she hadn't.

Skye scooted herself straighter. "Peter told me again at lunch that he liked it. His cousin did, too. Allie. She's a grade behind us."

"So, they're the ones you pay attention to. You can't let the *mulkvistit* get you down, *kultu*," Laurel said. *Mulkvistit* was a Finnish invective, *kultu* what Gran called Laurel in tender moods: golden, dear one. "That's a rule in life."

A smile flitted across Skye's face. "Quarter in the swear jar, Mom."

They trekked carefully to the trailer with the knarr atop the sled Laurel had found in Baldy's shed, and Laurel rewarded them with tacos for supper, one of Skye's favorite meals. Afterward they played Boggle beneath the glow of the gaslight that shone down on the table. Before each round, Skye shook the dice with gusto—the rattle made Harper bark every time—then flipped the egg timer and gave the command to go. By six she was teasing Laurel for making so many three-letter words; by six thirty her laughter had squeezed her cheeks into apples.

Laurel laid her pencil down half a minute into their fifth round. Skye's eyes flicked between the game and her paper; her pencil treadled steady as a sewing machine pedal. She glanced up. "What?"

Laurel smiled. "Nothing."

Skye bent back over her work. "You better hurry it up. You have, like, one minute left and, what? Two words?"

"Four. Hut, hot, shot, gourd."

"Wow, I am so impressed."

"Meanie."

"Hush, you're breaking my concentration."

Laurel stuck her tongue out and Skye pursed her lips as if she hoped that one day Laurel would outgrow such displays of immaturity. The gaslight hissed and flickered, bathing Skye in its buttery light that reminded Laurel of old Polaroid photos. Tonight, Skye wore a gray cardigan that pulled some over her belly, jeans that were a shade too wide and too long, and a giant pair of socks that had once been Sean's. Also, her hat and scarf. She looked frumpy and brilliant and happy, and Laurel felt happy, too. Everything was going to be fine. It wasn't just going to be, it already was.

# Sixteen

arper barreled toward Skye when she appeared on the track one afternoon midway through February. Laurel dropped the ax and waved, and Skye lifted a mitten. Her cheeks glowed red, her arms pumped. At the trailer, she shushed Harper's leaping with a gesture—when she patted the air, he settled and gazed at her in adoration. Skye took a sheet of paper from her satchel and handed it over. "Here. So I don't forget."

"What is it?"

"You're supposed to go see Mrs. Fox after school tomorrow."

Laurel frowned. "About what?"

"It's all on there. You have to sign it." She ruffled Harper's ears.

Laurel skimmed the paper, uninformative aside from stating the date and time Mrs. Fox wished her to appear. She zipped it into her coat pocket and studied Skye's round face. A thousand thoughts lived in her brown eyes, but she was quieter than normal these days. "How is school, anyway? You haven't said much since you took your boat in."

Skye unbuckled the bindings of the snowshoes Laurel had borrowed from Baldy's shed. "It's okay."

"I thought you might take your telescope."

Skye flashed a scornful look. "After the knarr? Um, no."

Laurel tapped her knee. "What gives, then?"

Skye put her nose to Harper's. She whispered something to him and Harper licked her neck.

"You miss Gallion."

"Yeah. But this isn't forever. Like I said, it's fine."

Laurel ran her hand along the ax handle. It and the leather gloves she wore for splitting were from Baldy's shed, too. It was strange to imagine his hands in the gloves before hers. Strange but good, as if she was carrying on with fundamental work he'd been stopped in the middle of. "Okay, good."

Skye nodded.

"So . . . what else?"

"Nothing else. I'm going in." She put a boot on the stair.

"Stay and talk a while."

"No, it's cold."

Laurel felt stricken. "Just tell me one thing you like about school."

"I already said. It's okay. It's school."

Laurel pressed her palms together. "Please, miss, can't you spare a scrap for a poor, starving mother."

Annoyance creased Skye's face and vanished, a cloud racing across the sun. "I like Mrs. Fox. She's kind of scary, but she has a good way of laughing. And we sit by tables instead of alone—it's different from Gallion, but it's cool."

When Laurel had dropped Skye off at school for her first day, she'd seen a girl raise her eyebrows at Skye's outfit, the purple velvet dress and paisley leggings. Laurel had yearned to swoop in and carry Skye back home to Gallion, and it had taken everything she had to stride down the bright hall full of student artwork and posters cheering the Waiska Warriors and out the door, leaving Skye behind. She couldn't admit that, though. "It's good, then, having more kids around?" she asked.

"Mostly. Peter's at my table. I like him and we always win the word relay Mrs. Fox does on Fridays. But sometimes I do wish I had my own space." She wrinkled her nose. "Like when you're trying to think hard about something? And nobody else is in the same mood? Then I wish I had my own desk."

Laurel balanced another piece of wood on the chopping block. She'd spent the day hauling it from a shed beside Baldy's cabin on a sled she found in his barn. The pile measured four feet by eight now. She would write "one cord stovewood" in the account book she'd bought at the gas station the day they pulled into town. If she could pay all this back someday, if a relative of Baldy's appeared, she wanted to be prepared. "Do you go to the meeting, too?"

"No. Just you."

"Do you want to wait for me in the library?"

"I'd rather come home and hang out with Frank and Harper. I want to work on some drawings."

"You'll be all right alone here by yourself?"

The annoyance flashed again. "It's an hour."

"An hour can be a long time, baby-cake."

"You do realize I'll be leaving for college or whatever in not that many years?" She clomped through the door.

Laurel stared into the snow-drenched trees, then rounded the ax up and brought it down on the waiting chunk of pine.


Mrs. Fox looked up when Laurel knocked, then glanced at the clock. "You're Skye's mother? Laurel?"

"Yes, I'm sorry." Laurel rubbed at a smudge on her sweater, a dollop of coffee from the cup she gripped in her other hand. She'd had to stop for gas or run out and had bought the coffee at the same time. She shouldn't have brought it in with her; it screamed careless, selfish, and sloppy, as if she cared more about her own pleasure and convenience than wasting someone else's time.

Mrs. Fox waved her forward. "Please, come in."

The teacher wore her mahogany hair twisted into a smooth bun that made Laurel wish her own wasn't hanging loose and stiff from the sweat she'd worked up shoveling the car out. She'd dug and dug, sweating until she was damp and bedraggled. She wound a hank of curls around her hand and squinted apologetically.

"Thank you for coming. Though with this weather, I'd have preferred to reschedule."

Laurel's face heated. Skye had appeared at the door at two instead of three thirty, but that the weather might affect this meeting as well as the children's schedule hadn't occurred to her.

"I tried to call several times. Is the number in your file correct?" The teacher read the number from the form Laurel had filled out when she enrolled Skye in school.

Laurel set her coffee cup on the floor; her coat slipped from her arm and knocked it over and the last sips dribbled onto the tile. She blushed and draped the coat over the chair, blushed deeper when it slid off again. "Yeah, yes, that's right," she said as she fussed with the parka. "It's a cell phone, we don't have the best reception back at— back where we live. I should have turned it on. I don't leave it on much, I hate to drain the battery, since we don't—" She managed not to say *have electricity*. Her cheeks burned. "I guess it didn't dawn on me."

"I see."

Laurel suspected Mrs. Fox did see, that she saw all kinds of things Laurel would've preferred her not to. She sat and wove her fingers together.

"Another time, check in if at all possible, please. You don't have a landline?"

Laurel shook her head.

"Well, try to make it a habit to turn your cell on if you get into an area that has reception during the school day. I feel better if I can reach a student's parent in case of emergency."

Laurel swallowed and nodded.

Mrs. Fox let a beat of silence pass. "Thank you."

"I'm sorry if I messed you up. It's just, you know, you set a time, I signed the paper."

Mrs. Fox narrowed her eyes. "It's a parent-teacher conference, not a summons."

"I know. I just—" The old Lakeshore-crew phrase ricocheted in her head. "Just" was a slippery, undefinable word and justice uncertain, though neither was anything to cry about. Life dealt cards; you played them. Laurel cleared her throat. "I assumed I had to come."

"And was that a problem?"

"No."

"Good." Mrs. Fox flipped a folder open and rested her hand on the papers within. Her nails were smooth and white tipped, and Laurel curled her own fingers into her palms. She'd loaded the stove right before she left and the log was caked with dirt. "I called you in because I want to talk about how Skye's doing. It can be difficult to change schools in the middle of a year."

Laurel leaned forward to explain that they wouldn't be here long, they'd head back home the minute they could, but she realized how flighty that would have sounded. She leaned back again.

"It can be challenging, but she seems to be adjusting. She's an excellent student," Mrs. Fox said.

"Yeah, I know, she's amazing. Me, I wasn't great at school. Aside from shop class and running; running was my specialty. Cross-country, I mean. Not from things."

"Of course."

Laurel smiled too widely, like a lion about to eat a child; she wanted to stop, but couldn't.

"At any rate, I wanted to go over a few things with you."

Laurel crossed her legs and uncrossed them when her skirt rode up. She spread her hands flat on her thighs and realized this showcased her dirty fingernails. She tugged at her cardigan, stowed her hands in her lap, fingers curled to hide the dirt, and made herself sit still.

"We've been administering the accelerated math and reading tests." Mrs. Fox slid a page around to face her. "Skye is reading at a twelfth-grade level."

Laurel considered explaining how they'd worn out Skye's first books, reading them so many times. *Corduroy. Goodnight Moon. The*

*Very Hungry Caterpillar.* Should she confess that they still read together, acting out parts and giggling like maniacs? No. This smooth, stern woman would think it childish. Mrs. Fox talked on; Laurel refixed her gaze.

". . . how much she likes science, and her math scores are high, too. She's a smart girl."

"I know. People always say so." Another stupid comment. She knew from her own observation, not from people informing her. Why must she sound so lame and ignorant now when it mattered most?

"What I mean is, she's exceptionally smart."

Laurel looked hard at Mrs. Fox. "And?"

Mrs. Fox frowned. "You don't care?"

Laurel lurched forward. "Of course I care. I'm asking, what's the problem, why did you call me in here?"

"I needed to touch base with you, make sure we're on the same page."

What page was that? The one where they were more or less squatting on a dead man's property? The one where they lived without electricity or running water, which was maybe illegal if you had a child? Or the page where they'd moved without warning and would move again before long? Laurel pressed her lips together to prevent any secrets escaping.

"Let me show you her ecology folder."

Inside was a book report with a sketch of two woodpeckers on the front. *Downy woodpecker,* Skye's neat handwriting had labeled the smaller bird. *Hairy woodpecker,* the label beside the bigger one read. Mrs. Fox turned a page and tapped something Skye had written with her French-manicured nail. Laurel nodded sedately, though she longed to leap at the woman and shake answers from her. More than that, she wished that she was not herself. It would be better to be someone else, someone smoother and smarter and more adept. Mary Lynn, for example, would have worn her going-to-town jeans and a clean flannel shirt and would have looked just right: down-to-earth and steady. Laurel, on the other hand, had understood when she checked in at the office and some random man winked at her that she was all wrong in the black skirt and spike-heeled boots and pink cardigan with the lace-trimmed T-shirt beneath. When she chose it, she thought the outfit was dressy, but then saw in his leer that it was sleazy and scrapped together. Now, she leaned closer to Mrs. Fox to listen better.

Minutes later, Mrs. Fox tapped Skye's papers back into their folder.

"So, what do I do?" Laurel had calmed as she gazed at Skye's handwriting. "How do I help her?"

"I don't mean for you to overreact to this."

"You called me in here, there had to be a reason."

"Just make sure she feels secure, that she's happy. This is an important age. I'd hate to lose her."

"*Lose* her."

"I only mean that she's so bright and unique. She's a very authentic character."

*Skye Hill is not a character*, Laurel wanted to shout. *She's a real girl, my daughter.*

"We want to foster that special spirit."

"How?" Laurel croaked.

"Encourage her. Which I'm sure you do. And, well . . . watch her." Mrs. Fox opened her desk drawer and pulled out packages of Ho Hos. "I'm sorry, I'm not explaining this well."

Laurel frowned at the treats. "What—"

"She's hoarding them—rationing them, I guess, might be more accurate. I found them in her cubby, I went through it. I hate to do that, but I thought I'd better. It took me a while to notice, but she only eats half of one each day. She cuts them with a plastic knife she keeps in a baggie. She's clinical about it, she—"

"But she loves Ho Hos. Do you think she's sick—is her stomach hurting and she didn't tell me? Is it an ulcer? Do kids even get ulcers?" Laurel snatched up a package, as if she could identify it, make certain that these were from Skye's lunches and not some other child who was behaving strangely. But every Ho Ho was identical.

"I wondered. I even wondered about anorexia."

"Are you nuts?" The moment the words were out, Laurel slapped her hand over her mouth.

Mrs. Fox smiled. "I realize it's not that. And I don't think it's a stomachache."

"So . . . what?"

"I'm not sure. I expect you'd know better than me."

Laurel gazed at the Ho Ho. It was smashed now at one end. She shook her head.

"It's only a part of the reason I invited you in, but I thought I should tell you."

"She's been eating Ho Hos in her lunch ever since she started school, one pack a day like clockwork. Why she'd start divvying them up now, I can't imagine." Laurel could not stop shaking her head.

"Mull it over, I guess. And in the meantime, make sure she feels safe."

Laurel's head snapped up. "You think I'd let anyone hurt her?"

Mrs. Fox held up both hands. "No."

"What then?"

"Just—make sure she's free to be herself."

An icicle spear of fury stabbed through Laurel. "Who else would she be?"

Mrs. Fox reached across her desk to touch Laurel's arm and Laurel was aware again of the dirt under her nails, her sweat, the stain on her sweater, the thrift-shop parka, warm but hideous, drooping off her chair. "The main thing I wanted to say today is that she's gifted. She has something special and it's important to support her. Especially right now. Children are vulnerable at this age."

Laurel remembered sitting on the stool in the corner of a third-grade classroom downstate because *Laurel refuses to focus on her times tables, class, and this is what happens.* Her long johns itched and her feet sweated inside her boots. She was so used to wearing them from Gallion that she kept forgetting her shoes. No matter where she was, she waited for recess, living it in advance. Downstate, she'd hide at the farthest edge of the playground, somewhere near a tree. In Gallion, she would burst from the school's double entry doors and race to the monkey bars. She'd scramble to the top, do a flip on each bar on her way back down. The whole time she sat inside she ached with an actual physical pang to move, to run across the grass, grip the bar, tense her stomach muscles, and flip. The blood rushed to her head as she dangled upside down and whatever was wrong—the times tables, the boredom of the classroom, the loneliness and awkwardness if she was not at home—drained away, leaving only joy. Was it like that for Skye?

Out of the blue, Mrs. Fox smiled warmly and Laurel imagined the good laugh Skye had mentioned. "The takeaway on this? She's great."

Laurel nodded and dragged her ugly parka across her knees, which never should've been showing. "I'm glad her test scores are so good and all. And, um, I'll keep in mind what you said, for sure." She smiled miserably. Every word she said came out wrong: she looked bad, she smelled bad, she sounded bad. It was as if what she thought of as her real self—her reasonably smart self, who was entirely devoted to Skye's well-being—didn't exist.

# Seventeen

All week Laurel rhapsodized to Skye about work: she loved the Best Western, so swanky and modern; her coworkers were fantastic; the tips were great! All this was stretching things. Work was work, her coworkers were as absorbed in their lives as she was in her own, and the tips were adequate. Nevertheless, she continued enthusing.

Also she asked Skye to face any bills she earned—Skye enjoyed turning them all in the same direction and smoothing their bent corners, a tradition as old as Laurel's busing days at Graham's—and upped her allowance from five dollars a week to eight. One day Laurel brought home a pair of figure skates a coworker was selling, an expensive brand, not cheap even secondhand, but new skates were something Skye'd wanted forever. Another day she splurged on strip steaks. She made a show of buying an extra box of Ho Hos on the same trip to Hahn's, and ate a package herself each night, though she didn't share Skye's taste for their waxy coatings and übersweet cream interiors. Beyond that, she didn't know where to go with her reassurances. She was the one who'd chosen this strange, hard route through the thicket of just-surviving to that promised land where things would be better.

Sunday evening, Skye leaned against the armrest of the couch, a notebook on her lap. She wrote a few words, then deleted them with hard scrubs of her eraser. She seemed serious but not anxious, Laurel thought. Though what did that mean? That she hid her worries well? "What are you doing?"

"Writing to Abby."

"Nice."

Skye made a face.

"Not nice?"

"I'm trying to figure out how to tell her I can't go to Endeavor next weekend."

"Endeavor?"

"It's the Endeavor Challenge."

Endeavor was a settlement along the water farther east. Like Gallion, it was only twenty-some miles away in a straight shot and yet unreachable by any direct route. Laurel tried to remember the details of the previous year's race. "Did Abby run it, or just her parents?"

"She and Hamish both ran. Abby won the junior division, Hamish took second in the ten-dog."

"Right."

"Last year we signed up to be bag checkers—we already memorized the list." Skye ticked items off with her fingers: "Compass, fire starter, knife, drop chain, trail map, bandages, headlamp, booties for every dog—" She dropped her hand. "It doesn't matter. I know I can't go. I just have to say it." She started writing again. This time there were no erasures.

"Well, wait, though. Wait, wait."

Saturday morning, a loudspeaker crackled. *First up in the twelve-dog race is Kendrick's Kennels, all the way in from Big Falls, Minnesota.*

Two dozen people clustered at the race's starting chute clapped and called out, *Yeah!* and *Go, Big Falls!* Skye grabbed Laurel's arm. "I can't believe we're here."

Laurel beamed. Once the idea dawned on her, it had been obvious: it was the answer, or anyway, an answer.

Skye ducked back into the car to tell Harper he'd have to stay put—*You can't distract the dogs here to run. You didn't like to be distracted when you were working, did you? But you are still my favorite dog. You're the best dog on the planet*—then ducked out and grabbed Peter's arm. "They're starting—we have to hurry. We're going, okay, Mom?"

"Okay, we'll catch—" But they were already jogging across the parking lot, a clearing plowed in Endeavor's grass airfield.

Jenny threw her hands over her ears to cut the noise of hundreds of dogs barking. "This is insane."

Half a dozen volunteers trotted a team up into the start chute, the dogs lifted by their collars so their front legs scrabbled at the air instead of finding purchase. *Mushing for Kendrick's is Noel Briggs. Noel was born and raised in Big Falls, pop-u-lation two hundred and thirty-six.* Another smattering of applause. Noel Briggs, in a long red

155

anorak with a fur-rimmed hood and embroidered mukluks, stood erect as her dogs strained and leaped in their harnesses; the volunteers gripped the rigging tight.

*This is Noel's second time at our race and her first time doing the sixty-mile leg. Let's wish her good trails.* The crowd applauded and Noel lifted a hand from the sled's handle. The race timer sat huddled on a pile of straw bales in the center of the starting chute, swaddled in a parka with the hood pulled up, snow pants, and giant-sized boots. He—or she, it was impossible to tell—counted the seconds down to zero, pointed at Noel, and called time. Noel pulled the brake and was off. The crowd cheered in its modest way and Noel gave one brief wave, her mind clearly only on the dogs and the trail. For her, the spectators and volunteers, the campfires and rigs, the canvas army tent where the Endeavor Rotarians were selling chili and hot dogs from giant slow cookers, had evaporated.

When she'd vanished, Laurel scanned the crowd for Skye and Peter. They stood with Abby and Corrine beside the family's rig. Peter stuck his hand out to Corrine, and Skye and Abby spun in a circle, clutching each other's arms. Soon Corrine handed each child a clipboard and they trotted into the melee of men and women and children packing gear and checking rigging. Laurel and Jenny headed for a bonfire, Jen practically skipping. "I'm so glad you called me. I wouldn't have missed this."

Laurel bumped her hip against Jen's. "I know, I'm brilliant, you can say it." When Skye had asked if they could invite Jen and Peter, Laurel had said of course. Her mental calculator raced at the cost, but she'd ignored it.

"We so should've done this when we were kids. Can you imagine the fun we would've had?"

Laurel let the impossibility of the suggestion pass without comment—who would have paid for the dogs and sleds and trailers and
travel?—and laid her head on Jen's shoulder. Their friendship was a
hot spring, healing and reviving.

"You okay?"

"Just tired."

"You've been working too hard. You need to move in with me," Jen
said.

"Oren would love that."

"He'd come around." Jen grinned. "Probably. And anyway, I'll bet
you'd move in near me, not with, 'cause I know I'd drive you nuts
within a week."

Laurel smiled. They were Oscar and Felix: Jen sloppy, Laurel neat.

Jenny tipped her head. "Would you actually consider it?"

"No, Jen."

"You don't think you'll get busted for camping out at—"

"No." Laurel worried about many things, but not that.

Jen tucked a stray lock of hair from Laurel's cheek. "You really
hope to send Skye to this camp?"

Laurel had told Jen about Cedar Lake the night before, after Skye
was asleep. "I have to. It's not just a camp, it's an education. Kids learn
there, they work with real artists, famous people, they drink it all in."

"Somebody's been reading too many promotional brochures."

"No, it's a good place. I talked to Ms. Bainbridge about it before we
moved and I've been doing some research. People say great things."
Laurel had taken notes when she looked the camp up on the school
library's computers and she carried the notes with her at all times now.

"'Phenomenal, amazing, life changing,'" Jen read.

Laurel refolded the paper and put it back in the side pocket of her satchel for safekeeping. "I want to do this for her." Ever since Skye wondered why things were so hard and whether they'd ever get better, she thought of nothing else. "She's so—"

"Amazing!"

"Yes." Tears welled. Laurel hated how emotional she got about things, but there it was. "Just once I want to give her something fantastic. At least one thing that she'll always remember. One thing that might, I don't know, set her on her way, change her life."

Jen caught Laurel's hand and they laced their fingers together the way they used to during the scary parts of movies. "Sounds big."

Laurel laughed, a single *hunh*. "Yes. It would be."

After all the teams left, people chatted around campfires and ate snacks from the Rotarians' tent. Laurel slowly consumed a bowl of chili and watched a field mouse skitter around in the trampled snow. It must've come from the pallet of campfire wood stacked near the bonfires. It acted lost and frantic and she wished she could catch it and tuck it into her coat.

Jenny tapped her arm, pointed toward a fire near the rigs. "Look at them." The children stood talking to a half dozen owners and handlers. Skye and Abby were laughing as Peter held forth on some topic, his hands outflung. The adults listened with interest. "They seem so grown-up. So capable."

Laurel nodded.

"The boy seems nice. Peter."

"They play chess together on the bus. Their social studies teacher said he'd start a chess club if they wanted."

"Nice."

They watched Abby tap her own chest, making some point. Peter squatted down and prodded the fire; Skye punched his arm.

Jen smiled. "Will this be her first romance?"

"They're just friends. So far, anyway."

Jen nodded. After a moment she said, "Abby's parents must be doing okay. That's a nice rig they're driving. And Abby's outfit." She whistled.

"She always has cute stuff."

"Not just cute. Top-of-the-line. I know those boots she's wearing; I wanted a pair. Even the kids' version costs two hundred dollars."

Laurel shrugged.

"I'm not saying anything bad about it."

"I know."

"It's just that I can't imagine being a kid and having that kind of stuff. We sure didn't!"

"No."

"I wonder how our lives would've been different if we would've. Easier, I'll bet."

"I don't know." She did, though. No amount of money could've made Jen's life easier with Big Jim around, and Laurel still deemed her own childhood—the pieces lived in Gallion, anyway—perfect.


At the motel they ordered delivery pizza and bought candy from the vending machines and watched movies on cable. Everyone was asleep by midnight, and by ten, they were all up and showered, even Jen. They wolfed down the continental breakfast included in the room rate, the children focusing on the waffles, then packed and walked Harper and smuggled Frank to the car. Jen pulled away and turned east, honking, and Laurel headed toward Crosscut. Taking Abby home was another amazing feat she would perform in this weary old car, but she'd wanted to make the weekend as perfect as possible for Skye, make it so Abby could stay over, and Laurel would be the one doing the ferrying instead of the other way around for once.

Soon the snow, which had trickled and spit while they packed, bucketed down. The visibility siphoned to the distance between power poles and the wind shook the car. Peter dozed, Abby stared out the window, and Skye took Frank out of her cage because she claimed Frank was frightened. Within moments Frank slipped out of her hand and disappeared beneath Laurel's seat. Laurel pulled over and Skye picked sunflower seeds from Frank's bag of mixed food. Eventually she coaxed the cowering creature out of hiding and returned her to her cage.

Laurel pulled off at a gas station twenty minutes later. She filled the tank and, when everyone had used the restroom and bought snacks, herded her brood back to the car. "Everybody in?" she asked when they were settled. She heard a chorus of yeses and stuck the key in the ignition. When she turned it, she heard only a click. She went still as mud.

"Mom?"

Skye's voice was tense; Laurel's good work was already turning to ashes. She smiled over the seat back. "No worries, I'll be back in a jiffy." She hopped back out of the car. Lifted the hood and fiddled with cables. Was about to try the engine again when an older couple approached the pickup parked beside her. "Need a jump?" the man asked.

"I think I do."

"Let's get 'er done."

He and Laurel attached the cables and moments later the Sable roared to life. Laurel gave the man a hug; his jolly-faced wife cuffed his arm. "Ever the charmer, you."

A few miles on, they were caught behind a plow. Abby and Skye complained because they could only go twenty. Laurel hushed them and strained to see in the wake of its flashing, circling red and yellow lights. Still, her mood could not be diminished, and finally the plow turned onto a drifted side road. She relaxed her grip on the wheel and switched on the radio. Peter was reading on his phone; he looked up and they exchanged smiles in the mirror. Half an hour later, the snow let up; she could see two power poles ahead instead of one.

They reached the stretch of swamp where Laurel had seen the eagle after Christmas. She hummed and peered at the hazy sun. How was it that Jen didn't like it here? It was so glorious, so peaceful and wild, safe in some ways but interesting and challenging in others. And these kids in the back seat—they were the next generation of northerners; they were sturdy and funny and kind. Life was good. Life was sweet. Sometimes it was even easy.

# Eighteen

I t's like summer, Mom."

"It'll be summer before we know it. The time changes tomorrow."

Skye tsked. "I hate losing that hour."

They swung hand in hand along the main road in the opposite
direction of town. It was too nice to stay indoors, and heading south,
even on foot, was an adventure. They had been nowhere but to school
and work since the race in Endeavor.

The snow was melting from the road; they could see blacktop for
the first time since they'd moved here. Laurel veered into the middle
and walked the yellow-painted line like a balance beam, her arms
stretched out. Skye waved a stick she'd dug from a drift, making de-
signs in the air. Did she draw the same indescribable satisfactions in

these small things as Laurel did? Was that a thing you could ever know about someone else?

Skye hurled the stick forward. Harper ran after it and she dashed after him. She circled back and lapped Laurel, pumping her fists and chanting encouragement as if she were both the race and the crowd of spectators. "Way to go, keep it strong!" She began doing jumping jacks. When she ran out of breath, she flung herself over at the waist and panted.

"What're you doing?"

"Exercising. Winter is making us fat and flabby, Peter and me and everybody decided."

"Really?"

"Mostly we just feel blah. It's been winter-winter-winter forever."

"Do you not like winter?" Maybe you couldn't know someone else. Maybe you could only ever know yourself—and maybe not even that, not for more than a moment.

An image of Ms. Trevor appeared in Laurel's mind, reading to them one morning senior year. Cold permeated the room—the boiler was out again—and Ms. Trevor perched on the front of her desk, a book cradled in her hands like a psalter. Brian and Louise whispered to each other in the back row, despite being the two most intellectual seniors, and Jen stared out the double-hung windows toward the cloudless February sky. Perhaps alone among her classmates, Laurel listened to their teacher. They'd been studying *To the Lighthouse*; Ms. Trevor was quoting Virginia Woolf's diary. "Woolf wants us to understand how complex we are. She says we are each 'a thing that you could ruffle with your breath; and a thing you could not dislodge with a team of horses.'" Ms. Trevor looked up; her eyes beamed at them with sharp intent. "Try to remember that."

Laurel had.

Now, Skye jabbed at the sky. "I like winter. But when the sun was shining yesterday? We all said we'd go crazy if we didn't get to, like, run a million miles right away. We thought of starting a boxing club and calling ourselves the Junior Warriors. I said we should have T-shirts. Pink ones instead of red, because pink is like a junior of red. Peter said okay, but they had to be salmon-pink, not pink-pink. Pink-pink was too girlie."

"That all sounds fun." The mental calculator started figuring the cost of a custom-made T-shirt.

"Yeah, but we won't do it. There's too much winter left, and it gets dark too early, and the roads are too slippery, and blah, blah, blah."

"Blah, blah, blah?"

Skye pulled a face. "That's what we all said our parents would say."

They reached a pine with a broken top. It had branched out at the snag and started a half dozen new shoots, little treelets that were sturdy and healthy despite the tree's trauma. Laurel studied the tree as Skye thwacked the nearby snowbanks with her stick, humming to herself and ambling from one side of the road to the other.

"What would you guys think about doing a preseason conditioning class?" Laurel asked.

"A what?"

"A conditioning class. Do some training, inside, so that when spring does come, you're in shape to run. That's what we did in high school—started in the middle of March, right before everybody went nuts from cabin fever."

Skye laughed. "Yeah, cabin-fever-y, that's how we all feel."

"We should see if we can reserve the gym. We could jog, do stretches and laps." What else? High knees, butt kicks, high skips. The idea was for Skye. But also, despite all the years it had been and the complicated things Laurel had felt about running, now she was the same as her daughter: spring-fevered and restless. The sun and the bare pavement under her feet made her want to move.

Skye stared at her. "You'd do that?"

"Why not?"

Skye frowned. "Because you don't run."

It was true. Laurel hadn't run since the day Gran died. But now she wanted to, or at least she wanted to help these restless children get in shape for it if they wanted. "Well, I've been busy. With you, so there. Anyway, what do you say?"

A smile spread over Skye's face. "I say yeah. I say cool."

Laurel walked the centerline balance beam again; Skye raced Harper to the road sign.

"What do you want to have for supper on St. Pat's?" Laurel asked.

"We always have corned beef and cabbage."

Laurel grabbed up her own branch with which to thwack snow-banks. "But I was thinking, let's do something different. Like—pizza. Or pasties! Great-Gran's pasties, the family recipe from the old country."

"Feen-laand!" Skye boomed, brandishing the stick.

"Great idea," Mrs. Fox said as Laurel finished explaining about the conditioning class on Monday. "I'll find out about the gym tomorrow, bring it up with the kids and get permission slips printed."

"Super!" Laurel smiled nervously. "Thanks."

"Thank *you*." Mrs. Fox wrapped a wine-colored scarf around her neck. "I'll bet you can start by next Monday. That'd be good. These kids are climbing out of their skins. Everyone is."

Laurel chewed at a thumbnail. "What about Skye and her Ho Hos?"

Mrs. Fox reached for her jacket. "She eats a whole one every day now, saves the second in the package."

"That's progress, I guess."

Mrs. Fox slid a coat button into its hole. "It's possible we've made too much of this. She might just be changing."

"Changing?"

"Maybe she's moved on to carrot sticks, or trail mix. Kids go through food fads. It was gummy bears when I was in sixth grade— we had to have 'em. Luckily my best friend's folks had the service station; she was our supplier."

"But why wouldn't she say? Why wouldn't she tell me?"

Mrs. Fox laughed at Laurel's plaintive tone. "Because she wouldn't want to hurt your feelings."

Laurel followed her out of the building, like a gosling trailing its mother. She felt young and befuddled. Also, strangely safe.


"What should we do until four thirty?"

"Dunno." Skye bounced her bootheels against the floor mats. Outside, sleet fell from a low gray sky. The first conditioning class would begin in an hour.

"Want to go to the library?"

"Nah. We do that all the time."

Laurel drummed her fingers on the steering wheel. The sleet fell and fell. A teacher hurried past, hunched beneath a giant blue umbrella. Aside from his pickup, the school parking lot was deserted. "We could take a drive."

Skye lifted a shoulder. "O-kay."

Laurel turned onto Pine Street. She eased past Hahn's Market and the Lutheran church, then slid through the blinker at the town's four corners. She steered into the curb. "End of drive. I don't think we better try going anywhere we don't have to."

"Yeah."

They stared outside. On the left was the Piney Tavern. On the right, a cobblestone building called Aurora Market. If that was around when Laurel was in high school, it had been off her radar. The bus would stop at the BP on the highway and she and Jenny would race inside for Gatorade and Twizzlers and the large-sized Symphony bars, which no one in Gallion carried. Then they'd ride up to Waiska for whatever event they'd come for, intent on candy, the boys vying for Jen's attention, and the upcoming event.

Nowadays, she wouldn't miss a place like this. The building was an old service station—was this the station Mrs. Fox's friend had smuggled candy from in grade school?—that still sold gas from the one pump outside, along with campfire wood, propane, birdseed, and yard art; a troupe of metal sculptures were positioned around the edge of the parking lot. Laurel pointed at a hippo made from a hot water heater. "I love that one."

"The crane's my favorite."

On the exterior of the building, painted signs advertised wild rice, books, and baked goods. In the windows, neons dangled. One read *Espresso* in pink script, another *Gifts*, a third *Tea*. Laurel turned the car off. "Let's go in."

Skye shot her a surprised look. "I thought we couldn't risk the temptation of this place because we had to save every penny we could lay our mitts on."

Laurel shouldered her door open. "We'll just look around. And we can afford some little thing."

Excitement zoomed into Skye's eyes. "We can?"

"Definitely." It would be another brick to cement in the wall she wanted to build between Skye and the idea that she must ration her Ho Hos.

Inside, a painting of a forest covered the entry wall, ending in a ferny glade on an open office door. Beyond it, a woman sat at a computer. Skye studied the mural and Laurel studied the woman. She leaned toward the computer and hit a key, and a voice came from the speakers, saying what sounded like "Nee-noon-dez-gad-ay." The woman repeated the word and the computer corrected her: *Ninoondezgade.*

The woman crossed her arms. *"Ninoondezgade."* But the computer flung the same word back, or anyway it sounded the same to Laurel. The woman groaned. When she glanced up at Laurel, Laurel quickly turned away so she wouldn't appear to be eavesdropping.

"Hi!" the woman called. "Welcome. What can I help you with?"

"We're just browsing."

The woman came toward her, smiling, and Laurel frowned. She seemed familiar. An angular face dominated by deep-set eyes. Black hair threaded with silver in a braid down her back. Medium-tall and skinny, skinnier than she'd been before.

But how would Laurel know that?

Then she remembered. She'd seen this woman in a picture, a framed picture in a room she had cleaned last August at the Lakeshore. Two women and a girl smiling with their arms around one another on a sunny beach. Laurel wasn't sure why she remembered the woman's face. But she knew she had been staring at the photograph when she'd told Skye she had to work late on Skye's birthday. She'd been examining the woman's features when she'd heard the disappointment in her daughter's voice. "Oh!" Laurel said now. "Hi."

The woman tipped her head. "Do I know you?"

"Do you ever go to Gallion?"

Pain ran across the woman's face. "I do." She blinked the emotion away. "It's a pretty spot."

"We're from there. I—I think I cleaned your room once."

The woman winced. "Bad day for a road trip. Not that I'm not glad you're here, you're the first sign of life in hours, but that's a lot of miles on these roads. I'm surprised you made it."

"Oh, no, we live here now. I work at the Best Western."

"We?"

Laurel glanced behind her, but Skye had vanished. "My daughter and I. She's around here somewhere; I'd better go find her."

Skye was sitting in a rocker near a gas log stove in the back of the store, reading a used book. Laurel tickled her neck with the feathered end of a dream catcher she intended to purchase. It was inexpensive as well as pretty, it would cement her message about being able to afford a treat, and most of all, any help they could get catching dreams, she'd take. "You can pick a treat."

Skye looked up. "What kind of treat?"

"I saw avocados."

Skye straightened. "No way."

"Yes, way."

"We should make our guacamole!"

Laurel had taught Skye how to make guacamole when Skye was so small, she had to stand on a chair at the counter to mash the fruit. "Great minds think alike."

"Oh, Mom! It's the same color as peas, but it isn't peas. It's guacamole-guacamole-guacamole, yum."

"Right?"

"Could there be chips?"

"There could. Even blue corn chips, if you so desire; I saw them near the avocados." Laurel reached into her bag and handed Skye a twenty.

At the register, Skye received their change and pulled the bills' corners flat before she handed them to Laurel. She beamed at the woman behind the counter. "I'm so happy you have avocados, you can't imagine. We're making guacamole. I'm Skye, by the way."

"I'm Naomi. Nice bag."

"Thanks. My mom made it."

"It's great."

"I know. My friend at school wants one." Skye squinted at Laurel. "Peter does, he asked me today."

"*Peter* wants one?"

"In darker colors, more for a boy, but yeah."

"Huh."

"Could you make him one? For his birthday? It's in May."

"Well—sure, I guess."

"His mom picked him up at school the other day. She said the owls on mine are whimsical and wise looking."

"Oh!" Laurel blushed. Sewing was a skill that humans couldn't do without, not if they lived anywhere that required wearing clothing or sleeping in tents or a thousand other things, but people didn't realize it. They didn't think about it now that almost everything was store-bought and machine-made—by someone else, someone far away, someone destitute in most cases—but it was true. Your whole life was held up by millions of stitches that were taken for granted unless you made them yourself.

"She hoped you'd put frogs on Peter's. They're frog clan, or anyway his dad is. And I said I would ask."

The bags were slow, fussy work. Choosing and cutting the many pieces, double-sewing the seams and ironing them open, designing the appliqués and hemming their edges so they'd never fray, anchoring in the zippers flat, getting the linings in—it all took forever. The result seemed simple, but doing it right required a huge amount of effort. "Wouldn't the other kids tease him?"

Skye rolled her eyes. "No, Mom. Peter's different. He's himself. Plus, he's cool." She said this as if these were two distinct points, and Laurel understood her to mean that Peter was cool as in popular, rich in social currency. She wouldn't have predicted that in a stocky, mannerly chess player who wanted to tote a messenger bag around school. "He does beadwork, you know, his dad teaches him. He's not afraid of art. He's into it. Plus, he thinks the girls will be jealous, which they will."

Laurel held up her hands. "Okay, I get it."

"Anyway, he wants one. You should do it. You should do a bunch; you should sew them to order. Yours are way nicer than these." She jabbed at a display of cotton bags that hung near the register.

"Skye!" Though it was true. You saw the bags Naomi was selling everywhere. Gift shops, convenience stores, gas stations, everybody had them. Twenty-five bucks and zippers worth about a nickel; linings made of muslin so cheap you could read a newspaper through it. You'd assume a slender vegan in a bright room that smelled of patchouli stitched them, but in fact children in a sweatshop in Asia, children younger than Skye, most likely, did the work.

Naomi prodded a bag. "I agree with you. I don't know what I was thinking, getting these in. They depress me."

"So, we're kindred spirits," Skye declared.

"I expect we are. Like you, I'm a big fan of guacamole. I have my own favorite recipe—"

"You have to use fresh limes. And cilantro."

"If you ever need it, just ask, I keep it on hand." She patted a small freezer beside her. "It comes in cubes, it's almost like fresh, and fresh is the real secret."

Skye nodded emphatically. "It is! You can almost never find it—we usually use dried, but fresh is way better."

A moment later Naomi handed Skye a small Ziploc containing four cubes of the frozen herb. Laurel protested that she didn't have to and Naomi said almost severely that she knew she didn't have to. Skye tucked the cilantro into their sack. "Thank you so much. That's generous of you, we appreciate it. And I love that you carry blue corn chips. I had homemade ones over Christmas? I was in New Mexico with our friends? And we ate at a café where they had their own recipe and cooked them every day. Those were the bomb."

Naomi laughed. "I'll bet."

"Anyway, thank you!"

Naomi's eyes were as warm as melting chocolate. "You're welcome. And *miigwech* to you, too. *Chi miigwech.*"

Skye stopped. "What's *miigwech*?"

"In Ojibwe it means thank you. The *chi* amps it up: big thank you."

Skye walked to the door repeating the phrase to herself. Laurel paused before she followed. "What was that other word you were saying earlier? It sounded so pretty."

Naomi made a face. "*Ninoondezgade*. It means 'I'm hungry.' And who isn't? Some way or another."

# Nineteen

A knock came on the door just past noon the following day. Harper barked and Laurel dropped the water jug she was using to fill Frank's dish. Her eyes darted around the room. Coats on the pegs, boots on the floor, a scarf Skye was knitting on the couch beside the satchel Laurel had started for Peter. A travel alarm clock ticked on the end table, framed photos lined the shelf near the ceiling (Skye's school picture, Mom and Link onstage in a pub, Gran holding up a trout), and Frank napped in her cage.

The knock came again.

What if Baldy had relatives after all? What if they were here?

Plants decorated the trailer's sunny spots; the smell of chicken baking filled the air; WCMZ played "Turn the Page" on Baldy's transistor radio. No way to claim she'd been here for an emergency pit stop and wasn't full-out squatting.

Laurel shut her eyes. Then she marched herself forward to answer.

Naomi stood on the step, aluminum-framed snowshoes dangling from one hand. "Surprise!" She smiled brightly.

"Wow, hi. I mean, come in."

Naomi pulled a piece of paper from her puffy blue jacket. "I found this after you left yesterday. I wanted to bring it in case you needed it. Swung past the Best Western, but they said you were off today, so I took a chance I'd find you here. Bea Fox thought you lived back in this way and I saw your car by the road."

Laurel nodded as if this didn't make her nervous. The paper Naomi handed her was an old shopping list on which she'd scribbled numbers budgeting for Skye's camp money. It was huge to her, but on its own the paper was nothing to make a person drive six miles out of town and hike half a mile up a snowmobile track to return. "Thank you. That's nice of you. Um. Would you like"— Laurel tried to think what she could offer. Water, milk, oatmeal, a shriveled orange.—"a cup of tea? I have Lipton's. Well. Not Lipton's, the store brand, I'm sorry."

Naomi pointed at herself. "Not as picky as the market might make you assume."

Laurel put the kettle on as Naomi's eyes wandered out the end window, across the plants and Skye's knitting and the satchel, to Frank's cage on the counter. She tapped a finger on the wire, making a *pshh pshh* noise. Frank sat up and eyed her. Naomi tipped a wan cactus blossom toward herself. "I never can get mine to bloom."

"It was my grandmother's, and her mother's before that."

"There's a responsibility. Mine I bought at Hahn's. No pressure if I kill it."

"My gran will haunt me if I let anything happen to this one." The plant was pale, its branches thin. It hadn't recovered from their trip to Endeavor. The water they'd left in buckets had a skim of ice over the top when they returned; the plants had looked breathless and stunned. Laurel gave one flat branch a consoling touch.

"I expect it gets cold for it sometimes, if you're heating with wood." Naomi turned to the cupboards where Laurel had taped up Skye's art projects: painted footprint owls on a branch, *Laurel* and *Skye* written in curlicue letters on their breasts; a pencil drawing of Harper. There was a collage of items that made Skye happy: a Mallo Cup wrapper, a cartoon dog cut off a birthday card, a photo of Skye and Abby and Abbott racing after a soccer ball, and one of Laurel and Sean and Jenny at a bonfire. Also several strands of Ramen noodles, a blue jay feather, three wheat pennies, and a desiccated brown-eyed Susan. Naomi touched a picture of Skye on a swing, then one of Gran standing beside the sauna with a cloche pulled low on her head.

The kettle whistled. Laurel poured the water and handed a mug to Naomi, and Naomi cozied her mug close. "I have a question, a proposal."

"You do?"

"What would you say to running the market next week?"

Laurel spluttered out a mouthful of tea. "What? Why?"

"I need to go downstate. I leave Saturday and come back the following Sunday."

"Oh. But I work at the motel. Four days a week, sometimes five. Even Saturdays now and then." Laurel made Skye go to town with her the two times that happened. Skye hung out at the school library, which was also the public library and open on weekends. It wasn't a perfect solution, but it wasn't terrible.

"My friend Sarah will fill in some, but she can't do nights; she teaches a language class at the college."

"On the reservation?"

Naomi nodded. "She can't do the weekends either. If you covered what she can't, I'd be set. It would add up to seventy hours or so—"

"But I don't know how your store works. How to run the register, what things cost, where things go—" What to say to anyone, how to keep from committing some irreparable error, especially when it came to math and the money.

"I'm sure I could show you the ropes pretty quickly."

Laurel bit at a thumbnail. She'd be working around the clock, but it might be good. She liked Naomi and it would be nice for a change, to be the giver instead of the receiver. And with seventy hours, she could put even more aside for Skye's camp fund. Next week was Waiska's spring break; it could work. It'd be boring for Skye to tag along the whole time—or almost the whole time; she was spending three days with Abby—but she'd survive. "What made you think of me?"

Naomi patted Harper's head. "I like you."

"You barely know me."

"I feel like I know you."

Laurel stayed quiet and Naomi sighed. "If you take the job, or even just stick around Waiska awhile longer, you'll hear it, so I'll tell you," she said, then fell silent.

Laurel waited. In the quiet, she heard the clock ticking.

Naomi breathed deeply. "My daughter died ten years ago. My daughter, and my granddaughter with her. They were swimming in the bay in Gallion. My daughter loved to go over there in the summer. A riptide caught them."

Laurel's hand flew to her mouth. "Oh, Naomi."

Naomi nodded.

"I'm so sorry."

"Thank you." Naomi's fingers wove around Harper's ears. "You wouldn't have thought it could happen. I wouldn't have even, and I grew up on the lake. It was a sunny day. Just another sunny day. Windy, though. It was windy, I will say that."

Laurel imagined losing Skye that way, or any way, and cast the vision out of her head. She tried to remember when it had happened, but couldn't be sure. People drowned every summer.

"I couldn't stand it." A gust of wind tossed snow against the glass. "My husband couldn't either. We couldn't help each other. We're divorced now."

Laurel said the only thing she could think of. "I'm sorry."

"Me, too."

"I can't imagine."

Naomi nodded, her eyes trained on the clearing. "You go on. But it changed me."

"Of course."

"Losing them broke me."

"Yes. I can see how that would be."

Naomi rubbed at her neck. "Eventually I mended, and in the mending, I changed. I don't mean I was a bad person before and I'm a good one now. That's not it. I'm different, is all. What matters is written on different pages."

Laurel nodded even though Naomi wasn't looking at her.

"I moved back up here after it happened. We'd lived downstate our whole married life—we met in college—but I had to be nearer to them. That makes no sense, I know."

"It does to me."

Naomi sighed. "So, I came back for that. Also, to keep the store going. My parents ran it as a service station. It was Avril's—my daughter's—life's dream to keep it going and expand it into what it is now. She had such ideas, such energy. Me, I thought it wouldn't work. All that specialty stuff, and in the middle of nowhere. Being from here, I knew better. But she grew up downstate, so she couldn't realize how it is, you know?"

"Sure."

"But she proved me wrong." Naomi turned. Her eyes were bright, but soon the brightness faded and the more inscrutable woman was left standing before Laurel. "Anyway. I dragged through my days; I kept the store open. People were kind and I made it through somehow. And now, the person I am after—"

Naomi stopped again. She shook her head as if whatever thought she was trying to express eluded words. She raised her hands, palms out; she was changing the subject. "I thought the extra work might be welcome. And you'd be helping me in return. I have things to do." She grinned suddenly. "I'm getting to be an old lady."

"No, you aren't!"

Naomi laughed. "I'm nearly sixty; I might only have thirty or forty years left. I realize it's a lot of hours at a bad time, the nights and weekends and all, but I would pay you well."

Laurel felt like different threads inside herself were channeling through a spool, coming out the other side knit together into a rope she could shimmy down to carry Skye to a better place. She had what was almost a vision: Skye at twenty-something, bursting through the door, wearing some outfit only she would dream up, holding an artist's portfolio. It was Skye home for a weekend from art school, a school she got into because of being a Cedar Lake alum, is what it was.

The paper airplane crashed into Laurel's forehead at five fifteen Saturday morning. She squeezed her eyes shut tight, then peeled them open to see Skye in the doorway, wearing her velvet dress and paisley leggings. She sniffed. Oatmeal wafted to her. Skye rapped the doorframe. "Rise and shine, daylight in the swamps. We can't be late for work on our first day."

Laurel groaned. Then she got up.

Sunday unfurled the same way: paper airplane, dressed daughter, cooked oatmeal. After breakfast they trudged to the car on their borrowed snowshoes, Harper dancing ahead on the trail, and arrived at Aurora Market twenty minutes early. All morning Skye bustled through the aisles, straightening products and noting any gaps or low stock. She greeted customers and warned them to be careful of the floors wet from snow tromped in on boots; she rearranged the dream catcher display and dusted the used books. In the afternoon she settled in the rocker beside the gas log fire and sketched a copy of the entry wall's mural.

Monday morning, they met Abby and Corrine at the junction of the highway and the road to Waiska; Wednesday afternoon Laurel returned to the junction during her break between the Best Western and the market and picked Skye up.

At the trailer Skye dumped her duffel in her room, greeted Frank, and spent twenty minutes scratching Harper behind his ears and on his belly until he was zonked out with happiness. "It was fun to see Abby and the dogs and everyone, but it's also so, so good to be home." She opened her book, something with a dragon on the front, and sipped the hot chocolate Laurel had made her.

Half an hour later, Laurel whisked a finger along her cheek. "Time to head back out."

"Oh, no, don't make me go. Not today. Today I just want to stay here. Please." Skye clasped her hands and Harper lifted his head to offer his own plea.

"Sorry, Charlie."

Skye waved toward the stove and the window; outside, a fluffy snow drifted down. "Everything is so perfect."

"I can't do it, sweet pea. You have to come with."

"I truly am kind of worn out."

Skye's cheeks were rosy and she'd been coughing in the car. She did look snug in her chair. Inside herself, Laurel wavered.

Skye laid her hand across her heart. "I'd be fine. I'd call if I needed anything."

"No, baby."

Skye came to the table where Laurel had been threading fresh wicks into the kerosene lamps. "I promise we'd be okay. What's going to happen? Nothing ever happens."

"It's not a good idea."

"It is, though. I still have homework to do and I concentrate best at this table." She patted the small table Baldy had wedged in beside the love seat.

"Skye—"

"I do! And Harper-dog will keep me company and protect me from anything scary."

"That word right there, 'scary,' is the problem."

"I'd call 911 in a real emergency. Which you know won't happen. I'll dust. And do the dishes."

"I don't want you heating water by yourself."

"Okay, but you could heat it up before you go and I'd do them right away. Instantly! And when you get home, everything would be"— Skye made a swirling motion—"squeaky clean!" She gave the gleaming smile of a TV housewife advertising dish detergent.

"Honey."

"Please."

Laurel teetered on the edge of the decision, then caved in. She tapped a finger on Skye's sternum. "I'm calling you." The phone worked if left in one exact spot on the window ledge. Usually. "A dozen times. And—"

"Be careful, I know."

At seven, Skye told Laurel to quit calling. "I'm fine!"

"The fire's okay? Nothing smells hot?"

"No. Harper and I are reading, that's all."

When Skye read to Harper, he always sat with his ears pricked forward and his eyes on her face, as if he were following the story. Maybe he was. "Make sure you turn the lights off when you go to bed. Make sure the lever's closed tight. Remember how I showed you?"

"I will, I do."

"If you have to turn them back on for some reason—and it had better be a good one—"

"Be careful of the match, be careful of the mantel. You've told me ten million times."

Laurel gnawed at a pinkie nail and didn't even try to correct herself. "You'll call me if anything comes up. Anything at all."

"Yes, but it won't."

Twenty minutes later, the phone rang. Laurel snatched up the receiver.

"Laurel Tree, it's me! Your BFF, your favorite woman, your very own Jen."

Laurel poured cheer into her hello, but she fidgeted as Jenny talked. She needed to keep the line open. Jen, however, was in a chatty mood. First, she recounted her adventures in accounting. "Full disclosure principle, objectivity principle, yuck. It is so boring."

"Huh." Laurel peered across the market's aisles. She wondered if Naomi understood those principles.

"And Oren, God. He is driving me nuts."

Laurel swiveled her gaze to the window. It reflected her worried face back to her. She needed to get off the phone.

Jenny's grievances about Oren seemed ordinary. Socks left on floors, coffee grounds spilled from the grinder and not swept up.

Laurel drew a spiraling circle on the notepad in front of her, then added overlarge ears. "Hmm."

Jen laughed. "I'm boring you."

"No."

Jenny groaned. "I'm boring myself. I have an idea. Let's go to the movies."

"What?"

"The movies! Tomorrow night, seven o'clock, the Majestic. It'll be like old times."

"No."

"What do you mean, 'no'? You haven't even thought about it."

"I don't need to. I have Skye, I have to work, it's winter, it's sixty miles one way. 'No' is the only answer there is."

Jenny's laugh tinkled across the line. "You're bringing Skye with, silly. No way I'm driving all that way without seeing my best girl."

Laurel closed her eyes. Refusing Jen was like leaning against a north-facing door in a blizzard. "Jen, no. It's too far, it's a school night, the roads are bad. And, I'm going to say it again, *I have work.*"

"Come on. You can blow work off."

"What? No."

"How many people have come in tonight?"

Laurel scowled. Two people had ventured through the door, one man and one woman; she'd sold a cookie and a loaf of bread. "Not a lot."

"Two, I'll bet. So, call your boss and ask if you can close early. Tell her you have a friend visiting. I'll bet she says okay."

Laurel said nothing. She did not want to drive to the theater in Crosscut tomorrow. It would be dark in both directions and most likely snowing.

Jen sighed. "Fine. Forget it. I'm putting you on notice that I'm mad, though. You're not getting out of it that easy."


Jen called again the next night. "So, you're there? At that gift shop or whatever?"

"Aurora Market, yes." Irritation tightened Laurel's voice. They'd been over this. But she made herself relax. Jen was Jen; Laurel was being bitchy. "I'm sitting at the register, doing a crossword." It was seven; like last night, Skye had told her to quit calling. The market was quiet; the shelves were dusted. At eight she would close.

"Good, I guess. I'm at the grocery—we're out of everything. Oren's called four times, he's totally micromanaging. 'Make sure you get the thin-crust pizza, the beer that's on sale in the flyer—' Like I wouldn't anyway."

The fruit smoothies churned in their tanks, pomegranate pink and spinach green. Jen always picked the wrong guy. Always. And Laurel was always the shoulder she cried on. "You're sure things are good?"

"Oh, yes, this is just us acting old and married. Bicker, bicker."

"All right, okay. Well, I have to—"

"Hang on." A cooler door opened, something banged, Jenny whooped. "Some guy is following me down the dairy aisle," she whispered. "I'm going to get him to ask me for my number. I can tell he wants to."

Laurel disconnected. Jenny would get the guy to ask for her number. She'd get him to ask and decide whether to provide it—probably she would—and who knew what would happen next. Laurel stood and pulled the smoothie canisters from their holsters.

At home, the lights were off and the fire burned low. Skye and Harper slept in Skye's bed, the patchwork blanket Laurel had sewn out of Skye's baby clothes drawn up over both of them.

# Twenty

I can't," Laurel said.

"You have to. You already crapped out on me for the movies, don't stand me up now."

"Jen, stop. Skye's home alone, it's winter, it's late. You can't ask me to drive to the bridge."

"Bring her."

"That's not so easy, she's not feeling great. Even if she felt fine, I'd have to hike in to get her, then hike back out. Please don't ask."

"I did, though. I am." Jenny blew her nose and Laurel thought she'd been crying and did not have a cold as she'd claimed. Across the street, a snowmobile clattered across the dry pavement. There was something sad about the sound.

Jen sniffled again.

"Tell me what's going on."

"Nothing! I just want you to come meet me. I'm at the—" Jenny took a breath. "I'm at the rest stop at the bridge. On the east side. Drive down. We'll go to that all-night truck stop and I'll buy you a malt. Double malt, extra sauce, the way you like. We'll get burgers, cheese fries, whatever you want, it's all on me."

"Jen, I'm at work, I can't leave."

"Since when does work come before us?"

*Since we're adults*, Laurel thought. "Naomi is depending on me. I like her."

"You like her? You like *her*? This is me, Laurel. This is us."

Laurel massaged her temple. "What's wrong, Jen?"

"Jenny?" Laurel whispered inside the cavernous women's room at the deserted rest area on the northbound side of the expressway. "Are you in here?"

Feet hit the floor and a stall door opened. Jen clutched a duffel bag; a backpack dragged her shoulders low. Her pant legs bunched at the tops of her mukluks as if she'd jammed them on fast; her coat flapped at the collar where the zipper was ripped. Laurel reached for her. "Oh, honey."

Jenny sobbed in a strangled, hiccuping way. Laurel always thought it would be better to let loose and weep, but she didn't say so. They had their roles: Jen lived; she burned like a fire. Laurel ambled alongside, the dopey homebody. When Jen stumbled, she called Laurel and Laurel came running. When Laurel needed an injection of energy and excitement, she turned to Jen. It had been this way since Jen swirled into their third-grade classroom and Laurel pointed at the empty desk beside her. Now she rubbed circles on Jen's back. "You're okay, it's over, you're coming home with me. And you'll see. Things will get better."

Jenny searched her eyes and Laurel nodded.

Five minutes later they inched along the snowy sidewalks toward the highway. Laurel carried the duffel and kept her arm around Jen. Jen walked with her eyes down, matching their steps, right for right and left for left. They waited for a break in traffic and crossed I-75, aiming for the lot on the southbound side where the Sable sat lonesome in a corner. Two officers walked out of the State Police Post that abutted the lot as they passed. Laurel pulled Jenny closer.

"Everything all right?" one of the men called.

Laurel nodded. "My friend left her bag in the bathroom. Sorry, I guess we're not supposed to walk across the highway like that."

"She find the bag?"

Laurel gave a thumbs-up. The officers nodded, and Laurel marched Jenny faster.

She was about to slam her trunk shut over Jenny's duffel when headlights bounced toward them. "Get in the car." If it was random guys out to harass them, she wanted to be ready for a quick getaway. She was trying to remember how to get out of the lot without getting on the expressway when Jenny said, "It's Oren."

Laurel squinted into the headlights. "Get in the car," she said again, but Jen didn't.

The truck stopped; Oren climbed out. He was a big guy, plump and muscular. Short dark hair, a square face. "Jenny!" he called. "I was looking for you in the rest area. I thought something happened."

"Something did happen." Laurel's voice wavered, but she met Oren's eyes. Jen had finally told her the story. She had talked Oren into coming to see Laurel and Skye for April Fool's Eve. *I wanted to surprise you. But then we got into a fight about which lane to use getting off the bridge, and it turned huge. I told him to get off at the rest area and he did, but we kept fighting. I hopped out to go to the bathroom, and he yelled at me to get back in and I wouldn't, and he took my stuff out and threw it after me. He pulled away, he left me here—* "Here" had turned into a three-syllable word as Jenny struggled not to give in to tears.

"You left her there," Laurel told Oren. "You threw her stuff out."

Oren glanced at Laurel briefly before looking back at Jen. "Come on, Jen. Let's go home. Get in the truck, we'll figure this out."

Jen hugged herself.

Oren inched closer. "I'm sorry. We were both being stupid, and you made me so mad."

Laurel stepped forward. "Sorry doesn't fix anything."

"Stay out of this," Oren said.

Laurel took another step forward. "Are you going to make me?"

Jenny grabbed Laurel's arm. "Don't. It's okay, we're only talking."

"Jen. Let's go."

"No. Give me a minute."

Laurel stared at her. Oren gazed at her, too, his face scared and sad.

A moment later, he nuzzled Jen's neck as Jen's shoulders shook. "I'm sorry, I'm sorry," he whispered; Jen said, "Me, too," each time. Finally, she turned to Laurel. She ran a hand through her hair. "Oh, God. What a mess." She stepped closer and put her arms around Laurel

189

and her embrace was as muscular and sure as always. "Thank you so much for coming. I don't know what I'd have done if you hadn't."

"Jen. Don't be an idiot."

Jenny gripped Laurel's forearms. "I'm okay now. I am. I'm sorry I dragged you down here, but that's what we're here for, isn't it? For anything? For everything?"

"I want you to come home with me."

"I'll get you that malt. I'll tell Oren, we'll all go."

Laurel shook free. "He dumped you; he drove away." She smoothed Jenny's collar. "He tore your coat. You can't go with him."

"Like Oren said, we were both acting like idiots. It was a bad fight, and it wasn't fair to drag you into it, but it's okay now."

"It's not okay."

"It is." Jenny nodded and the tassel of her stocking cap bounced.

Oren lifted Jen's duffel and backpack out of Laurel's trunk. "You got your answer. Thanks for coming to help Jen, but leave it now." He strode to his truck and threw the bags in.

Jen turned to follow and Laurel caught her hand. "You don't have to do this. Why are you doing this?"

Jenny clasped Laurel's fingers. "He came back."

The fur balls on one of her mukluks were tangled. Laurel wanted to reach down and untwist them. "Jen. Stop and consider. Choose a different answer."

Jen shook her head.

"But why would you go with him? He left you on the expressway."

"But he came back. He came back because he loves me. He knows me, and he still loves me."

Laurel's heart was a chunk of firewood split down its center. "That's a terrible way to think. You don't have to think that."

Jen smiled merrily. "Stop. I'm okay, and I'm going, all right? I'm sorry I called!" She pulled her hand free and jogged toward the truck. Oren started it and Jenny was caught in the headlights. He leaned over and opened the passenger door, and Jenny climbed in.

Laurel drove home with the radio off. She wanted silence. No music, no talk, nothing.

She'd been furious at Oren when he roared up. It was bullshit behavior, leaving Jen, tearing her coat, making her cry, then coming back and saying *I love you, baby, I'm sorry.* She understood the wrath of the smiting God so many people believed in. He knew right from wrong. So did Laurel. Oren was wrong. Jen must leave him.

But then she saw Oren slump as he waited for Jen to decide, the tight way he hugged her when she walked back to him, and she had felt, though she hadn't wanted to, sorry for him. After that she'd been mad at Jen. The original drama queen, famous for yanking people's chains and acting oblivious of the consequences, always getting involved with guys who were messed up some way, never anyone who was just nice. Laurel's unwanted sympathy for Oren didn't make her think Jen should get back together with him. She felt sorry for him, but that didn't change the fact that Jen should walk away. But Jen wouldn't. She'd light the match and call the fire department and dash right back into the blaze.

For a long stretch of miles Laurel fumed at both of them.

Then, finally, at neither. She just felt done. Their problems were theirs to solve. Maybe they would, maybe they wouldn't. It was up to them.

She stopped for gas an hour north of the bridge. She opened her phone as she walked back to the car with coffee, but there were no missed calls. Skye must be asleep. They'd made their plan before Laurel left: Skye would call every half hour until she went to bed, more if she wanted. Laurel would be home within five or six hours, no later than midnight, for sure. She glanced at the phone's clock. She was on schedule.

She turned north on the Waiska road, shifting in her seat. She had to pee. Five miles went by, then ten, and then she couldn't wait any longer. She steered onto the shoulder and scrambled into the ditch and peed, though it was snowing so hard she could've gone right out in the open and no one would've seen even if they did come along, which they wouldn't. Back in the driver's seat, she turned the key.

Nothing happened.

She tried again.

Nothing.

Laurel swore and pounded the steering wheel, then stared into the darkness. After a minute, she dragged the sleeping bag out from behind the seat where she always kept it and zipped herself in.

Wind buffeted the car; snow clawed at the windows. The road ahead stretched empty: she remembered two camps and zero year-round residences. Cell service died for miles in either direction, too. Laurel snuggled the bag closer around herself. Someone would come along. And Skye had called for the last time before Laurel reached Jenny and the bridge, sounding peaceful.

"Hey, Mama," she'd said. "It's me, checking in."

"All quiet on the western front?" Laurel had struggled to keep the anxiety out of her voice.

"Yes."

"Good!"

Skye yawned. "Stop worrying, you're waking me up. I'm going to bed now. I'm not calling again, so don't get freaked out when I don't."

"Got it," Laurel had said.

Now she shivered and imagined warm things: Gran's sauna, the potbelly stove in the back of Belle's, a dirty motel room with painted-shut windows in the middle of August.

Three hours later, a crew cab pulling a snowmobile trailer passed, then slowed, stopped, and backed up. Four men climbed out. They were on their way to the Best Western; they'd heard about the storm and drove north on the spur of the moment, hoping to get the season's last good riding in. Within minutes, they'd hooked cables to the Sable's battery, and when the car groaned to life, they trailed Laurel home. At the pullout, she waved them off with thankful sweeps of her arm. They honked, picked up speed, and vanished. She strode along the track. It had hardly snowed here. That happened sometimes: pouring in the snowbelt, dry a few miles out. She moved fast, her flashlight bobbing.

Its beam caught something on the ground as she came upon the trailer. A charred chunk of wood lay in a shallow bowl that its own heat had made in the snow, Baldy's gloves beside it. Laurel snatched them up and ran, sliding, up the stairs. Harper jumped on her the instant she opened the door, whining and scrabbling. The room smelled of smoke. Laurel put her hand on the stovepipe. Cold. She yanked the door open. A few embers glowed in the bottom.

"Skye!" Laurel ran through the kitchen and her room to Skye's. The blankets lay smooth. "Skye!" She ran back into the living room. "Baby! Answer me!"

She cast the flashlight beam over Frank's cage, the counter, the couch, then hurried to the bedrooms. Empty. She hurried back to the living room. On the couch the throw lay crumpled with a book on top and Laurel saw it in her head: Skye nervous, reading to Harper to reassure herself—too much like that April night with Sean. "What happened?" she whispered.

Harper whined. She kept the flashlight roving.

The beam caught the white of a sheet of paper. Laurel grabbed it from the table.

*Ms. Hill, Your daughter had trouble with the fire. She was unable to reach you and became alarmed. She called 911 and we rode out and assessed the situation. We have taken her with us to the station in Crosscut. Please contact us as soon as possible.* A deputy had signed his full name with precise block letters and printed a phone number below.

Laurel trotted for the door, slamming her hand against her top coat pocket as she went. The phone wasn't there.

She sank into the chair.

Remembered swinging Jenny's bag into the trunk and leaning over to push it farther in. A tiny plunk she paid no attention to at the time now thundered in her ears. It had been the phone dropping out of her coat.

# Twenty-One

The caseworker wore maroon slacks and a white blouse with an orange tint. Her water must be hard; hard water left its greasy film on everything. Laurel's own ivory sweater was tinged gray for the same reason. She perched on the edge of her chair. The woman said a few things—none of it was sinking in. "Skye will be in the foster home for at least two days," she finished. Laurel wanted to sweep the name plaque that read ANDREA PHILLIPS, engraved in white letters on brown plastic, off her desk.

She clenched her hands. "Why? Why so long? It's already been all night."

Andrea Phillips pushed a loose strand of hair out of her face. "We need time to investigate."

"Investigate."

"Ms. Hill. Skye is ten years old. She was alone, in a remote area with no one to call on, unable to reach you, dealing with fire."

Laurel swallowed.

The caseworker nodded at her. "We'll talk to people in your community. Teachers, friends, neighbors. We'll visit your home. We have to determine the severity of neglect."

Gray light fell through the window, making everything look as hopeless as it was. The carpets smelled of industrial cleanser and despair. "But Skye is my life."

"I realize this is upsetting. But we have to be satisfied of your ability to provide a secure environment for her."

"Things aren't perfect, but foster care—no. She needs to come home."

"Maybe. But not yet."

"But school starts back up tomorrow."

Ms. Phillips rubbed her eyes. Laurel had been informed that it was Ms. Phillips who had contacted a foster family on the emergency placement list and taken Skye there overnight. And now at nine on a Sunday morning she was in her office. It was her job, yes. But it had to be exhausting. "Is there someone Skye can stay with?" she asked. "A close family friend, a grandparent?"

Laurel thought of Mom, somewhere on the back side of Cape Breton Island. Jenny—but that was no good. Mary Lynn in New Mexico, or Naomi downstate. Downstate and soon to be disappointed in Laurel. "It's just the two of us right now."

"Then you'll have to let the process take its course."

Laurel's hands shook. "But you have to believe me. Skye is everything to me. I wouldn't put her in danger."

"But you did. She could've been hurt."

"But she wasn't. She wasn't, she knew what to do, we went over it a hundred times, and she's been building fires forever. Beach fires, I mean. And I was always there—" Until she wasn't.

Ms. Phillips shifted her shoulders as if they ached.

"Ms. Phillips, please."

The caseworker placed a hand on a file folder that lay before her. Skye's file. "It's obvious you love your daughter."

"Of course I do."

She sighed. "I see a lot of positives here already. I called Beatrice Fox this morning. She says Skye's grades are good, she seems well taken care of, her clothes are clean—as clean as any ten-year-old's, anyway—and that she doesn't seem tired or hungry when she comes in. Her attendance is regular, although Mrs. Fox has some concern about—"

"Of course she's not hungry! And of course her attendance is regular. She loves school. Do you think I wouldn't send her?"

Ms. Phillips's expression turned exhausted. "I'm sad to say there's no 'of course' about any of it."

Laurel clenched her satchel. Inside were her envelopes of cash and the deposit slip for Margie's money and the piece of notebook paper with the testimonials about Cedar Lake on it and, ridiculously, a magnet that had come in the mail from Mom last week. *Leap and a net will appear.* Jen was right. The magnets were stupid. *She* was stupid.

Ms. Phillips reached toward her. "You mustn't think I'm against you. We take very seriously the relationship between a parent and a child, and poverty itself cannot be a reason for removal. Your living situation isn't necessarily at issue, not if your daughter is happy and healthy and well taken care of. But we have to ensure the safety of the child. We can't do this quickly. Terrible things happen to children."

"Not to Skye! I would never hurt her. Never. It was stupid of me to go when my friend called. We had a plan, but—" Laurel faltered; her heart hammered. "I know it wasn't a good one. I would never do anything like it again."

"You have to realize that stupidity on your part, as you call it, affects Skye."

"I do realize it. I found my phone. It had fallen out of my pocket, into the trunk. I just, I didn't notice at the time." She had been so wound up with Jen's drama. An unworthy cause. Laurel clenched her fists. "I'll be more careful of it from now on, I promise I will, and I bought a new battery for my car this morning. I'd been putting it off; they're expensive, you know? And I kept hoping I'd fixed the problem. I hadn't, but now I have."

Ms. Phillips massaged her temple. "Nonetheless, we have to look into it. It's a process. I'm sorry."

The office window overlooked the highway. Beyond it was the Crosscut junkyard. The bucket of a derelict cherry picker reared up over the roof of a school bus; a fire truck with brush growing through its ladders listed to one side. "What about Harper?" Laurel asked at last. "She loves that dog; she needs him."

"I'm afraid the foster family won't take a dog."

"Can I bring him to see her?"

"I imagine so. I'll try to arrange it for Tuesday."

"*Tuesday.*"

"Or Wednesday. In the afternoon. After school, or during lunch." Ms. Phillips picked up her pen. "You can phone to check what I found out. I'll give you my number and Skye's case number. If you talk to the receptionist, you can . . ."

Laurel's head buzzed and her skin turned clammy; Ms. Phillips's voice sounded tinny and faint. She closed her eyes until her head cleared. Then she slid the paper with Skye's case number on it into her satchel.

# Twenty-Two

Skye sat with her arms wound around the swing's chains; Harper lay on the ground at her feet. Laurel squinted into the sun, pushed herself on her own swing with one toe. The playground of Crosscut Elementary swarmed with kids; ten minutes remained until the bell signaling the end of lunch hour would ring. Shouts rose like sparks from a campfire; herds of children stampeded across the slushy soccer field. Students mobbed the swings closer to the school, but the only person near this set was the playground monitor, who stood talking on a cell phone.

"So how is this school?" Laurel's voice emerged thin. She cleared her throat. "Do you like it?"

Skye tapped her fingers on the chain's links, then rubbed them as if testing them for weak spots. She was a prisoner searching for an escape route. "It's okay."

Laurel's hands and feet were cold, her armpits damp. She'd lost the ability—the right—to talk to her own daughter. "Do you— Have you met anybody nice? Anybody you like?"

"Nobody talks to me much because I'm a foster kid."

Laurel froze. "You're not a foster kid."

"To them I am."

"That's a bad reason not to talk to someone. And a few days doesn't make you a foster kid. This is just—" That word again. "It's temporary." She straightened the collar of Skye's coat. "Zip up, it's cold even with the sun."

Skye didn't move. Laurel reached to tap her shoulder, then changed her mind. "Did Ms. Phillips come and talk to you?"

"Yesterday."

"How was it?"

"I told her we're fine and I want to go home."

"She's coming to see the trailer tomorrow. I'll bake something, it'll smell good. Like they say to do if you're selling a house. Bread, or cookies."

Skye rubbed Harper's belly with the sole of her boot. "Well. Don't burn them."

Laurel caught the scent of Skye's hair. It smelled of bananas instead of coconut. "Do you like having that television in your room?" Skye had told her about the television on the phone. Also, that her roommate had been in foster care for a year, but that she might go home soon because her mother was getting out of jail.

"We're not supposed to have it on after nine, but Katy sneaks it after Mrs. Janson goes to bed."

"Do you want me to say something?"

"No. It'd only make everybody hate me more."

"Skye! I'm sure nobody hates you."

Skye ground her foot against the earth. "No, you're right. Nobody cares enough to." She dropped beside Harper. "I wish we were home," she told him. "Oh, Harper-Harps, don't you wish we were, too?"

"Back in Gallion," Laurel said. A bank of clouds had blown in while they were talking. In Gallion, the day would be beautiful; in Crosscut, it was grim.

Skye glanced up. "I meant Waiska." She blew into Harper's ear; he twitched it in a way that made her smile, though sadly. She leaned over to touch her forehead to his flank. "I'm sorry for messing up."

Laurel stopped her swing. "What are you talking about?"

"The fire. I should have been able to do it."

"Skye, no, it's not your—"

"If I hadn't messed up, everything would be fine. I wouldn't be here; you wouldn't be missing work."

"Stop. You do not need to worry about my work, my work is fine. And more important, you did not mess up. This is my fault. I made a bad choice."

"You had to go to Aunt Jen," Skye said simply.

Laurel shook her head. "No. I thought I did, but I didn't."

"That's friendship, though, going when the person needs you."

Laurel frowned across the playground. "Sometimes yes, sometimes no. In this case, no."

Skye leaned closer to Harper. "I miss the sound the woods make," she told him. Her hand smoothed and smoothed his ear. "In the morning, especially. You know that time before you even know you're awake yet? Before you have to start being you and doing stuff, and you can kind of float? I like listening to that sound, the whirring. It always makes me feel—" Her hand stopped and Harper bumped his nose into it.

"Makes you feel what?"

"Huh?"

"You were saying about the wind."

Skye climbed back onto the swing. She pushed herself off and tipped her head far back. "It makes you feel big, I guess. Or, it makes you feel small, but in a good way. A pine in the yard here sounds the same way. I listened to it this morning and yesterday, too, before anyone else was awake." Suddenly, she leaped from the swing. She scooped up a stick and threw it for Harper; he loped after it and she followed.

The playground monitor advanced toward Laurel, glowering. "Get that dog on a leash! What are you thinking?"

After a startled moment—such a thing would never have mattered in Gallion, or Waiska either—Laurel scrambled off her seat and hurried after them.

Laurel waited for three o'clock at the gas station across from the school, feeling like a kidnapper. Still, it was easier than checking in at the office and saying who she was: Skye's unfit mom, who'd put her in danger and lost custody of her, but had been granted two brief visits on this stingy, dreary day.

Finally, Skye appeared outside the school.

Laurel hurried to meet her and they walked toward the foster home. A dog roared from behind a fence; a car zoomed past and threw slush onto their pant legs. Laurel held Skye's hand tight.

"Abby called yesterday," Skye said as they arrived. The house was two stories, painted cream and brown, with a porch across the front.

"You must've been happy to talk to her."

Skye pulled her hand from Laurel's and stuffed it in her coat pocket. The way she stood, her face set but her eyes full, her elbows jutted out and her weight on one hip, she looked like her father when Laurel told him she had to get going, goodbye, and (inanely) thanks.

O.A.R. had been playing "That Was a Crazy Game of Poker" on the Trackside's jukebox the night they met. It was the Friday after Thanksgiving and every corner of the house had echoed and stabbed without Gran in it. Laurel drove to the bar as fast as she could in the newly empty world. Once there, she swayed on the dance floor, a ten-by-ten square of tile with a never-used drum set at the edge, letting her sadness lift out of her for a while. *I say oh, you say ah, I say revolution and you say jah,* O.A.R. sang. And then she noticed a guy swaying nearby, dark complexioned and stocky with friendly eyes.

When the song ended, they sat at the bar. His name was John Child. He was twenty, from Detroit, a student at the University of Michigan. He wanted to be a trial lawyer, but he wasn't sure he had what it took. The past summer he'd worked in a law firm.

"Wow," Laurel had said, impressed.

He had laughed. "As a secretary, more or less. I wasn't great at it. But I didn't get canned and it'll look good on my law school applications. I'm a senior now, I have to consider that, what looks good, what'll get me in. If I can get in at all." He shook his head in an elderly way that made Laurel smile. He pointed at a skinny redhead leaning over the pool table. "I'm kicking back over break, though. Up here hunting with that guy. My best buddy. I've got some family up this way—we spent Thanksgiving with them."

"I'm at Northern." It startled her how fast she lied. And why did she? To change the subject away from holidays and family and because she was ashamed. She'd been at Central for one year on a track scholarship. She tried to like it, but in fact she was doing poorly in her classes and missing home. She'd already had to drop calculus before she flunked it. When Gran died the month before, everything that was barely holding together collapsed.

She told John Child none of that. She rewrote the story of herself so that none of it would be true. At least for an hour, she wouldn't be a brokenhearted girl whose gran was gone, a girl who blamed herself enough that the regret would wake her up in the middle of the night for the rest of her life, a girl now so apraxic—a word she'd learned in General Biology before she flunked it—she could barely get her clothes on the right way. If only she'd come home from her run sooner that October afternoon. If she'd gone to get the firewood when Gran asked instead of putting it off. Maybe Gran would still be alive.

"You all right?" John had touched Laurel's arm.

Laurel tightened her hands around her beer bottle. "Let's dance."

Later, they had sprawled in the back seat of John's car, a blue Neon full of the kinds of things you'd expect from college guys on a hunting vacation. It had been pleasant in a hectic way to be so close to him, but the event itself was confusing. It wasn't how she ever imagined things going. Afterward she scrambled into her jeans and pullover, yanked her coat and boots on, said, "I have to go," and vanished. By the time she knew she was pregnant, their encounter seemed hazy, almost beside the point next to the fact of this baby on the way, this being, this spirit. Laurel called the registrar's office, but there was no John Child listed. Had he been lying? Or had Laurel misunderstood, misremembered? Either way it hadn't seemed very important. She'd grown up without knowing her own father. Her parents' marriage had been so brief that her mother had changed her name back to Hill almost before the ink was dry on their marriage certificate. And besides, her new love consumed her. Skye Elva Lynnette Hill—Lynnette for Mom and Elva for Gran—showed up and took over everything. Maybe, if Laurel admitted it, she hadn't wanted to find Skye's father. Maybe she'd wanted Skye all to herself. Now, faced with her poor marooned daughter, she saw how wrong that had been.

Skye kicked the ground. "They're moving, Mom."

"What?"

"Abby's moving. To Alaska. After school ends. The neighbors complained and complained about the dogs barking, plus it'll just be better there. They can train better for the Yukon."

"Oh, honey."

Skye pulled her mouth one way and then the other. "What'll I do, Mom?"

Laurel brushed bangs away from Skye's face. Her hair needed trimming; the new cut she'd gotten in New Mexico with Mary Lynn wasn't so new anymore. "You'll be sad. But you'll keep in touch, and after a while, things won't seem so bad. Different, but okay, that's how they'll seem."

A girl opened the front door. "Hilda says to come in and wash up and change. We're going to her mom's for dinner. We're supposed to wear a dress or something." The door clapped shut.

Skye cast Laurel a beseeching look and Laurel pulled Skye's sweatshirt straight. She'd worn the same shirt the last night Laurel had seen her at home, before the incident with the fire and the sheriff. Her jeans were the same, too, though Laurel had given Skye's favorite clothes to Ms. Phillips that first day: the paisley leggings and purple dress, Gran's cloche, her chukkas. "Why the ho-hum clothes?" she asked.

"It's just easier. The other kids tease."

"Let them tease. Your outfits are awesome. They're you."

"I'm tired, Mom. I'm tired of how much work it is to be me. And I'm not me here, anyway. I'm not me anywhere but home."

Laurel grasped her shoulders. "That's not true. You're you wherever you go. I can't believe you'd think otherwise."

"I don't know why not. It's what you always say."

Laurel stood and cradled Skye's shoulder, and after a moment, Skye slumped into her. The girl thrust her head out again. "It's time to change *now*."

# Twenty-Three

L aurel pushed her cart down the dairy aisle at the Crosscut grocery, stopping every few feet to set butter and milk in the basket, cheese and eggs. Yogurt was on sale; she drew Skye's favorite flavors from the cooler: raspberry, lime, and vanilla. Skye was coming home today and Laurel wanted to make everything perfect for her.

In the next aisle, she pulled canned beans and tomato puree off the shelf, vinegar and mustard. She studied her list as she rounded the end cap. When she looked up, Jen was standing nearby, surveying the cereal options, wearing flip-flops despite the bright chilliness of the day. Laurel tightened her grip on the cart handle. "Jenny."

Jenny turned, tapping the toes of her right foot. Laurel saw that her nails glistened red; she wore a narrow silver toe ring. "Well, look who's here."

Laurel hadn't returned Jenny's calls since the night at the bridge. Her anger had shot back triple-strength when she found Skye gone. Now, though, faced with actual-Jenny, some of it evaporated. Not all, but a chunk calved off the main glacier. "You look good. You look fantastic."

"I'm glad you think so," Jenny said icily.

"I wish I could find my flip-flops. It's so warm today. Out of nowhere, right?"

Jenny rolled her eyes.

Laurel stepped closer. "What're you doing?"

"What does it look like?"

Laurel wanted to hug Jen. She also wanted to shake her. "Are you okay?"

Contempt washed over Jenny's face. "That's how you want to do this, all nice and polite? All righty, then. I'm great, how are you?"

"I'm okay."

"Really."

Laurel nodded. It was more complicated than a simple yes, but for now, a yes would do.

"What I heard was, they yanked Skye out of that trailer you're squatting in and shoved her into foster care. That certainly sounds great."

Laurel's anger flooded back. "She's there because of you."

"Me."

"Yes, you. Your call, your crisis, your drama. I came to get you and Skye had trouble and you didn't even—" Laurel shouldn't have been surprised, was the thing. For years the boyfriend before Oren knocked Jen around whenever his mood turned sour. And every single time, Jen called, Laurel went, and then Jen changed her mind when he apologized and pleaded.

Jenny snatched the Cheerios down. "I can't believe you. You're the one living in the woods like some hermit, taking all kinds of chances, and it's my fault when the shit hits the fan."

Laurel wanted to yell, but Jenny's hands were trembling. Laurel knew they'd be cold because they were always cold. Cold hands, warm heart, they used to say to each other about it. They'd been such little old ladies. "It *is* your fault. But it's mine, too. I should've done things different. Differently. Anyway, she's coming home today—the caseworker came yesterday and okayed it."

"Really. How'd you explain the trailer?"

"I said it belonged to my cousin."

"And she bought that."

"Why wouldn't she? And Baldy wouldn't have minded, I know he wouldn't. He invited us to stay there."

"When he was alive."

Laurel wound a strand of hair around her hand. "No one minds, even if they do suspect something. I'm not hurting anything."

Jen shook her head. "Only in the U.P."

Laurel's ears rang. "What?"

"You are just like your mother. Traipsing around, singing your songs, always believing things will work out in the end."

"I don't sing—"

"God, don't be stupid, not about Skye. My brother's different, he's an adult, he'll survive, but Skye—"

"Jen. Sean and I—that was never right."

"He loved you. You got rid of him when you got bored."

"That's not true."

"Yes, it is."

"No." Laurel didn't want to say more, but maybe she had to. "You know Sean's had a hard time since he got back from over there." He'd been in Iraq, then Afghanistan. The longer he was home, the worse things got.

"Good of you to dump him because of it."

Laurel sucked in a sharp breath. "Listen. I left for Skye."

Jenny froze. "No, no way. Not Sean."

"No, not like Jim. But still bad for Skye."

"I don't understand." Jen's voice was subzero.

On its own what happened might have seemed like a minor incident, a moment lounging in a crowd of moments, not hurting anyone. But when you were living it, it was enormous.

A late-winter blizzard had hit in April. Town was busy with snowmobilers and Laurel was working long hours at Belle's. She had come home at two in the morning one Sunday and heard Skye's voice when she stepped in the door. She tiptoed through the foyer to see Skye on the couch beside Sean in her pj's; she wasn't in bed, the way she should have been so late at night; instead she was reading to Sean from one of her chapter books, running one finger along the text, while Sean stared forward in silence. By the deadness of his face, Laurel guessed that his silence had gone on all afternoon and evening. He'd been sinking lower and lower over those last few months. She had tried every way she could to jostle him back to them, but nothing worked.

She had cleared her throat and Skye had looked up. "Mom!" She slid off the couch and ran to Laurel. "Sean and I are reading this!" She waved the book and Laurel tried to take it from her, but Skye wouldn't let go. "No! No, I have to finish, we're almost done, we started right after dinner." She had broken down sobbing.

Laurel had never told Jen that story; she hadn't wanted to hurt her more than was necessary. "I had to go," Laurel told Jen. "For her sake."

"You're pathetic." Jenny's voice shook. "He was depressed. You think that excuses you?"

Laurel clenched the cart handle. "It was like living with endless darkness. I couldn't get through to him. I did try. I love him, too, you know."

"Oh, yes, that's obvious."

"I do. But not romantically."

"You don't even believe in that. Romance." Jen put bitter quotes around the word. "How many times did you tell me it was a crock? That any two reasonable people with good intentions and a little in common could love each other?"

Laurel had said that, but she wasn't sure if she believed it anymore. She wasn't sure she didn't, either. She only knew she couldn't pour herself into making things work with Sean. Skye came first. "Skye was trying to fix it, Jen. She was trying to fix something so big and broken—I had to think of her. I had to."

Jen crossed her arms.

"He's doing better now," Laurel said softly. "He must have told you he met someone, somebody online. He told me when I ran into him at the post office before Christmas."

"Like that'll last. She lives in Idaho."

"It might. He seemed really happy."

"That doesn't excuse you. And good job protecting Skye, by the way. That worked well."

Jen rammed her cart past Laurel.

"Jen, stop."

Jenny stopped.

"I'm sorry I haven't called." Jen had called six times on Monday. Laurel was too angry to even listen to the messages. She still hadn't listened to them. That "done" feeling she'd had in the car remained. It had seemed permanent until this exact moment. "I know you called, but I was mad. I was furious. They took Skye; everything was a mess."

"You can say that again."

Laurel leaned toward her. "Are you okay? What are you even doing here? Visiting your mom?"

Jen's smile shimmered with rage. "Yeah, no. I'm living with her. Which I swore I'd never do again, for any reason, ever. But she answered my call when you didn't. So. Good thing Big Jim's history, eh?"

To her credit, Faith had left Big Jim when Jen finally told her what he'd done. "But what about Oren? What about school?"

"I quit."

"Jenny, no!"

"Shut up."

"Jen."

Jen stepped closer. "Do you not get it? I needed you."

"What happened?"

"None of your business."

"Please tell me."

Jen raised a stop-sign hand. "Too little, too late. I'm done."

Laurel stepped backward. "Oh, what, forever? What about Skye?"

Jenny's eyes blazed. "I love that girl, I always will. You tell her that for me."

"And what? I'm supposed to explain that this is a message you're sending along but that you don't actually want anything to do with us anymore?"

"You always think the rules of life don't apply to you, but they do. There are actions and consequences, and everything does not have a happy ending. Wake up."

"Jenny."

"You're a dreamer and dreamers are dangerous. They're naive and people get hurt."

Laurel couldn't speak.

"You always have to march to your own drummer. But guess what? You're the only one in the parade. You and Skye, and Skye's being dragged along for the ride. Your ride."

Laurel gazed into Jenny's basket. In its bottom sat corn chips, a bottle of ketchup, a half gallon of milk—organic—and a box of ice cream bars, which must have been melting. She could've picked the items out for Jen herself, though she wouldn't have known to get organic milk. That was new. She looked up and Jenny closed her eyes. When she opened them, she said, "A good parent makes sacrifices, Laurel. That's the bottom line, the golden rule. And you just don't. The sad thing for Skye is how much you lie to yourself about it."

Laurel gripped her cart hard to keep herself upright. *Gran*, she wanted to cry. *Mom!* She wanted to burrow into them and sob like she had when she was five and fell off the slide at school. And yet of course Jen was right.

"You know what'll happen next? You'll get caught squatting and DSS won't like it and it'll be goodbye, Skye. For good." Weariness rolled off Jenny in waves, waves that would drown Laurel. "It might be better if Social Services never lets her come back. She's probably better off almost anywhere else but with you."

214

Laurel's dazed eyes wandered to the oatmeal. They had the steel-cut oats here now. They never used to. Bob's Red Mill. She gazed into Bob's smiling face beneath his jaunty cap. She smelled Jen's perfume as Jen brushed by. It was flowery and pretty, like Jenny. A moment later, she went back to taking groceries off shelves: waxed paper, sandwich baggies, dish soap. Toilet paper, paper towel, tampons. She stopped in front of the laundry detergents. Tide, Purex, Arm & Hammer. All in bright bottles, all making promises of cleanliness and renewal.

She dropped her hands from the cart. Strode through the first set of doors and into the lobby where the carts were stored, through the second set of doors and outside. She made a hard right and sailed onward. A half second later she stubbed her toe on a curb. The pain was so shocking that she doubled over.

Eventually she straightened. Tears leaked from her eyes and she let them leak. The cool spring sun poured over her. She rubbed at her face and the movement reflected off the grocery's tinted windows. She turned. There she was: Laurel Hill, terrible friend, callous lover, failed parent. She proffered a wobbly smile. Her face was splotchy, her eyes sunken. Every positive slogan she'd ever plastered to her refrigerator scrolled through her mind, and each was revealed as ridiculous. The truth flamed inside her: She was broke, and she'd always been broke and always would be. Also broken. She was not equal to the world; she couldn't function in it. She could not—would not?—ever see the truth of things. She was selfish, she was shortsighted, she failed the people she cared about the most. Without meaning to, to be sure. No bad intentions, no evil deeds. Just stupidity and blindness. Look how she'd failed Gran, running instead of going to get the wood when she'd known how stubborn Gran was: Gran would get in the pickup and do it herself before waiting through another day of

Laurel's promises. She'd lost Gran years before she would have had to. She lived with that truth, but she would never forgive herself. And now she was hurting Skye, neglecting her despite her Herculean efforts to do the opposite.

Laurel sank to the curb. Across the parking lot, a man in a green windbreaker herded a trolley of carts, his head tucked against the breeze. A stray sack cartwheeled from behind a truck and he bent to grab it, losing his hold on the carts. They trundled toward a line of cars and he nabbed them just before they smacked the grille of a blue Dodge.

Had this been his dream in life? Bagging groceries, chasing trash, wrangling carts? More likely he was doing what he had to: working a job, earning a check, taking care of himself and his family. That's how life was. How it had to be.

Laurel yanked her phone out of her pocket and dialed a number that hadn't changed since she was a kid, a downstate area code, a Grand Rapids exchange. A minute later, Uncle Milton's voice boomed in her ear. "Hel-lo," he said in a two-syllable song, same as always. "What can I do you for?"

"For Pete's sake, kid, haven't I always said you can come here?" Uncle Milton's voice was gently exasperated.

"Yes. You have. Thank you."

"We'll tuck Skye into the sewing room upstairs—it's just her size. Suze won't mind; she doesn't use it. You can bunk in the basement 'til you get your feet under you. It's unfinished, but it has its own entrance. That would be handy." Laurel wouldn't wake everyone up, coming and going at all hours as she would have to. "When will you come? When school lets out in June?"

His saying "June" made June rush up like a hard stretch of pavement. "Yes," Laurel whispered.

They worked out the details before the bank of clouds streaming in from the west disappeared over the sky's east rim. One morning the past fall a page in Skye's science workbook had reminded Laurel that these marshmallowy piles of clouds were called cumulus. They predicted fair weather, which was ironic.

"I'll put you on one of my crews cleaning a building downtown," Milton said. He chuckled. "Thirty floors of nothing but mirrored glass. Quite a sight to see, but hell to keep clean." In time, he might put her in charge of it. Even to start, he would pay her more than she'd ever made. "And that car of Mother's has to be near death."

"Pretty much."

"I could use another one for the fleet. You go to the Ford dealer in Crosscut and pick out something." An Escape would be sensible, or a Fiesta, but whatever color she liked was fine, though black would show the dirt. "Whenever you're ready, you let me know, and I'll see to the details."

"Okay. Thank you." Inadequate, but what else could she offer? She didn't know how to repay him. Laurel ended the call and stared across the pavement; in the distance the flags at the rest stop on the highway flapped. She shoved herself to her feet and headed into the store. Each lift of her foot required enormous effort, but in time she arrived at her cart. She began pushing it through the aisles.

Even if she was broke, and broken, and even if everything was about to change in ways she'd never wanted—had already changed in ways she'd give anything to undo—Skye still loved peaches and Harper was almost out of kibble and Frank needed sunflower seeds.

She placed the cheapest bottle of laundry detergent in the cart. A bag of apples, a head of lettuce, two onions. A sack of potatoes, a loaf of bread. The only thing she didn't buy was aspirin, though her hand hovered over the jumbo-sized bottle for a while. But she might as well feel her pain. Masking it didn't do any good, it just let you keep dreaming.

# Twenty-Four

Skye gazed out her window, humming a song Laurel didn't recognize. She leaned forward in her seat. "Everything's changed. I was only away for a week. Not even."

Laurel couldn't answer.

"The snow's all munchy."

The crunching motion she made with her fingers and thumbs mimicked the settling of the snow, the way it pockmarked after a string of warm days, like a ground cover of Rice Krispies treats. "The sun was out a lot," Laurel admitted. "It didn't feel all that warm, though."

"It feels warm now."

"It's better." Laurel yearned to keep at least one fingertip on Skye at all times, but she kept both hands on the wheel. The tires swished on the pavement. Otherwise all was quiet. She'd stopped turning the radio on since the night she went to get Jen. Music made her feel things, it let her out of the cage of herself, it made her think of the past and of the future, and she didn't want that. She didn't deserve it, was the truth.

Halfway to Waiska, they glimpsed an animal running in the trees, a fox or a coyote. Skye gasped. "I missed these old woods," she said gravely. She began humming again, leaving off long enough to call, "Hello, bears! Hello, deers!"

"You're something else."

Skye glanced at her.

"Something good," Laurel clarified. "Where'd you come from, anyway? The stars?"

"Mom, that's dumb."

"No, it isn't."

Skye examined Peter's satchel as she ate her eggs Monday morning. It lay folded on the table, a needle trailing dark green floss poked into it. "I thought you'd finish it while I was gone," she said.

"I have until May, right?"

"But I thought you were making bags for Naomi's."

Laurel wiped at a splash of egg on the stovetop. She'd called Naomi that first morning to tell her that there was a family issue and she couldn't do her shifts. Naomi said it was all right, but Laurel disagreed. She wasn't about to go sashaying into Naomi's store and talk about selling crafts, even if she wanted to make more satchels, which she didn't. "I'm letting that idea go."

"No!"

"It's one of those things that just won't work out." Laurel adjusted the magnet stuck on the side of the fridge that claimed *Perseverance will take you places talent can't even dream of.* Then she pulled it off and dropped it into the wastebasket.

Skye didn't notice. She smashed the last bite of egg onto her bread. "I can't decide what to wear today."

"Something you love." Laurel wanted to ask if it would be strange, going back to school after missing the week and whether she worried what her classmates would think, but she wasn't sure how to bring it up, or whether she should.

Skye arched her brows. "Probably a good idea. Dress for success."

"Are you—are you nervous? About what people will say and wonder?"

"It's nobody's business. I'll probably tell Peter what happened, but mostly I'm just going to catch up and be happy I'm home."

When her door slid shut, Laurel peeled all the magnets off the refrigerator. She shoved them into a plastic bag, fishing the first one from the garbage. It seemed mean to pitch them; she'd drop them at St. Vinnie's next time she was in town. Someone else might give them a good home. Someone smarter than she was.

Skye came out in her purple dress and paisley leggings.

"Oh, pretty. You always look great in that outfit."

"Thanks." Skye frowned. "Where's everything off the fridge?"

Laurel scooted her hand over the bag. "They're here."

"I like those magnets."

"Sure, I'm just—I'm cleaning."

*"Now?"*

Laurel was due at the Best Western at nine. Luckily, she hadn't lost the job, taking Monday and Wednesday and Friday off, too. "Well begun is half done, right? And maybe I won't put them all back up when I'm finished. Less clutter."

Skye shrugged into her coat. "Yeah, well, be careful, okay? Don't throw the baby out with the bathwater."

Over the next week, Laurel tried to relax into the routine of their lives. It would be disrupted—ended—soon enough, but for this last brief while, it was simple. She cleaned rooms. She fixed easy but nutritious dinners. She read or sewed while Skye did her homework in the evenings. Twice Peter came home with Skye after school; once she went to his house. This sleety afternoon they were playing Monopoly. They were like brother and sister in the way they flared into squabbles and subsided into harmony. They looked alike, too. Their ears curved the same way, Laurel realized, watching Skye bang her playing piece along the board.

Peter rolled the dice and moved his iron ten squares. Skye rolled and marched her Scottie three. Then it was Laurel's turn; she was the thimble. "Move for me," she told them. She dipped chicken in flour. A thigh, a breast, the wings and legs. While the bird baked, she'd get the asparagus ready to steam. She'd bought a pound at Aurora Market earlier that day. Guilt dragged her steps every time she walked inside, but it would be pathetic and weak to avoid the place. Laurel had shot Naomi an apologetic smile as the bells on the door jingled behind her.

Naomi had been leaning over a magazine on the countertop; red-framed reading glasses perched on her nose. She looked up. "Stop that. You look like a kicked dog."

"I feel bad about what—"

"Good grief, girl, how many times are you going to make me tell you? Closing was no problem."

Laurel nodded, but she knew otherwise. She skulked into the produce aisle for the asparagus and carried it to the register.

Naomi took Laurel's money and poked the asparagus into a sack along with a square of cilantro and two cookies. When Laurel began to protest, she held up a finger: no, hush. "Don't take this wrong, but your hangdog act is getting tedious."

"I'm sorry," Laurel mumbled.

Naomi's expression was rueful. "Just say thank you."

"Thank you." Laurel avoided her eyes.

Naomi sighed. "Bea told me more about what happened. You must have been stricken."

"It was my own fault."

"What I've found is that life happens no matter how careful you are. And even if it was your fault, it doesn't change your grief. Loss is loss."

Laurel gave a tiny nod.

A man approached the counter with a pound of coffee. When he was gone, Naomi grabbed an index card and scrawled her phone numbers on it in Sharpie. She reached across and tucked the card into Laurel's coat pocket. "My dear, I am not mad, or sad, or anything like that. Closing was fine; it was no big deal. Call me sometime. If you need something or if you don't. And bring Skye to see me soon." Laurel nodded and mumbled another thank-you. She grabbed the asparagus bag, but Naomi put a hand over hers. "Beating yourself up forever won't do any good. I learned that from experience."

"You didn't do anything wrong."

"But I did. I named her Avril, to begin with. She hated it. Weird, she said. Pretentious. Why not call her plain old April like a normal person?"

Laurel almost laughed. "But that's—"

"I didn't let her pierce her ears until she was twelve; I wouldn't let her date until she was sixteen; I never bought her a Cabbage Patch doll. Oh, and I once missed her school play because I got caught up at work. I laughed too loud at jokes; my spaghetti was runny; I was a timid driver. Plus, I didn't believe in this place."

"But, Naomi, none of that caused—"

"But I regretted all of it. Anything that had ever upset her haunted me like Marley's ghost. Kept me up nights, scrolled through my head on endless loops."

"But that's dumb." Laurel's hand flew to her mouth. "Oh, God, I'm sorry."

Naomi grinned. "It is dumb. But those were my feelings. Even if I'd been a perfect parent in every way—I wasn't—I'd have had them. And regret isn't all bad. It can teach you things. After a while, though, it doesn't serve any purpose."

Laurel nodded, though she didn't agree that their situations were similar.

"Make sure you bring me things to sell. And I want you to consider working here this summer."

"I don't think—"

Naomi put her hand up. "Don't answer right now. Mull it over."

Laurel had dropped her gaze. "We're moving when school lets out. I'm sorry. Please don't mention it to Skye. I want her to enjoy everything these last two months."

Naomi hadn't said anything more.

Now Peter carried dishes to the sink after dinner. "That was delicious. A real treat."

Where had he learned this sweet formality? From his parents, surely. "I'm glad you enjoyed it." Laurel took the stack of plates from him.

Later, he retrieved his hat from Skye's bed, a gray porkpie with a black band, what a sleuth in an old movie might wear, and slung his backpack over his shoulder. "Thank you for having me over. Dinner was delightful."

"You're most welcome."

He and Skye jogged down the steps toward the car. Skye's laughter floated back to Laurel and a bolt of optimism flashed through her: Peter would be a doctor, or a lawyer like his cousin D.J., who he often talked about. D.J. grew up downstate but now lived in Sault Ste. Marie and worked as an attorney for the tribe. Peter wanted to do something like that; he wanted to be a spokesman for his people. Skye would be a fashion designer or a screenwriter or a marine biologist. They would be happy and generous and fulfilled, good citizens of the world. Skye would remember these days as if from a great distance, like peering through the wrong end of a telescope. As for herself, Laurel would remember each moment; she would savor every second.

"You sound down, baby-girl." Mom had been in cell range since the middle of the week and since then they had talked almost daily.

Laurel stood on tiptoes to see inside the trailer, then sat again. Every afternoon Skye had been rehearsing for the school talent show and banishing Laurel outside. Laurel hoped it wouldn't be much longer.

Her butt ached with cold. She brushed a hand over a patch of winter-green. "I'm okay. But it was horrible, putting her through that. I'm an idiot. I suck."

"You are not and you don't. You're going through a rough patch, is all. Listen, I think I should come home."

"No, you can't, not now." An Irishman who played the penny-whistle had heard Mom and Link in the Cape Breton hinterlands and wanted them to come over for a month. "Across the pond," he called it; Mom laughed every time she repeated this. Ireland, Scotland, Wales, and the north coast of England were on the itinerary. It was all on a shoestring, but it was a legitimate lineup of pub dates on a whole other continent, with studio time at the end. It was astonishing.

"It's rinky-dink, really."

"No, it's fantastic."

"But, baby, you and Skye are more important."

"Truly, we're all right. We'll see you afterward. The time'll go by in a flash."

"I don't like your plan to move to Milton's. I'm sure he and Susan will be good to you, I hear what you're saying about the schools and all, but, Laurel, have you truly stopped and thought?"

She yanked up a wintergreen leaf. "I have. It's what's best."

"I can't imagine you two down there, all hemmed in, and Milton and Susan are—oh, honey, they're good-hearted, but they are about as humdrum as people come. All nine-to-five and the latest gadgets and no shoes on the carpet or God forbid up on that white couch Milton had to have. Every weekend it's off to the mall—"

"Mom. Stop. Stop picking on them, they're nice."

"Nice, yes, but oh my God, so conventional."

"No." Laurel's voice was rough. "This is what's wrong with us. We're dreamers, and dreamers are dangerous."

After a silent moment Mom said, "That's what you really think?"

"I don't know!" Laurel punched the moss. "And no, I don't want to move down there, but Skye will be so far ahead of where she'd be if we stay here. Imagine the music and art and sports they'll have there, the level of education, the level of everything. I realize Uncle Milton and Aunt Suze bore you, but the fact is they're steady, and that's not the same thing."

"It isn't?" Mom said, all innocence.

"No, it is not. They're secure, and they're willing to do this, and I can't give her what they can."

"I don't agree. Not that they're not nice, and steady, but that the cards they're holding trump what you have in your hand."

Laurel rubbed her eyes.

"Sweetie, Milton and Susan don't want what you do out of life. I'm serious now. I'm talking about the whole foundational philosophy of existence."

"And I'm talking about a decent car and a steady paycheck and good schools."

"But they don't even remotely see things the same way as you do. It's apples and oranges, round holes and square pegs. You've worked so hard to give Skye the life you believe in, the experiences—"

"Such as getting taken into foster care?"

"That's one. Not a great one. But there are a thousand others to balance it out. What you've tried, and done, it matters. Skye could do anything because of you. She's the real deal."

"She'll still be the real deal," Laurel said tiredly.

"Yes. But sometimes hardships make people stronger. Skye might become a hero in this bad old world. You ever consider that?"

Grateful tears sprang into Laurel's eyes.

"Don't give up now."

Laurel smeared her tears dry with her sleeve. "I'm not giving up. I'm moving."

"To the *suburbs*. And you'll be working nights and living in the basement and more or less turning Skye over to them to raise. Does that make sense?"

Laurel stared across the clearing. What a mess she'd made of everything.

"You know that condo where they live doesn't allow dogs."

"I know," Laurel whispered. "But it's what I've decided." She would have to pay to have Harper boarded.

"I'm going on the record to say I'm against it."

"So noted." A breeze stirred. The wind chimes hanging near the kitchen window rang lonesome and wistful.

Mom sighed. "It's not that I don't know how you feel."

Laurel doubted that.

"I don't think I ever said this to you before. I know I didn't. But it's a good thing your gran was there all those nights I was gone, and all those years."

Laurel folded the leaf of wintergreen. She rubbed the edge on her wrist, like perfume. A trick Mom had shown her way back when.

"I shouldn't have done what I did. Always chasing the dream."

"But, Mom, I was so proud of you." Despite everything, it was true. "And we had so much fun. Remember how we staged a mini Woodstock out in the pasture and the whole school came?"

Mom chuckled. "That was a good time."

"Remember how it rained?"

"It poured."

"But you stayed up there on that stage we built, playing backup for Jen."

"The show must go on; I thought you all better know that. The rain comes and you say, *Hey, rain, there you are.* You don't fold up your tent and go home at the first setback."

"We did know it. We learned it without even knowing we did. I had a fantastic childhood."

"But your gran was the one who—"

"Gran was great, too. I mean, obviously. But you were my mom."

"Thank you, baby. That's sweet of you to say."

Mom's voice was sad and Laurel leaned forward. "You loved me. It was so obvious I never even thought about it, I totally took it for granted."

"I wanted you to. But, God, I was flaky."

"Creative," Laurel amended. "A free spirit."

"I think you're too kind."

"You didn't have to be a magazine mom. That would've been gross."

Mom snorted.

Laurel smoothed the surface of the leathery wintergreen leaf with her thumb. "You were you, and you were great," she said, feeling her way along the words. "No kid ever had more love than me."

"Well," Mom said. "I'm glad." Then, "So how is your situation with Skye any different?"

# Twenty-Five

Snow poured from dense, low clouds all weekend, but on Monday the temperature rose and everything turned sloppy; the dirt roads were soupy muck. This discouraged no one from attending the spring talent show. The children produced skits and recited poems, sang songs and performed dances. Three girls in bright dresses sewn with rows of metal cones—*ziibaaska'igana*, the program helpfully informed the show's non-native speakers—skipped and spun through a jingle dance; Peter stomped out a grass dance wearing moccasins, fringed leathers, and a tunic beaded by his father with fleur-de-lis. Afterward everyone clamored into the gymnasium for treats.

Laurel greeted people she knew from the Best Western and the market; she congratulated Junior Warriors on their performances.

Naomi, elegant in a plum velour sweater and porcupine quill earrings that swayed as she walked, came toward her, beaming, as Laurel was about to pour herself a cup of punch. "Skye did a great job!"

Laurel grinned. "She's a force of nature." Her smile faltered as shame rushed up like an overlingering guest who couldn't be budged. "I want to say again that I'm so sorry—"

Naomi held up both hands in refusal. "Stop. Apologizing. And cash your paycheck, you're messing up my balancing."

"Naomi, no, I don't want it. I didn't even finish the job." She'd told Naomi this again the day before, when she stopped by the market for milk on her way to Peter's to pick up Skye. She apologized; Naomi brushed the apology off and tried to talk her into staying; she even had a lead on a house in town Laurel could rent.

"Cash it. And bring me something to sell."

Laurel smiled perfunctorily.

"I don't care what. Satchels, skirts." Naomi tugged on the wraparound Laurel wore. As a teen, Laurel ran them up whenever she found a big enough piece of fabric on sale, even made them from old sheets or draperies if the pattern was cute. "It'll be summer before we know it. I'm sure your stuff would go. And remember, Sarah is leaving soon."

For her dissertation, Sarah was developing a strategy for preserving and teaching the Ojibwe language. She would head to northern Canada for a year, to interview and record elders in remote villages; she wanted to rent out her house while she was gone.

"It'll be affordable." Naomi singsonged the last word. "She doesn't want to leave her place empty and I don't want to be the one having to water her plants all the time. So many plants! I told her you'd be perfect for it."

"I'm sure it's nice, but we're going as soon as school lets out."

Naomi's face clouded. "I wish you'd stay."

Laurel looked at her helplessly. When a couple came near and picked up snack plates, Naomi put a smile back on. "Think about it." She touched Laurel's arm and hurried off, her heels clicking.

Laurel poured her punch. Mrs. Fox spied her from across the room and beelined toward her. Laurel clutched her cup. She hated being the parent whose kid had been in foster care. But it had happened. All she could do now was ensure it never happened again.

Mrs. Fox arrived. "Wasn't she grand up there?"

"That poem!" Skye had recited "Stopping by Woods on a Snowy Evening," her hands loose at her sides like she wasn't afraid of a thing in the universe.

"An oldie but a goodie." They studied the refreshments: salami on crackers, cheese cubes on toothpicks, celery sticks with peanut butter smeared down their middles. Also, grapes and melon and every dessert imaginable. Laurel had brought a jar of stuffed olives and another of pickled asparagus spears from Aurora Market. Both were empty. Waiska Consolidated Middle School's spring talent show had sparked people's appetites.

"How did she pick it?" Laurel asked.

"She found it on her own."

"I'm lucky, having her. It's like a shooting star falling into your hands."

Mrs. Fox gave her a dry smile. "It's not exactly random."

Laurel swirled her punch. The fact was, Skye had been born special; she'd have been special if she'd been left on a rock in a desert and adopted by wolves.

Mrs. Fox plucked a cheese cube from its toothpick. "What are you two doing this summer? We're putting together a program for the kids—day hikes, museums. Skye should—"

"We're moving downstate when school lets out. To Grand Rapids."

Mrs. Fox's hand with its cube of cheese stopped halfway to her mouth. "Wow. I didn't see that one coming."

"My uncle owns a cleaning business; they do offices. I'll be working for him."

"So, night work?"

Laurel nodded and Mrs. Fox grimaced.

"Don't say anything to Skye. I haven't told her yet."

Mrs. Fox frowned. "Why?"

Laurel pressed the bridge of her nose. "She'll like it once she gets adjusted, but maybe not right at first."

"No. I meant, why move?"

Laurel would have thought this was obvious. "It's a good job."

"Cleaning offices."

"Yes! It's honest work and somebody has to do it."

"I meant working nights."

"It's decent money, and year-round. My uncle's even leasing a car I can use. I'll be able to buy Skye things—"

Mrs. Fox snorted.

Laurel frowned. "—and pay for lessons, for extras. Grand Rapids has good schools, some of them win awards, even, and my aunt and uncle will help me take care of her. My aunt does their business's bookkeeping from home, so she's there all the time."

"Skye seems happy right where she is. What will a different school offer her she doesn't already have? Or your aunt and uncle either?"

Laurel's frown deepened. "Everything. They have every activity known to man down there; she'll be busy every minute. She can do theater if she wants. Take art classes. The school she'll go to has a lacrosse team, even, a good one. They won State last year."

"I wasn't aware Skye yearned to be a lacrosse champion."

"You know what I mean."

Mrs. Fox gazed at Laurel over the tops of her glasses. "I don't believe I do."

Laurel swallowed and said the truth. "She'll be secure, and that's what I can't give her. Plus, she'll have options there that she'll never have here; it'll make a huge difference when it comes time for college. It'll—" Laurel stopped, frustrated and flustered. All she said was true, but it didn't sound convincing. "It will all just be better for her."

"With you working nights."

Laurel dropped her eyes to the toes of her boots. They were no more appropriate for a school talent show than they'd been for a parent-teacher conference, and they didn't go with her skirt, but they were all she had. Another type of situation she wanted to prevent for Skye. "She'll have my uncle and aunt."

"No," Mrs. Fox snapped. "Don't be stupid."

Laurel blinked.

"Well, I'm sorry, but it's not a good reason. Another school, whatever, maybe. But that's a wrong reason. This is her home."

"It isn't, though. We were only ever here temporarily."

She turned to face Laurel directly. "What I mean is that you are her home. Don't you know that? She's a great kid. A lot of that is your doing."

Laurel speared a few grapes onto her plate. It was nice of her to say, especially that last part, but Beatrice Fox had no idea what it was like, being them.

The sun blared for the rest of the week. The snow melted to a thin crust in the open areas and birds sang in the mornings. Soon the icebergs along the lakeshore would shrink and break loose from one another, drifting away like islands and vanishing over the horizon and into the deeps.

"Rise and shine," Laurel told Skye at eight on Saturday morning. "Adventures ahead, dress accordingly."

Skye sat up. "What adventures?"

Laurel considered being cagey and teasing and decided this wasn't the day for it. "We have to haul our stuff out of Whittle's. I promised Niels." Plus, she'd decided to tell Skye about moving. She'd put it off long enough.

"That doesn't sound fun at all."

"We'll make it fun. We'll buy a frozen pizza at Phil's and bake it for lunch."

"Could we add pine nuts to it? Naomi has them in the market and, Mom, they're delicious. Mary Lynn ordered them on a pizza we ate in Albuquerque, at a place she found off a little alley. It was heavenly. It had lots of basil on it, fresh basil, and the pine nuts—"

"Yes. Now come on, get up. It's a long drive. It'll take a few trips— we might do two today, I don't know."

"Grah!" Skye swung her legs out of bed.

By nine they were on their way. Laurel put her window down as they bounced along Tin Camp Road. "Oh, smell that! Spring." She inhaled deep, and so did Skye. "I'll bet the trilliums are out. I'll bet there're tons in that stand of maples down toward the highway."

"Can we stop and see them?"

"We'll do more than that. We'll revel in them, we'll bask."

"We'll stop and smell the roses!"

Would smelling the roses soften the blow Laurel would deliver? She hoped so. She hoped Skye's memory of learning about the move would always be tempered with the beauty of the spring wildflowers.

# Twenty-Six

They filled the car with boxes at Whittle's, and on their way back, Laurel had the idea to drive by Gran's—Mary Lynn's—to see their old homestead. They drove up Plank Hill and down Iron Road, and then Skye was banging on the dashboard and pointing at the Subaru in Gran's drive. "Mom! It's Mary Lynn and Sam, they're back, they're early!"

Skye ran up the steps and flung the door open. "Sam! Mary Lynn!"

Mary Lynn stood on a stepladder pulling a platter off the top shelf of a cupboard. She wore jeans and a flannel shirt and had a red bandanna tied over her hair. She gripped the plate and made her way down. Her face was bleak. She hadn't heard them over the piano, which Sam was playing loudly in the other room.

Skye darted forward. "Mary Lynn!"

Mary Lynn's head jerked up. For a moment her expression remained lost and hollow. Then cheer bloomed. "Look what the bobcat dragged in."

They said the things friends did when they hadn't seen each other in months. All the time they talked, Mary Lynn packed tins and boxes and dishes. Skye watched her swaddle a mug and nestle it into a box. "What are you doing? Are you getting new dishes?"

Mary Lynn studied the bowl she'd picked up as if she didn't recognize it. "Just sorting things out."

"Why? What's going on?"

Laurel stepped closer, placed a hand on Skye's back.

"Are you moving?"

Mary Lynn set the plate down. She swiped Skye's jawline with a fingertip. "I am, my little lingonberry. There's been a change of plans."


"I'm heading back to my room for a bit." Mary Lynn folded the top of a box together. Sam had wandered in and run himself a glass of water and he leaned against the counter. He appeared the same as ever: affable, distant. He was the distracted host at a party being put on by his wife, only now his wife wouldn't be his wife anymore. Mary Lynn would be his ex, a state of affairs she had explained in as few words as possible: people change, paths diverge. "No!" Skye had cried; "Yes," Mary Lynn had answered firmly. Skye frowned, then focused on Barnum, who'd wandered in.

Laurel had squinted at Mary Lynn. "But you're the one leaving?"

"I don't want the house. He does."

"I'm surprised."

Mary Lynn shrugged. They watched as Skye dragged a piece of string across the floor, trying to lure the cat close. "He likes the quiet. Nothing distracts him from his playing here."

"But what about you? What about the bed-and-breakfast?"

Mary Lynn glanced at Skye, but just then Barnum streaked up the stairs and Skye followed. Mary Lynn sighed. "The B and B was our dream together. You wouldn't think so now, but it's true." Her voice was matter-of-fact. "But since the surgery, he's not the same. The surgeon said his personality might change, but he didn't dwell on it, and we sure didn't. We never thought it would happen to us."

Laurel nodded. You never did think certain things could happen to you.

"He's not interested now in anything that used to matter to us. He only wants to play. As for me—well. It's no way to live, reminded every minute of how it was versus how it is. I need a fresh start."

Then Skye pounded downstairs and Sam appeared from the parlor and the conversation ended.

Now Mary Lynn lifted her jacket off a peg. "It's time for a break."

Skye flung her arms around her waist as if Mary Lynn was boarding a ship bound for America, and Skye was being left behind in Ireland to starve on potatoes. "But we just got here."

"I know, but I have to pace myself. Pack a bit, rest awhile."

Laurel tugged Skye away from her. "We'll get out of your hair. Skye was hoping to see Abby, so we'll go back there. Plus, I planned to swing by Belle's before we head out, and the Lakeshore, and Phil's." Say her farewells, was what she meant to do.

"Mom, I haven't seen Mary Lynn in so long!" Skye said.

Mary Lynn studied her. "I know what. How about your mom does her errands and you come to the motel with me? I'm staying at the

239

Breakers. I have some sandwiches in a cooler there. What do you say
to a picnic?"

Laurel finished her rounds earlier than she expected. From half a
block away, she spied Skye and Mary Lynn atop one of the picnic tables on the Breakers' lawn. Skye talked and Mary Lynn leaned forward with her head tipped. Laurel wanted to listen, too. To hear who
Skye was when she ventured out alone. She ducked behind the
Owens' toolshed.

"My friend Peter and I are building a fort," Skye said. "We hauled a
bunch of branches to the spot where we want to make it—it's by this
lake where me and Mom live."

"Oh, there's a lake?"

"It's more of a mud puddle, but we like it. There are cattails, and
turtles now—they crawled out of their mud—and frogs. They are so
loud at night. Peep-peep-peep-peep all night long, that's all you hear."

"Mm."

"It's nice, though. It's like the earth is alive and that's its voice, you
know?"

"I wouldn't have thought to put it that way, but it sounds exactly
right."

"It's all the frog babies, cheeping for their mamas. That's what Peter said. He's *omakakii*—that's frog clan in Ojibwe—so I guess he
should know."

"Oh?"

"Yeah, frog clan people love water, it's their element. Frog clan's a
subset of fish clan, and fish clan people are teachers and healers.

They also love water, and they can be, like, gentle with people. With how their feelings are being."

"Huh."

"Although, being frog clan isn't some guarantee. I mean, not all Smiths are smithies anymore, right?"

"Right."

"And Millers aren't all millers, or Bakers bakers, and Hills don't all live up on a hill, even if at one time they did."

"I suppose not."

Laurel shifted. A pebble had worked its way into her holey sneaker. By the time she'd wiggled her toes around the stone and nudged it onto the ground, the subject of Skye and Mary Lynn's conversation had changed. "Oh, don't you worry about me," Mary Lynn was saying. "I'm a lonely old horse, but I get along."

Laurel peeked through the boughs of the lilac that grew beside the shed. Skye looked at Mary Lynn with her eyebrows raised and Mary Lynn gazed into the empty swimming pool. The cement had cracked years ago, and the Owens hadn't yet seen clear to spend the money to fix it. Skye patted Mary Lynn's hand. "You're too hard on yourself."

Mary Lynn smiled. "You think?"

"My mom's the same way. She worries a lot."

"What about?"

Skye rolled her eyes. "Me. Me, us, where we live and what we eat, did I take my bath, am I getting my sleep, am I happy. All that kind of stuff."

A smile flickered across Mary Lynn's face. "That's her job, I guess."

"Yeah. But ever since that thing that happened—"

"What thing?"

Skye grimaced. "It's over; she should move on. But she keeps worrying about it."

"Whatever it is, I'm sure she'll work through it."

"I certainly hope so."

Mary Lynn grinned. "I wish my mother and I would've been half as close as you two."

Skye scowled. "Didn't you get along?"

"I was an odd duck. Peculiar. It's a tiring thing, both for the duck and the duckee, I guess."

Skye made a face: she was unconvinced.

"I wear myself out sometimes. I suppose I wore my mother out, too. She didn't bargain on getting a hairpin like me for a daughter."

"What does that mean?"

"I guess that we were such opposites. She was dainty and proper and she lived to entertain—"

"You do, too!"

Mary Lynn snorted. "Smarty-pants. But it was a different sort of entertaining, all very la-di-da. She loved shoes and jewelry and—"

"You like shoes. You like those hiking boots you bought last fall especially, your Wolverines. And your sneakers."

Mary Lynn poked Skye's nose. "Not the same and you know it."

Skye shrugged, not conceding the point.

"My mother was regimented. Traditional. Our set had certain expectations. I didn't meet 'em."

"Hmm."

Mary Lynn chafed her own forearms. "I do think she tried to understand me, as well as she could. She was always very—civil."

"Civil?" Skye looked baffled, and Laurel wanted to hug her. She wanted to hug both of them.

"Polite. Correct." Mary Lynn sighed. "We didn't have much in common. She was a dedicated golfer. She cared who married whom and what they received for their gifts, where they were taking their honeymoon. And I didn't." Skye gazed at Mary Lynn; Mary Lynn made a discontented noise deep in her throat. "It doesn't bear rehashing. Suffice it to say, we didn't understand each other. Unlike you and your mother. I envy you two."

"Yeah, my mom is cool. Without her I'd be"—Skye gave the rueful headshake of a middle-aged lady contemplating unfortunate outcomes—"a mess."

Mary Lynn raised her brows.

"I'd be so boring, I think. Or else—" Skye waved a hand. "Half-baked."

Mary Lynn laughed in her guffawing way, and Laurel stepped around the lilac. "Hey, you two. Here I am."

# Twenty-Seven

Laurel leaned against the rock while her phone tracked for a signal Sunday morning. The clearing sparkled under the just-risen sun; the pines and birches glowed. The trees struck her as extraordinary this morning. They were intricate and beautiful and they reminded her of Mary Lynn's paintings in the B and B.

The phone found service and rang; Uncle Milton boomed a hello in her ear. "Milt Hill here, what can I do ya for?"

Laurel began to explain.

"Well, that's fine, that's good. I did wonder, and Suze did, too," he said when she finished. "But Mother knows best, that's what I said to myself. The rule still applies! What we'll do is run up for a visit in July. We'll get ourselves a room and stay a week, let Skye show us the sights. You, too, if you can, though I guess you'll be snowed under with work. I know how that is. I remember that first summer I worked at Johnson's, pumping gas—we did still pump gas back then, my girl!—and boy, was it hopping."

Laurel listened to the story of Uncle Milton's first job. She laughed as she always did when he described falling asleep behind the tire display one August night when he was supposed to be sweeping. She thanked him profusely before they hung up. Next she dialed Naomi, then the Best Western, and then Sarah, in Canada.

Sarah's house was modular and cream colored with dark green shutters. Outside, a small yard bordered a disused garden plot. Inside the floor plan was open—an actual open floor plan, unlike Harv's—with the kitchen and dining room and living room all flowing into one another. A tiny laundry room and three bedrooms, two small and one larger, framed the central living area.

"Mom! Come see." Skye stood at the pantry cupboard. She rolled a shelf out, pushed it back in. "It's on wheels."

Laurel plunked a box of utensils on the counter. "Awesome, right? I thought we should—"

But Skye didn't wait for her to finish. She was off, poking her head into one of the bedrooms. "Can I have this one? The view is all trees and woodpeckers." She turned her head. "It'd be inspirational, I think."

"Sure."

Skye galloped to the other small bedroom. "But the light is nice in here."

A square of sunshine fell across the floor. Harper sat down in it with a sigh, lay on his side, and groaned.

245

"You won't miss the trailer too much?"

The house was empty, aside from the plants and the bare minimum in furniture. Luckily, Hugh would bring over their own in a few days. Another big favor this old friend was doing; she'd have to make him a meal, or buy him a gift. A new Clash T-shirt, maybe. Or else a book. "I will miss it. But this is nice, too." Skye surveyed the room as if assessing it for a sketch. "I don't know which is best."

"You don't have to decide right this minute. And I thought, whichever one you don't use, we'll turn into a project room. You can have an art table; I'll set up my sewing machine."

Skye smacked her hands together. "Yeah."

Laurel mulled over ideas as she tromped back and forth with boxes. Skirts would be quickest to make. Aprons, too. She had a lot of fabric (she never had been able to resist a bargain) and she could get plenty done in the next few weeks. Fifty or more, if she worked at it. Hours would dwindle at the motel in April, even here; it would probably be slower until the middle of June. And if it stayed busy, she'd stay up later and sacrifice sleep for a few weeks. She hefted a tote full of sprigged calicos onto her hip. She could do a reversible apron with a patch pocket, a different material for each side, the pockets contrasting. It wouldn't take much extra time to add a button for decoration. A detail like that could sell a piece.

She bumped inside and dropped the boxes on the counter. If she asked twenty dollars apiece and made fifty pieces in the next few weeks, she'd earn a thousand dollars and have almost no new expense in it. The important thing was that with a thousand extra dollars, she could, without question, send Skye to Cedar Lake.

———————

After Skye was asleep that night, Laurel carried a notebook to the kitchen island. She yawned and rolled her shoulders. The days were long, compared to winter. More could happen before dark descended. Anything, practically. Even this, the creation of a message she didn't know how to articulate and hardly even how to feel. She gripped her pen, hoping that the truth, clear and sharp edged, would appear in her head. Maybe it was like oil and ran in a pipeline that could be tapped into and siphoned. Probably it wasn't. Probably it was like water, a river, always changing, twisting and turning, sometimes even running over its banks.

Sarah's fridge hummed; Frank shoved at her bedding. Laurel stared at the paper, willing herself to say something real to Jen.

An image of them rose in her head. Bored and restless one March night, lying at opposite ends of Jen's bed, needing something to do and some way to change their vast, implacable, slushy world. They had proposed ideas and rejected them: no movies in Crosscut, no cruising Gallion's one pathetic main street, no prank calls—so junior high!—no sewing. "Never any more sewing," Jen commanded. "Never, ever. Sewing's dead to me." No baking, either. "Please, no baking, I can't take any more of your experiments." That hurt. The last thing Laurel baked had been red bean cakes, in honor of the Japanese exchange student who'd stayed with her and Gran the previous summer. The pastries came out all right, considering they had to use kidney beans instead of adzuki, and Laurel had thought she and Jen were having fun as they stirred and simmered and mashed. In revenge, she had dared Jenny to drive her silver Fiesta out onto Granite

Bay. Mike Mulligan's mudder was parked out there next to his shack; the idea was bold but not insane.

Jenny had said no.

That surprised Laurel, and pleased her; she was never the more daring one. "You're chicken?" She'd rubbed her hands like a diabolical TV scoundrel.

"Oh, no way, I'm going one better. Why risk the Fox?" The Fox was what she called the Fiesta.

"What do you mean?"

Big Jim had been snoring in front of the TV while Jen worked the truck key from his pocket. Laurel lurched with fear, but she had to go along. She had to tiptoe out, creep into the passenger side, murmur instructions to Jen. *Watch the fence . . . There's somebody coming . . . Turn your lights off.*

The two of them had jumped up and down, clutching each other and shrieking, after they'd managed to park the truck a hundred feet beyond where anyone was fishing. Jen passed Laurel a fifth of brandy. Laurel took a drink and handed it back. They downed the whole bottle; they hugged each other fiercely; they howled like coyotes over a kill. Laurel yelled as loud as Jen, but even as she did, her mind jogged ahead to returning the truck to the driveway. They could get under the covers, lay cold feet to warm shoulders, whisper and relive this moment, but be safe. "We rock," she whispered, as if the screaming hadn't been a tip-off they were out there. "We're amazing. But I'm freezing, let's go."

"No, not yet."

Jen had raised her arm and flung Big Jim's key into the darkness.

The snow, whirling in scattered tornadoes across the bay, swallowed it.

"Are you crazy?" This time, Laurel's whisper was fierce. Taking the truck was risky, but throwing the key away was genuinely dangerous. "He'll kill you."

Jenny's smile was honey. It was tulips in spring, hot cocoa with marshmallows, it was puppies and kittens. "I hope he does know it was me. If he says anything, I will, too."

Laurel's gut tightened. She had known forever, known without knowing, but still she asked, "About what?"

"Nothing, forget it. Come on, let's go."

They were back in bed before Big Jim ever woke up.

Jen had told Laurel that night what Big Jim had done to her when she was twelve and thirteen, before she started keeping a knife under her pillow. They talked and talked, promising to always tell each other everything and never let each other down. At last they fell asleep, Laurel letting herself hope that somehow everything would be all right. Jim must have an extra set of keys somewhere. They'd find them, sneak out, get the truck back in the driveway somehow.

But before dawn, a wind came in and shifted the current and moved the ice. The truck drifted away, left all the fishing shacks behind. Just as dawn broke, it went through.

Even then they had been lucky. The truck's drowning was blamed on a band of snowmobilers who'd been lifting sleds all across the U.P. They'd been taking machines from in front of bars and loading them into a trailer, never to be seen again. If they'd do that, people said, they could easily have hot-wired Jim's truck; he'd probably just misplaced his keys.

Jenny was gleeful at their success and before long Laurel came around to her point of view. Stealing the truck was symbolic and strong. It was the best, most daring and meaningful action they'd ever taken, one that could never be equaled but which they must spend the rest of their lives trying to equal.

Hunched over the kitchen counter in their borrowed home, Laurel began to write.

> *Dear Jen, You were my best friend for a long time and I was yours. For me, nothing can ruin that past or lessen what we meant to each other. I hope we can be that close again, but I don't know if we can. I want you to know that I understand the things you said in the grocery store. You were right about some of them. But the thing is, you were cruel in the way you said them.*

Laurel stopped writing, remembering the time she and Jeff accepted Jenny's dare to steal Ms. Trevor's car, though it hadn't been stealing really, but only moving it a few blocks over from where Ms. T. had parked it. Ms. Trevor was a good sport about it once they confessed, but Laurel still flinched whenever she pictured the confused look on Ms. Trevor's face when she came out of her house that morning. Laurel and Jeff and Jenny—but not Sean, he had thought the prank was stupid, that Jenny was only trying to get even with Ms. T. for giving her a bad grade on her *Scarlet Letter* paper—had hid in the bushes across the street. Ms. Trevor wore an old bathrobe and men's slippers and she looked really awful. *Très mal Trevor*, Jenny'd said in a way that even then Laurel thought was mean. Ms. Trevor held her hand over her eyes like the sun was shining in them when it wasn't and rubbed at her hip in a tired way. Laurel had watched with her heart sinking. Maybe Ms. T. did drink too much sometimes, but who wouldn't, in her shoes? She lived with her mother, who was still alive then, and took care of her, which everyone knew wasn't easy, and tried to make bands of half-feral teenagers care about prepositions.

So, yes, Jen harbored a mean streak. But that wasn't all there was to her, or to anyone. Laurel began writing again.

> *The one thing I always had and Skye always has is love. That is the greatest thing I have to give her. Love and life. Sometimes we lead a messy, risky, poor way of life, but it is ours. Sometimes it's a work-in-progress, but sometimes it has to be.*
>
> *Remember that poem we learned in Ms. Trevor's class? "Valentine"? Remember how much we liked it? "Not a red rose or a satin heart. I give you an onion. It is a moon wrapped in brown paper. It promises light. . . . I am trying to be truthful. Not a cute card or a kissogram. I give you an onion. . . . Take it."*
>
> *I miss you, Jen. I'm sorry I wasn't there when you called. I hope you'll forgive me. I hope we'll forgive each other. But you can't be mean like you were in the grocery. That's my limit, and this is my onion. I hope you will take it.*

She signed her name and read it over and wedged *Love* in above *Laurel*. She slid it in an envelope and walked the three blocks to the post office, dropping Skye's camp application in the outside box along with the letter.

Back at Sarah's Laurel brought out the two magnets she'd gotten at Phil's when they went in for the pizza. The first was a pink Upper Peninsula magnet that read *Yooper Girl* in white letters. The other showed waves breaking on a beach. *What lies behind us and what lies before us are tiny matters compared to what lies within us*, it claimed.

Laurel wasn't sure if she agreed with that one hundred percent, but one of her new goals was to own magnets she questioned, or at least to question the magnets she owned.

# Twenty-Eight

L aurel!"

Laurel whirled around, caught in the act. "Sam! Hi."

"To what do I owe this pleasure?"

"I, um," Laurel started. She had woken before dawn possessed by the need to go to Gallion. She still had totes of cloth in Whittle's and she'd promised Niels to move everything out by the time the ice was out. That would be any day now. Also, she needed the fabric. Skye had spent the night at Peter's and Laurel wasn't due at work until afternoon; there was nothing to stop her. She hadn't given Sam much thought as she drove up Plank Hill. He'd be asleep, or else playing his piano. She decided that she would poke her head into the sauna, wander through the garden and the family burial plot, see if

Gran's crocuses were up. She cleared her throat. "I was just looking around."

"Uh-huh."

Laurel clasped her hands in front of her apologetically. "I should go."

"No, don't. The coffee's brewing—stay and have a cup."

"I don't want to barge in."

He hiked a thumb over his shoulder. "Barge away."

Inside, Sam refilled his mug while Barnum twisted around his ankles. Laurel shucked her boots off, scooted them onto the tray beneath the coat pegs, rested her hand flat on the floor for a moment.

Great-Aunt Pam always cried when she told the story about laying it. Her chin would tremble, her eyes would fill. She'd dab at the tears with a tissue, as if they were water splashed from a cup, nothing important, and go on with her story. She never complained. Never said, *Oh, it was so terrible, poor us.* Only that they'd done it, and how. Sifting through the ashes of the burned house, prizing nails from charred bits of wood, pounding them straight. She always laughed through her tears as she described how hard it was to hold a nail with their fingers so cold, how often it went flying and had to be scrounged out of the snow. Her tears would be dry by the time she reached the happy ending: they had done it. She and Gran had fit together the floor of the new house—raised by their brothers and neighbor men—slowly, a few inches of progress at a time.

Sam sprawled into a chair. "Grab yourself a mug. Mary Lynn left a few."

Laurel filled a cup and sat. The kitchen and mudroom looked

naked without Mary Lynn's Michigan collection, but at the same time, more familiar, as if Gran's prosaic hand was back at work.

Sam didn't make any move to start a conversation, so Laurel didn't either. Far below, waves chopped and rolled. The view was endless, forever in a window frame. Waiska would never have one like it. She shifted her gaze to Gran's now-empty bird feeder. The roof had fallen apart a few years back, but Mary Lynn had repaired it last summer. Sam followed her gaze and grimaced. "I drove to Crosscut yesterday. I meant to get seed, but I forgot."

"They have it at Johnson's. Phil's, too."

"I'll try to remember. Probably won't." He rolled his eyes.

Even now, after he'd made Mary Lynn so sad and lost interest in their dream, Laurel couldn't dislike him. What would the point be? Sam hadn't chosen to change. The change was foisted on him and he accepted it.

"When I got back, I had two messages on the machine, people wanting to stay. I didn't know what to do."

"Call them back. Tell them you're not renting rooms anymore."

"Yeah, no. I erased the messages."

"You didn't!"

He shrugged.

"Mary Lynn did a good job, Sam. People loved the place."

"Probably I should rent to them, just go for it."

"You're kidding."

"It wasn't so bad, having people around."

Outside, the water churned; whitecaps decorated the waves. How she loved this place. This house, the bog, the lake, Plank Hill, Johnson's and Phil's and Belle's, the Road Ends Here sign at the end of the point, their campfire spot on the beach, her friends, her history, her whole family's history. As ever, covetousness struck her. She willed this away and sipped her coffee.

She loved it here and always would, but she would love it from afar and learn to love new things. Already she loved the cobblestones of Aurora Market, the hot water tank hippo. She loved seeing Peter walking around Waiska with his frog satchel. She loved Sarah's shiny refrigerator, of all things. Laurel smiled at Sam. "So, how are you doing? How has it been, being here alone?"

"Huh. Well. Lonely." Sam filled his mug again and stirred in cream from a blue ceramic pitcher. It surprised Laurel he'd take the trouble to use it instead of pouring from the carton. He remained a cipher, a puzzle she still half wanted to solve. Parts of it, anyway. "I like it here. A charming house, clean air, unbeatable views. As we used to say in our brochure. But I didn't realize how different it would be, without— well. Without Mary Lynn."

"Ah."

"It was her idea to go, you know." He leaned against the counter. "I know it's my fault. I understand that I'm not the same person I used to be, though to tell you the truth, I can't remember that person. But that doesn't change the fact that I didn't want her to go." Sam studied his feet.

Laurel noted that on this chilly morning he could afford to turn the heat high enough to keep them bare. "You'll get used to it. You'll adjust," she said.

"I wouldn't mind some help, though."

She frowned. "Are you—are you suggesting something?"

"I'm not great at taking care of myself. I forget things. The birds are hungry, I don't understand the washer, I do the dishes but almost can't be bothered. Oh, and I'm a lousy cook."

Laurel smiled. "Cooking isn't hard. You're capable of learning the basics."

"Doubtful I'd ever work up the interest. But I had a thought, just now. Any chance you'd consider a position as a sort of housekeeper?"

"A housekeeper?"

"A manager, then?"

She narrowed her eyes.

"Restart the motor on the B and B, is what I mean. Get some life around here, for the summer and fall, anyway." His voice was hopeful. "Maybe it wouldn't bother you the way it did her, with no history to make you sad. And there's room, or could be." He waved toward the outdoors. "I'll add on."

Laurel embraced her mug. The relief of the idea washed over her like warm water: doing work she liked well enough, doing it here, at home. To have the house, the sauna, the view of the lake, the clothes-line with laundry flapping, the tangle of raspberry bushes behind the barn. She could become that old woman she'd always envisioned, the old woman who'd spent her whole life in this spot.

"I'd pay you a fair wage, plus room and board."

Laurel's thoughts raced. What would happen after autumn? And what about Harper? Sam was still allergic to dogs.

"I'm not a bad guy. Clueless possibly, but not bad."

Laurel clasped her hands together to stop them from smoothing and smoothing at the scorched spot on the table. She'd lost control of the wood-burning tool during her pyrography phase in the sixth grade. On the counter was another burned spot, where she set a hot pan down without a trivet in high school. It had upset her, but Gran was philosophic about it: it would be a little story the house would always carry with it. Laurel pressed herself backward until each chair slat pressed against her spine. "Oh, Sam. That's an interesting idea, but I can't."

He cupped his hands over his ears as if refusing to hear her.

"Thank you for the offer. Really. But I've made other plans for us, in Waiska."

"Ugh, Waiska. You don't want that. You want this." He gestured to the window, the picture-perfect view of the lake.

Laurel closed her eyes. "It's not so bad there."

Sam snorted.

"It isn't. People are nice and I have an okay job, plus I'm selling some of my sewing. I'm even hoping to take some classes. The college on the reservation isn't far; I picked up a catalog last week. They're offering a coaching course this fall, and I could maybe get some financial aid. We rented a nice place, and—"

"Drab," Sam cut in. "And classes. Hell, take 'em online."

"The main thing," Laurel plowed on, "is that Skye's doing great. She's made friends; she's doing all kinds of activities; her teacher has some cool summer field trips lined up."

She trailed off. *Home.* They could come home. She would welcome people into Gran's house, make them feel happy and known, which was what most people wanted, in life and on vacation, as far as she'd ever seen. She would welcome them to Gallion, the best place on earth. She could have this view every morning. And she could be creative here. She could get Sam to replace Mary Lynn's Michigan collection and buy some old Stormy Kromer advertising while he was at it; they made the hats in Ironwood now. She sighed and Sam smiled as if he knew that she'd come around in a few more seconds.

Laurel flexed her feet on the floor, the floor that didn't belong to her any longer and wouldn't even if she accepted Sam's offer. The floor Skye would tromp across on her way to school as the lone sixth grader. There would be no Peter, no chess club, and no Junior Warriors. She sat up straight, jerked her chin in a crisp nod. "You should offer the job to somebody else. Lydia Makin might be good at it, talk to her."

Laurel knelt by Gran's headstone when she reached the far edge of the graveyard. Music thundered from the piano. She expected this was simply the music Sam wanted to play next, not that he had feelings to work out about her or his rejected proposition. Like he'd said, he forgot things. She rested her hand on Gran's stone. Rain drizzled down her neck and seeped under her coat collar; she was a plant being watered. She felt herself settling into the earth, sensing her roots, spreading down into the rocky soil.

After a moment, she patted the stone, pulled herself up, and drove back to Waiska.

At Sarah's, she watered the plants and washed the dishes. In the project room, she cut out an apron but soon was up again, adjusting the window blind and her chair cushion, wiping a smudge from the glass and dusting the bookshelf with a scrap of flannel. She'd done the right thing, turning Sam's offer down, but it didn't feel right. It felt sad.

She needed a different project, something mindless and physical.

Almost without thinking, she went into her room and opened the carton-filled closet, rooting among boxes until she found her blue nylon running shoes with white stripes. Gran had bought them for Laurel the last spring she was alive, and Laurel had put hundreds of miles on them by the end of that October. The last day she ever wore them, Gran died. Laurel tugged at the laces. She jammed a hand into each and wiggled her pinkies out the holes on the sides. She'd always worn her sneakers to nubbins. She stood up. Trash day was tomorrow. She'd throw out the shoes.

Halfway across the house, however, she stopped. Frank rustled in her bedding; the fridge hummed. Laurel lifted the shoes to eye level.

Ten minutes later she stood in the drive wearing sweatpants and a hoodie from high school, black with *Gallion Bobcats* written in green script across the chest. She pulled her ponytail tight and took a few experimental jogging steps. Her feet whapped the gravel in an old familiar way and Laurel smiled. Then she set off.

She passed half a dozen houses, an ice cream stand that wasn't yet open for the summer, the hardware store where an old-timer was wavering down the steps. She turned the corner where Aurora Market and Piney Tavern sat kitty-corner from each other and headed south, jogging past a bait shop and the Department of Public Works building.

A pileated woodpecker hammered near the top of a snag a quarter mile on. A raven called, tiny leaves peeked from the maples' red buds, and Laurel was running. Running!

She tipped her face to the sun. A flock of cranes flew overhead, crying out in their rattling voices.

# Twenty-Nine

S kye, tie your racing skates on, the boat sails at one."

Laurel had finished packing the car with their overnight bags, including a dilapidated black flight bag Mom had used for diapers when Laurel was a baby. Mom had mailed it to Laurel recently, along with a hammer and a note wrapping its handle.

*Look what I found!* Mom's excitable scrawl exclaimed. *I was digging around for an old jacket I want to take (across the pond!), and there it was—THE HAMMER, your inheritance!*

*You know there's no way for me to say how sorry I am I lost Gran's place. The bills piled up, and when I broke my leg—well, you know.*

*But, sweetheart, remember—as wonderful and special as Gran's place was, it is not what makes you strong.*

*You make yourself strong, Laurel Hill. YOU are where the magic is.*

*And the stories the old folks passed down every generation—those are
what's important. Not everyone could have laid that scrap-wood floor
in the middle of January, but my mom and Aunt Pam did. And you
can, too. Here's the hammer.*

The hammer was a clunky reminder, and a silly one, but one Laurel required. It was difficult to accept that Mom was right, but maybe
she was.

"Skye, you have Harper's leash?"

"You've asked me that four times already. We won't need it—Mary
Lynn told me no one would care if he wanders around on the ferry.
But it's in my pocket."

"Okay. I guess we're ready."

"Cool." Skye sauntered out the door as if traveling to Beaver Island
for a weekend getaway was routine. She was acutely aware of her status
as an almost-sixth-grader now that only a week of school remained.
Laurel had debated her missing a day, but Skye persuaded her. "When
do we ever do anything like this?" she asked at supper the night Mary
Lynn called to invite them. "We might never get the chance again."

She was right. Also, Laurel had the money for Cedar Lake. Not a
dollar to spare, but she had it. The day Skye's acceptance letter had
arrived, Laurel opened a checking account at the Waiska branch of
Up North Federal, emptying out her envelopes of cash. Cedar Lake
was near the town the Beaver Island ferry departed from; they'd go
pay in person. It would be fun to surprise Skye that way. Now she
grabbed the bag with Harper's bowl and kibble in it, and another
with the sandwiches she'd made for them, and took one last circuit
through the house: plants watered (Gran's cactus seemed more
cheerful now that it was warmer), beds made, dishes draining. Naomi
was babysitting Frank, so that was okay. As she stepped through the

door, she flicked the kitchen lights off and on. The click of the switch gave her a surge of satisfaction every time; it was a jolt of physical proof that she was doing right by Skye.

After two hours of driving and many rounds of "I spy," they came to St. Ignace. They passed the State Police Post—Laurel tried to ignore the memory of coming here to rescue Jen—and crossed the bridge oohing and aahing: It was so high! The water was so sparkly! An hour later, they were in Charlevoix. Laurel concentrated on the lane of traffic flowing along beside her, the cars passing fast. Unlike her, they knew where they were going. "Is it far to the ferry dock?"

Skye pulled out the map she'd printed at school. "It's three blocks from . . ." She inspected a street sign. "Here. Across the bridge, on the left. Mom, watch out! Cars."

She pointed at a cross street; Laurel hit the brakes.

Skye exhaled from puffed cheeks. "Okay. You cross the bridge and go over the channel and we'll be in the downtown." They did this even as she spoke. "Wow, it's busy."

Laurel wiped a sticky palm on her jeans. People wandered everywhere, tourists gazing into shop windows at T-shirts and fudge.

"Go slow. The ferry office should be right . . . there."

Relief blasted through Laurel, though the next scary thing was turning left with all this traffic.

"Don't worry. Stop, and everyone will stop behind you."

"Right." Laurel flicked on her blinker, eased down on the brake. No one rear-ended her, horns didn't blare. After a minute, a gap opened in the oncoming traffic.

Once parked, she sagged against the seat. Skye bounced up and down, her map-reading maturity evaporated. "Mom, we're here, we made it."

Laurel grinned. "Yes, we did."

They followed a crowd of people trailing through a set of glass doors and down a shallow stairway to the ticket office. Laurel bought their tickets from a woman wearing an emerald-green vest and a white shirt who said boarding would start in a few minutes. In the meantime, they had to move the car to a lot a mile away; a shuttle bus would bring them back.

"But—" Laurel lifted her chin toward the dock where the big white boat waited. Workers pushed luggage carts up its ramp; a woman in a green polo snapped ropes into place.

"You have half an hour yet, don't worry." The clerk slid a map across the counter. She directed Laurel to get back on the main street, head a mile south, hang a left, and park at a school. The shuttle would be along. Did they have luggage?

Laurel surrendered Skye's duffel, and the clerk snapped an ID tag around its handles. She herded Skye back outside, realizing as she hurried toward the car that she'd forgotten to check her own bag. There wasn't time now. She shooed Skye and Harper into the Sable, but the car wouldn't start when she turned the key.

Laurel swore and Skye pulled out her phone. "I'll call Mary Lynn. I'll tell her we can't make it."

"No." Laurel smacked the steering wheel. "No way. You're going. If I have to push this car over the dock and drown it, you're going."

Skye gaped at her like a small, surprised fish.

Laurel pointed at the phone. "Call and ask her what we should do."

Skye opened her mouth but didn't speak.

Laurel tapped her hand. "Hurry, they're boarding. Ask her to help us figure out how to get you there while I stay here and fix this."

The mechanic emerged from the bay, wiping his hands on a rag. Laurel had tried the key a few more times in the ferry dock's parking lot. She lifted the hood and jiggled wires, but the car was mute. She wanted to kick it, or light it on fire. Instead she went back inside and borrowed a phone book and called a tow truck. A mechanic showed up, wearing a light blue shirt with *Don* embroidered on the pocket. Now she clasped her hands in front of her and Don grimaced. "The good news is she started right up when I tried her."

"You're kidding."

"Nope." He made a key-turning motion. "Vroom! The bad news, or maybe it's good—I turned her off and couldn't get her to go again. So, what you've got is an intermittent problem. Worst kind there is."

Laurel closed her eyes. "Yeah."

"You don't know what to do. Is everything okay or isn't it? There's no trust left, see?" Don stuffed the rag into his back pocket. "My guess is it's a ground fault. Best thing you can do is leave her here and let me try to find it."

Laurel bit her thumbnail. "How long might that take?"

Don pulled a face: he couldn't guess.

"I don't live here, though. I was going to Beaver Island. I'm from up north; my daughter has school, and I have work."

Don made another face, this one of pained sympathy. "Tell you what. When were you going home?"

"Monday."

265

"Leave her here, I'll work on it over the weekend, try to figure it out. If not, we'll rent you a ride." He waved toward the station's Rent-a-Wreck sign. "Or you could buy a new one. New-to-you, I mean." He pointed at another line of cars. Each had a price written on its front window in colored soap: a sedan was thirty-two hundred, a small SUV sixty-five.

"Yeah, no. If you fixed the Sable, that would be—" A cavalcade of adjectives paraded through her head; great, excellent, phenomenal, fantastic, vital, critical, crucial. "Good."

"Going to cost you extra, being the weekend."

"Sure, I get it." She should have stayed in Waiska. She hadn't been on the schedule at the motel, but she could've gotten herself there if she'd tried. "How much?"

"I'd wager a grand. Two at the outside."

Laurel paled.

Don grimaced. "It could be less, could be something simple I find quick."

"Is . . . is it even worth it? If it's a lot?"

"Hard to say. But these Buicks can run forever if you take decent care of them."

"I do. I try."

"It seems solid. If it was me, I'd fix 'er. But honestly, it's a crap-shoot."

Again, Laurel bit at a fingernail. "Fix it," she said.

The ferry chugged into St. James Harbor midway through the next morning. Laurel gripped the rail, peering until she saw Mary Lynn and Skye, who had gone on ahead without her the previous day. Skye leaned against Mary Lynn and Mary Lynn held her close, squinting toward the boat. Laurel swiveled her gaze to the village that hugged the shore, postcard pretty, like something out of a children's story. A grim feeling overtook her. She put on a smile and waved.

They walked north from the dock, one block, then two, and half another. Mary Lynn stopped at a water-blue house with white shutters. Window boxes brimmed with geraniums; a screened porch on the side invited lounging in wicker chairs and chaises. In front was an open porch with pillars; on it a wooden swing swayed in the breeze, its chains squeaking. "Here we are." Mary Lynn pushed the gate open. "Home sweet home."

In the foyer, the air was cool and smelled of lilac and lemons. Lemon Pine-Sol, Laurel's expert cleaning-lady nose said. A woman stepped into the hall, a basket of flowers over her arm. Her hair had a windblown look that Laurel guessed had been expensive to achieve. "I was sure I heard the boat. You must be Laurel. It's nice to meet you. I'm Christine." She held out her hand and Laurel shook it; Christine's palm was cool and dry.

Mary Lynn's father appeared from the den. He was tall and athletic looking, and when Laurel shook his hand, she felt how damp her own was. "I'm Christopher," he said, looking fondly at his wife. "With matching names, what could Christine and I do but get together?" Laurel mumbled a laugh.

Mary Lynn grabbed Laurel's bag and cut off her mother's inquiry about the trip, the unfortunate need for car repairs, Laurel's potential thirst for a beverage.

"Thanks, Ma." Laurel saw Christine flinch. "We'll be back down in a jiffy. I want to show Laurel her room."

"All right, but, Skye, you take these." Christine lifted laundry from a side table, the outfit Skye had been wearing yesterday, a white T-shirt dress and blue leggings. "And good news, I coaxed that stain out of your top."

Skye had spilled the pop Laurel let her have as a treat when Laurel hit a pothole on the drive down. "Oh, thank you! I found this at St. Vinnie's last fall and I hardly even wore it yet—I'd be bummed if I wrecked it already."

Christine smiled down at her. "We wouldn't want that. Off you go. I'll make lemonade, shall I?"

"Yum, super, back soon! Toodles." Skye waggled her fingers.

"Toodles." Christine waggled manicured fingertips in return as Mary Lynn blinked.

In Laurel's bedroom, three long windows were hung with gauzy curtains. An ivory chenille spread covered the bed and six pillows graced its head; in the corner a lamp with a stained-glass shade cast elegant shadows onto the wall. Mary Lynn dropped Laurel's bag, and the hammer—such a stupid idea to lug it with her—thunked on the hardwood. She led Laurel to the bathroom, which had a claw-foot tub with a thick towel folded over its edge, looking majestic and inviting. "Take a bath, take a nap, whatever. Make yourself at home."

"Yeah." Laurel cleared her throat. "Yes. Thank you."

Mary Lynn excused herself to work on dinner, and Laurel let Skye lead her to her own room. Decorated in shades of gray and lavender, it overlooked the landscaped backyard. Like the rest of the house, antiques abounded; Skye's lamp was of the naked-lady variety. "It's so nice." Laurel's smile was weak, her nod like a bobblehead's.

"I know. It's so sweet and peaceful. Mary Lynn said it's mine any-time I visit." Skye tossed her clean clothes on the bed. She tugged her bandanna off and shook her hair out, then grabbed a silver-backed brush from the bureau and brushed vigorously. When she'd knotted her bandanna again, Laurel followed her back along the hall. Skye pounded downstairs and Laurel followed at a snail's pace, gripping the rail.

Laurel endeavored to appear intelligent at dinner, prepared by Mary Lynn with Skye's able assistance, as she put it, the two chefs grinning at each other. The meal involved courses—Christine and Skye car-ried out soup and a salad, followed by braised salmon, crunchy French bread, and asparagus tips—and cloth napkins and specialized spoons and forks. Christopher poured wine, and for dessert there was a lemony-pudding-ish something on the way.

Christopher asked what Laurel thought of the wine, its bouquet.

"It's nice. Flowery." Laurel smiled over the rim of her Pinot Noir glass, an item she'd never known existed until she loitered near the sideboard with Christopher before dinner while he deliberated over the choices, not only of wines but also of goblets, which he referred to as stemware. She hoped "flowery" was correct and that her eyes didn't show how much she felt like wailing.

On the porch later, Lake Michigan's big, clear light making eve-ning seem like day, Laurel learned that Mary Lynn's parents had met at the University of Michigan. Christine had been born in Petoskey and Christopher was from Bloomfield Hills. He'd grown up right near Cranbrook Academy, the school Jen had suggested for Skye all those months ago, back when Skye and Laurel were still living at

Harv's place in Gallion. "A fine school. A young firecracker like Skye would thrive there."

Skye giggled.

Mary Lynn dropped her hiking-booted feet from the porch rail with a thunk. "So, I'm diving back into the B and B business," she said, changing the subject.

Laurel was grateful for the diversion. "You are?"

"My folks are selling this house; they've been mulling it over for a while. I'm taking it over—I'll run it in the summers and fall."

Naturally things would run smoothly for her; even a marriage and life dream crashing wouldn't slow her down long. And Laurel was happy for her. She liked Mary Lynn. In fact, she loved her, with her big heart and goofy grin and endless curiosity. "That's great. What'll you do in the winter? Stay here?"

"I'll go back to the mainland, find a condo. Or a house. Some kind of weatherproof box, anyway. Who knows?"

"You never know what will happen," Laurel said, though, regarding herself, she did. No matter how hard she tried or which way she turned, Skye faced disappointment, even if she didn't know it. Despite Laurel's profound desire to be a great mother, ultimately, she wasn't.

When Skye began yawning, Mary Lynn said bed might be in order for a certain someone under the height line, holding her hand out as if she were the sign at a carnival ride. Skye kissed everyone's cheek; the screen with its ornate wooden frame clacked behind her as she shuffled off. Christopher excused himself soon after, and Christine followed.

Walkers passed; Laurel overheard the words "dinosaur" and "massage" and wondered what the conversation could be about. A woman on a bike dinged her bell at a boy meandering along the center of the street eating an ice cream cone and Laurel leaned against a porch column. "It's lovely here."

She turned to find Mary Lynn studying her. "Listen. I'd still like to help Skye get to Mesquite Canyon, the camp we visited in New Mexico. If she decides she still wants to go."

"Oh—" Laurel was ambushed, defenseless. Where was her gun, her bow and arrow? She was so flustered she didn't mention the payment to Cedar Lake.

"She seemed taken with it when we were there."

"I know she did."

"I think she'd enjoy it." Mary Lynn sounded timid.

Laurel sank onto a curlicued iron chair.

Mary Lynn started the porch swing swaying. "I want to help." She glanced at Laurel. "I know things have been rough. And I thought— I wanted—" She closed her eyes for a moment. "I hoped I could sort of adopt Skye for the summer. She seems happy here, and we'd have such a good time."

Laurel's throat closed. "Won't you be busy getting ready to open your new B and B?"

"Busy, yes, but mostly around the house, in the yard and my office."

"You already have an office?"

"I call it that. My parents redid the attics for me when I was a kid, turned them into an art studio. I have lots of space and all the supplies you can dream of. We were actually playing around this morning, designing logos—" She broke off. Her face was earnest. "Oh, Laurel. She's so talented."

"I know," Laurel whispered.

Mary Lynn took a breath. "So yes, I'll be busy, but Skye could help me. In fun ways, I mean. I won't make her wash dishes and scrub floors."

Laurel blinked sudden tears away. "Of course not."

"She could help with the decorating and the design. The menus, the colors, even the advertising, the whole gestalt." She waved her hand, including not only the house and yard but the whole island. "She's a natural."

Laurel's head swam.

"It'd be a kick for me, and I know the hours you log. It's remarkable, and admirable. But."

She didn't finish. She didn't have to.

"She's really something. And I could—well, I'd be happy to put her in school in the fall. Friends of mine run a Waldorf school up the shore. It would be perfect for her. She'd thrive, and I would be happy, more than happy, to help get her there."

Jenny's accusations in the grocery store roared into Laurel's head. They'd been waiting in the wings, not banished the way she'd thought when she wrote that letter: *You kid yourself. You're a dreamer, and dreamers are dangerous. Some things never change.* Uneasy, Laurel stood and wrapped her arm around a pillar. Clouds had rolled in over the lake and stuffed the sky full. Rain began falling. The heavy drops fell slowly, almost one at a time. Laurel reached out to catch a few.

"I wouldn't be taking her from you." Mary Lynn spoke softly. "I'd just be helping."

Laurel caught at another handful of raindrops.

"What—what do you think?"

Laurel kept one arm wrapped around the pillar to steady herself.

She was about to speak when Skye appeared. She came and leaned against Laurel and Laurel stroked her hair. "You okay?"

Skye nuzzled her head into Laurel's hip, put her hand around Laurel's wrist.

"Did you have a bad dream?"

Skye shook her head.

Laurel sat back down and Skye climbed onto her lap. She yawned and snuggled in. "It was dumb when you couldn't come yesterday. It wasn't fair. It's your vacation, too."

Laurel nuzzled her nose into Skye's hair. "You had a good adventure anyway, right?"

"Mm, yeah. It would have been better if you were with me."

"I'm with you," Laurel whispered.

Skye's mouth gaped into a yawn, her nose wrinkling.

Laurel rocked her from side to side. "Want to miss the boat on Monday, play hooky, hide out here and pretend we're islanders, living the good life?"

"Mm-mmm, no. We have Junior Warriors on Wednesday, and on Thursday me and Peter are going fishing after school. If it's okay with you."

"It's okay with me."

Soon Skye was dozing. The coconut scent of her hair filled Laurel's nose.

Mary Lynn watched them. "It's only an offer."

"It's an amazing offer. And tempting."

She smiled sadly. "But."

Laurel nodded. "But she can't stay on the island this summer. I won't send her to New Mexico either. And she can't enroll in your friends' school this fall. Not this year. Someday, yes, if she wants. But not right now. She's too young."

Mary Lynn held steepled hands against her mouth: plea, surrender, or maybe only waiting for what Laurel might say next.

"It's true that things are hard sometimes. It's also true that we're all right. And I'm her mom. I have things to teach her. We have things to do." Trails to hike, stars to watch, books to read. Mostly they had time to spend being together, alive on the same square of earth. "This place seems wonderful. I mean, an island! I'm sure your friends' school is great, too. But for now, I'm Skye's island, I'm her school."

Laurel lingered at Skye's bedroom door in the morning. Skye breathed deep; one leg stuck out from her blanket. Laurel patted the doorframe and padded along the hall.

In the kitchen, Mary Lynn gazed out a north-facing window at the sliver of Lake Michigan and the sky, which shimmered grayish pink with sunrise. "Hey ho," she whispered when she saw Laurel.

"Hey."

A red enamel teapot whistled. Mary Lynn poured steaming water into a French press. She stirred the grounds with a spoon, plunging it up and down in a way Laurel suspected would make Christine wince, and turned the dial on a kitchen timer. "Five minutes to Coffeeville!" She made a hooting sound like a train whistle and Laurel smiled. Mary Lynn pulled a pottery mug from a glass-fronted cupboard. "You want some?" Her hand hovered near a second cup.

"It smells heavenly."

Mary Lynn trickled cream into a pitcher, arranged spoons on cloth napkins, filled the two mugs with hot water to warm them. When she was finished, she leaned against the counter to contemplate Laurel. "You're up early. Sleep all right?"

"Yes, great." She had, to her surprise. "I'm a morning person, is all."

"Me, too."

"It's a good trait if you're running a B and B, right?"

Sorrow filled Mary Lynn's eyes, but she smiled. "Abso-tively."

Laurel swallowed. "Also, I was hoping to find you. I wanted to ask . . ." She hugged herself. "I want to ask you to help me send Skye to an arts camp here in Michigan. Cedar Lake accepted her; it isn't far—"

"I know where it is! I yearned to go there as a kid, though I never told my folks. I didn't have any special talent—"

"I doubt that."

The timer rang. Mary Lynn thrust the plunger down in the coffee-pot, her eyes narrowed, her expression intent. "Oh, it is. I'm crafty, but there isn't a genuinely creative bone in me, nothing unique."

"That's not true. You pay attention to every space you're in and make it beautiful."

Mary Lynn tilted her head.

"You do."

"Hmm."

Laurel nodded.

"Well. Thank you." Mary Lynn slid a mug of coffee toward Laurel. "So, Cedar Lake."

"I've been saving all winter for it."

"Why didn't you say so sooner? You should've said last night."

"I wanted to do it by myself. I wanted to give Skye something awesome, something important, something she'd never forget. And never forget it came from me."

Mary Lynn looked chastened. "Sure, I understand."

Laurel sucked in a preparing breath. "I don't have enough for the fee now; I'll have to spend most of what I had saved fixing the car— the mechanic left a message on my phone. So, I'm doing this awkward thing and asking for help."

# Thirty

After school let out, Skye rearranged her room at Sarah's, then rearranged it again. She doted on Frank and Harper; she played with Peter and Allie and the other Junior Warriors; she set her telescope up so she and Laurel could look at stars and meteors and northern lights. In July she went off to Cedar Lake. When she returned, she corresponded with the friends she'd made there using her flip phone and the market's internet. Also, she began work on a new art project, an arrangement of objects, the largest pieces the bulbous fender of an old truck and a rusty metal chair with bullet holes in it she and Peter had unearthed in the woods. Placing them with exquisite care in the middle of Sarah's backyard, she declared them an installation.

While Skye socialized and created, Laurel worked and jogged and fixed nutritious, sometimes even ambitious, dinners. She purchased a zester at Aurora Market and bought hard hunks of Parmesan there, too, lifting the unconscious embargo she'd placed on the stuff back in Gallion; she took a summer accounting class that met twice a week and signed up for the coaching fundamentals course in September. She made a satchel for Peter's mother, Drew, and one for a nurse from Drew's work, and three more for Aurora Market. The bags would always be time-consuming, but practice had made her quicker.

"At last!" Naomi had said when Laurel carried a craft-filled tote into the market on a July day midway through Skye's time at Cedar Lake. She gestured to the few imported purses that still hung near the register. "Let's get these out of here." She grabbed an index card and wrote *Clearance Sale!* on it in red marker, then drew a stick figure jogging, a bag bouncing on its hip. She studied it for a moment. "I have a proposition for you."

Laurel tensed. Naomi might want to stop buying things outright; she might want to go to consignment. But that would be okay. Her things were selling; she'd already made six more skirts and ten more aprons.

"I wonder if you'd consider managing this place."

Laurel blinked. "What?"

"Manage. Take over. Be me."

A nervous *hunh* had popped out of Laurel. "I couldn't be you."

"Be yourself, then."

"That's flattering. And I'd like it. A lot. But the nights and the weekends—with Skye I don't see how it's possible."

"We'd hire someone, or two someones. Plenty of college-age kids would work."

In Gallion there wouldn't have been plenty of any age person wanting to work. There'd have been almost none. Naomi's offer was tempting, but Laurel did not want to be anyone else's charity case. Asking Mary Lynn for help had been hard enough. "So . . . why not hire anyone before?"

"I didn't want to. But now I do. I want to hire you."

"But—"

"I'd stay involved, but you'd be in charge of the day-to-day operations." Laurel's shock must have looked like dismay; Naomi leaned toward her and hurried to sell the idea. "You could change it up, if you wanted. Make it yours. Put in, I don't know, double fudge brownies, or have poetry readings. Skye could give art lessons; you could teach sewing. But me, I'd like to step back a bit. I have other things to do."

"Oh. Wow."

Naomi waved a finger at her. "I know what you're thinking."

Laurel startled. "You do?"

"You're wondering if I'm seeing someone."

Laurel hadn't been thinking about Naomi at all in this conversation, only about herself. She blushed. "Are you?"

Naomi laughed. "My ex-husband!"

"Oh. Wow!"

Naomi grinned shyly.

"How . . ."

"He had a colonoscopy in March. That's where I went when I asked you to fill in. He always was shy about those kinds of things, 'body things,' he calls them, and when he asked if I'd go with him, I couldn't say no. And—it just happened." Naomi added a row of zigzagging footprints behind the running stick figure on the index card.

"That's great."

Naomi's eyes sparkled. "He's coming to visit in August. It'd be great if you could steer the ship by then. What do you think?"

Laurel had straightened her shoulders as the bells on the entry door jingled to announce a customer. "I think the answer is yes."

Laurel and Skye strolled down Tin Camp Road, soft dirt rising in puffs with each step. Laurel wore one of her wraparound skirts with sandals; Skye was in fraying shorts and a jean jacket with her pink bandanna tied over her head. She broke into a jog, the lichen crunching under her feet, then flung herself into a handstand and tottered forward. She made six steps, counting loudly, and tumbled to the ground; Harper dashed in to lick her face. She wrestled free and pulled her camera, a birthday gift from Mary Lynn, from her pocket. She aimed it at Laurel. "Ms. Hill," she said in a deep voice that startled Laurel. "Can you tell me what brings you out into these woods today?"

"Oh!" Laurel brushed at her hair, as if Skye were a real reporter and she was anxious to look her best. "We're celebrating."

"What's the occasion?"

"Life! The new moon, a passing green comet."

Skye made a roll-it motion with her free hand.

Laurel smoothed her skirt. "I have a good job and I'm taking classes up at the college. And my daughter is a general all-around superstar. An artist, an athlete, a scholar—"

"Any romance in the air?" Skye cut in.

Laurel blushed.

"Everybody loves a romance."

Laurel cleared her throat. "I've been seeing someone, an old friend."

"Oh, that's lovely," Skye cooed. "What's his name?"

"His name is Hugh," Laurel said sternly.

"How did you happen to start seeing him?"

"Hugh has also returned to school. We enrolled at the same college."

"And would he be part of your celebration today?"

"Possibly. Later on, after he's done working." At the Piney Tavern, mopping floors and making pizzas and burgers and cleaning beer lines, as he'd done at Belle's. But now everything was different.

"And what else brings you out here today aside from life, nature, and this budding romance?"

Laurel aimed skeptical eyes at Skye, but Skye only blinked. "We're here to thank someone who helped us in a time of need."

"We?"

"My daughter and I."

"Oh, you have a daughter, how nice."

Laurel laughed and Skye shot her a scolding look. "You don't think so?"

"I do. My daughter is so smart. And funny—she cracks me up."

"That's nice, you're very fortunate. Now, can you tell us something about this land we're walking on?"

"The land belongs—belonged—to an old man called Baldy. He's the one who helped us. He gave us shelter."

"Baldy. That is a very unusual name. Was it the one his parents gave him?"

"No. That name came later on, when it suited him better."

The camera lens buzzed closer. "Was that the main thing about him?"

"What?"

"His lack of hair, his baldness. Was it *him*, the most particular thing about him?"

The lens was a watching eye. Laurel wanted to get her answer right. "No. Baldy . . . Baldy was interesting. Complicated."

"Oh, yes?"

"He was a little crazy—" Laurel paused. The breeze hummed in the pines, and high overhead, cirrus clouds wisped and streamed. She shook her head. "Cancel that. He wasn't crazy. He was probably wiser than most people, though he'd have said he was just a guy who lived in the woods."

"Hmm."

Laurel angled toward her. "He made art out of his life."

"I see."

"His parents named him Baldwin. Baldwin James Chapter; Baldwin was his mother's maiden name." Someone should remember that. Even if his son never showed up—he probably wouldn't—someone should remember Baldy's name.

"And how do you know that, if you wouldn't mind telling our audience?"

Laurel gestured at the pines and birches.

"Mom!"

Laurel relented. "He told me. He was a friend."

"Ah, a friend. Friends are important." Skye turned the camera on herself and nodded sagely, then turned it back on Laurel. "And where is Baldwin Chapter now?"

"He's dead."

Skye lowered her camera. "That was harsh, Mom. How about saying, 'He passed away'?"

"I thought this was live journalism, the raw, uncut stuff." Mrs. Fox had the class revved up about media projects this fall, and interviews were Skye's new passion.

Skye put her hands on her hips.

"Fine. Fine, fine."

Skye lifted the camera again. "And where is Baldwin Chapter now?"

"In the graveyard in Waiska."

Skye sliced at her neck.

"I didn't say dead, did I?"

"Do it right!"

"Okay, okay."

"Where is Baldwin Chapter now?" Skye boomed.

"He passed away," Laurel said meekly.

"That's sad. But turning now to cheerfuller news"—Skye pointed the camera at Harper—"here is Harper M. Dog, *M* for 'Marvelous.' Many consider him the best former sled dog in the universe. Harper-dog! Say hello!"

Harper dipped his head.

"Harper, sit," Skye said.

Harper sat.

"Harper, shake."

He lifted his paw.

After Skye threw her arms around him and kissed his nose and recorded him raising his other paw, they continued walking. The track had a ridge of grass up the middle and limestone rocks with fossils in them embedded in the dirt. Laurel had never imagined that the rocks existed during the winter, though of course they had always been there. They'd been there for so long it was unimaginable. She nudged one with her toe, picked it up, and touched the outline of a tiny, ancient clamshell. Skye did another handstand and made four steps, tumbled and stood and did two, then wandered into the woods. When she returned, she walked beside Laurel, humming.

Laurel waited for her to come back to the interview, but after a grouse burst out of the brush and Skye caught her startled reaction on video, she ran ahead of her, calling out landmarks, capturing them on film. The tall pine that marked the halfway point between the trailer and the main road; a gnarled stump that had always looked like a sitting coyote in the dusk of morning. A huddle of black spruce that Skye declared "so sweet," which the trees were, the way they grew toward one another, their soft needles mingling.

An hour later, Skye poked at the campfire she'd built. Smoke drifted above the trees and Harper snuffled at the base of a pine, his tail swinging in meditative sweeps.

"We'll prob'ly live happily ever after now, right, Mom?" Skye glanced at Laurel, and Laurel squinted upward. The moon shone white and cotton-ball clouds floated high overhead. One shaped like a teapot blocked the sun for a moment, then ambled east and left the sky clear. Moments later, another blew in. She shot Skye a crooked smile. Happiness was a net—that was it. You had to build a life that happiness would snag in. When it did, you took it up and used it. Ate it, salted it, relished it. Then you put the net down again. Nothing guaranteed you'd haul it up full every time. You wouldn't. But sometimes happiness would catch, and you'd have what you needed, at least for a while. Long enough to tide you over until the next time.

"But won't we, Mama? Live happily ever?"

Laurel bundled Skye into her arms, gently bumping Skye's skull with her chin a few times—clunk, clunk, clunk—and said, "Oh, I would think so, definitely."

Later yet, Laurel's eyelids drooped. The fire crackled; pine sap popped. The mud-puddle lake lapped at its gummy shore and Skye played somewhere nearby with Harper. She heard music as if from far off—a dream—and smiled dozily. *Hi, Gran,* she thought. *How are you? Down here, we're okay, we're fine.*

"Mom! Wake up!"

Laurel opened her eyes. Skye and Harper ran toward her as the music swelled louder. "We have company. It's Peter and his dad and his uncle who's visiting. I forgot to tell you I invited them."

A pickup stopped at the edge of the clearing. Peter and his father climbed out opposite doors as someone—the uncle—dialed the radio tuner.

"David John," Peter's dad called. "Get your butt out here; quit fiddling with the tunes." The tuner settled. The announcer at WCMZ made his perennial promise to be *Your station for hits from the sixties, seventies, and eighties.* A man hopped from Peter's side of the vehicle and stopped short when he saw Laurel.

They stared at each other.

Laurel stood up.

ELO began singing "Evil Woman" and the man grinned at her, his eyes gleaming with cheer.

Laurel managed to formulate one thought: Life was so unexpected. Anything—*anything*—could happen. Today, *right now*, Skye was meeting her father. Her family—her tribe, her world—was expanding.

# Acknowledgments

Many people helped me in myriad ways as I wrote this novel. I've rounded up a few and listed them in alphabetical order. Many more remain unnamed—friends, family members, diner customers, readers, librarians, booksellers—and my thanks go to them as well.

For reading and commenting, sharing knowledge, and offering moral and logistical support, I thank: Mariann, Mark, Matthew, and Peg Airgood; Heidi Bell; Laura Bontrager; Susanna Campbell; John Corbett; Jenna Derusha; Phil Downs; Paul Dry; Lon and Lynn Emerick; Elladiss, Kevin, and Rebecca Fuge; Pat Grasser; Pamela Grath; Jean Guth; Rachael Guth; Genie and John Hayner; Terri Kapsalis; Patti Kucinskas; Gary Michael; Sarah Miller; Marcia O'Brien; Terri Poliuto; Kay and Stan Powers; Robyn Ryle; Julia Sippel; Lisa Snapp; Aaron Stander; Lillian Tschury; Mary Vecellio; Taylor Weeks; and Karen Wolf.

# ACKNOWLEDGMENTS

As ever, I appreciate my agent, Joy Harris, and my editors at Riverhead, Sarah McGrath and Alison Fairbrother. They gave my work careful attention and were patient as the book and I traveled a long, winding road. (Danya Kukafka's insights also provided treasured encouragement along the way.) I'm very grateful to the copy editor, Sheila Moody, who gave the manuscript its final close reading, as well as to scores of people I'll never meet who move a book out into the world.

Finally, thanks to my husband, Eric Guth, for understanding my writer's nature and for reading *Tin Camp Road* with painstaking focus.